LIKE MOTHER,
LIKE DAUGHTER

Miss Diana Forsythe's mother, Flavia Forsythe, was the most celebrated actress in London. But the famous Flavia Forsythe was determined that her daughter not follow in her footsteps.

Instead Diana would be the most respectable of young ladies, following the most respectable of occupations. Diana would become a teacher, safe from the temptations that her own striking beauty and the scandalous aura of the stage would subject her to.

But now in teaching an unpolished lord to become a flawless dandy, Diana found herself playing a role more demanding than any her mother had ever essayed.

Diana was acting the part of the perfect pedagogue to a man who must not suspect that she was a young lady in love. . . .

Lessons In Love

Ellen Fitzgerald
Lessons In Love

Ⓢ
A SIGNET BOOK
NEW AMERICAN LIBRARY

SIGNET TRADEMARK REG. U.S. PAT. OFF. AND FOREIGN COUNTRIES
REGISTERED TRADEMARK—MARCA REGISTRADA
HECHO EN CHICAGO, U.S.A.

SIGNET, SIGNET CLASSIC, MENTOR, PLUME, MERIDIAN AND NAL BOOKS
are published by New American Library,
1633 Broadway, New York, New York 10019

First Printing, July, 1986

1 2 3 4 5 6 7 8 9

PRINTED IN THE UNITED STATES OF AMERICA

Part One

1

Applause resounded through Richmond's Theater Royal and seemed almost equally loud in the green room. Diana Forsythe, sitting in the corner of an Empire sofa against the far wall, idly fondled its crocodile-headed arm and smiled as she heard her mother's name shouted by one-half the audience while the other half was screaming just as loudly, "Julia, Julia, Julia!" that being the name of the role she was playing in *The Midnight Hour*. Pride broadened Diana's smile. Julia was the youthful heroine of the play, and from the pit Flavia Forsythe did not look any older that the eighteen summers she was purported to be. Certainly, she bore no resemblance to the tired, harried woman who had chased Diana from her dressing room a good half hour before she was to make her entrance.

"Your mother does not want anyone in her dressing room before she goes on." That had been the injunction of Mr. Gifford, who had been passing when a ruffled Diana had emerged. "She needs that time to get into her role," he had added. "She is entirely remarkable, I think. She can look any age from sixteen to sixty, and almost without artifice, do you not agree, my dear?"

She had agreed and had mentally ignored the contrary devil that usually drove her to disagree with anything Mr. Gifford said concerning her parent. She dispatched a grimace in the direction of the door to the stage and Mr. Gifford, currently taking bows beside Flavia, in his role as the marquess, Julia's suitor. She removed her hand from the sofa as hastily as if the crocodile had clamped wooden teeth upon her palm. "She couldn't," Diana moaned under her breath, and tried to think of more reasons than her dislike of Mr. Gifford for her mother to refuse any offer other than that of remaining with the company for the next year.

"Sure'n he's a foine man," Moira, her mother's elderly abigail and dresser, had pointed out on more than one occasion.

"I am sure he's nothing like Papa," a young Diana had been wont to pout. "Why may I not be told Papa's name?"

"It is herself will have to tell you that, miss."

"But she will not, Moira, and I want to know!" A younger Diana had stamped her foot and glared at Moira. She had subsequently received a smart box on the ears for that bit of impertinence.

"It will do you no good to hear it, though you're more like him than I care to say," Moira had retorted sharply.

The years had not softened her opinion on that count, nor had they dulled Diana's curiosity regarding her anonymous parent, whom she must resemble. She knew that had to be the case, for her mother had golden hair and huge blue eyes set in a lovely, piquant little face. She also had a beautiful figure—but she was small, and that she was so commanding on stage was due mainly to the artful way in which she held herself. Diana, on the other hand, was at least a head taller, with green eyes, and curling black hair. She was also much slimmer than her mother—a forest nymph as opposed to a goddess. That was the stated opinion of Silas Hornby, the elegant young actor who usually specialized in second leads—Cassio to Mr. Gifford's Othello and the like. Be that as it may, a younger Diana had made up stories concerning the sudden appearance of a slim, green-eyed, ebony-headed gentleman among the elegant young bucks and beaux who came backstage whenever her mother performed. However, this flight of fancy never had so much as a feather of reality, and to this present moment, Diana remained in ignorance regarding her father's identity. Undoubtedly it would have pained both ladies had they known that their combined silence had given rise to suspicions that, if aired, would have pained and angered them.

At two months past her eighteenth birthday and employed as a pedagogue by the Earl of Marchant ("pedagogue" being a term Diana preferred over governess), she knew a great deal more about life than she had, say, even nine months earlier, when she had completed her final year at Miss Prentiss's School for Young Ladies in Bath. It was only too easy to become worldly in the Marchant establishment. Lady Aurora, the earl's sister, adored knowing the latest *on-dit*, and through bits of information dropped by the earl and his cronies, she was remarkably *au courant*. Lady Aurora did not hesitate to share her knowledge with her various friends, and whenever those damsels were not available, she took her two younger sisters into her confidence. They, of course, dutifully passed it along to Diana.

Consequently, Miss Forsythe was now aware that most of the thespians at Covent Garden, Drury Lane, and the Little Theater in the Haymarket were less dependent on their salaries than on the various gallants who vied for their attention. Diana had been extremely surprised to learn that one of these actresses, Mrs. Dorothy Jordan, had been living with the Duke of Clarence and had, it was rumored, borne him eight or nine children—possibly even ten, no one was sure of the number.

Diana had questioned her mother about Mrs. Jordan only to have her deny any knowledge of the lady or her circle of friends. She had been quite unusually angry with her daughter for a streak that she did not hesitate to describe as "unhealthy curiosity." Her attitude only served to strength her daughter's suspicions in regards to her mysterious father. Though Flavia Forsythe enjoyed as blameless a reputation as any actress in England, Diana suspected that some eighteen years ago when seventeen-year-old Flavia Forsythe had been the toast of London, some gallant—possibly or probably, a titled gallant—had succeeded in sweeping her off her firm little feet.

The fact that his name never passed her lips gave strength to that suspicion.

"She dared not bare the name of her seducer," was the quotation that coursed through Diana's mind. She could not remember where she had heard or read the line—probably she had found it in one of the plays her mother was always receiving from indigent but eager young authors. It was, she thought, very apt. Her mother must have been seduced and abandoned.

"Abandoned?" Diana whispered.

She frowned. Such a situation was not easy to envision. Men, faced with the beautiful and famous Flavia Forsythe, were totally bedazzled. Even though she never gave them so much as a morsel of encouragement, they flocked around her like so many starving chickens, quarreling over a handful of grain—fowls that, at the blink of an eye, were ready to turn into fighting cocks dueling over the lady's multiple charms. If anyone had been abandoned, the likely candidate would have been her father.

Diana mentally nodded. The seducer must have been abandoned. That was a very pleasant thought. The honorable or baronet or viscount, earl, marquess, or duke had been left to mourn while Flavia Forsythe went on to new triumphs upon the Dublin stage and, upon leaving Ireland, a series of other stages as well.

And will she now ally herself with an actor? Diana sighed. She also had an interior groan at the thought. Yet, aware that her feelings, if divined, must be considered disloyal, she mentally added, An actor not of the caliber of say a Kemble or a Kean. Other than that, Mr. Gifford— George, she had always loathed the name of George, even though it was borne by the present Prince Regent, his father, great-grandfather, and great-great grandfather as well—but other than that, George Gifford was handsome, a very good actor, and in his private life, sober. As far as she could discern, he hailed from a long line of yeomen and merchants, the salt if not the spice of the earth and . . . Diana's cogitations came to an abrupt conclusion as a

very tall young man suddenly appeared in the doorway.
She gazed at him wide-eyed. He was easily two or three
inches over six feet in height with shaggy dark-brown hair
and eyes of the same shade. His garments were of no
particular style. They sufficed only to cover his large
frame. Yet, for all that he was good-looking—more than
merely good-looking, extremely handsome. His nose was
straight, his mouth . . .

"I beg your pardon," he said tentatively.

Her inventory interrupted, Diana said, "Yes?"

"Do you know where I . . . I mean, is this where I
would find Mrs. Forsythe?"

"She is still onstage," Diana said, recognizing his symp-
toms immediately and concealing a smile. "She will be
here presently, though. You can wait if you choose."

"Oh, I should," he said quickly. He cast a nervous
glance around the room. "I seem to be the first one
back."

"You are that," Diana acknowledged. "Most people
wait until the play is at an end."

He flushed. "I am sure they do, but I wanted to be the
first. She is so very beautiful, Mrs. Forsythe."

"Indeed she is," Diana agreed.

"And young."

"That, too." Diana suppressed a second smile.

He moved farther into the room. Diana noticed that he
strode rather than walked, suggesting that he was more
used to country roads than small chambers. A bull in a
china shop was an apt analogy, she decided—very apt, she
amended as he bumped into a table, knocking it over and
sending a little vase to the floor.

"Oh, Lord," he muttered as he quickly set the table on
its legs and scooped up the vase. He added sheepishly,
"It's not broken."

"It would be small loss if it were," she said kindly. She
indicated a chair beside her. "Would you care to sit here
until Mrs. Forsythe comes in?"

"I would, thank you." He sat down immediately. "There

. . ." He grinned. "The rest of the furniture will be out of harm's way for the nonce."

Diana concealed a look of surprise behind lengthy black lashes. She had not expected him to be sensitive to his awkwardness. "It's very old furniture." She shrugged.

"All the reason why it should be treated with respect." He revealed white teeth in a broader grin. "Are you a member of the company?" he asked interestedly.

"Yes, I am," Diana decided to say.

"But you are not acting tonight."

"No, not tonight. I am resting tonight."

His eyes gleamed with interest. "Have you been in the theater a long time?"

"All my life," Diana asserted.

"I believe that most actresses do start very young."

"Some do. I did," Diana said blandly. She was beginning to enjoy herself.

"I expect you've played Juliet?" he hazarded.

"Oh, yes, and when I was fourteen."

"Really?" He regarded her with surprise and admiration.

"But," Diana continued before he could ask her any leading questions about the role, "my favorite part is Angela in *The Castle Specter.*"

"Indeed? I do not believe I am acquainted with that work."

"Really, you're not?" Diana injected considerable surprise into her response. "It is very popular. My, er, Mrs. Forsythe acted in it to great acclaim only last season. And it has been in her repertory for years."

"It could not have been *many* years," he responded. "Not at her age."

"When we speak of years—we mean seasons," Diana said loftily.

"Oh, of course." He looked relieved. "And what name do you play under?"

"Diana Dane," she answered glibly. "And might one know your name, sir?"

"Sabin Mallory."

"Sabin? I expect that must be a family name."

"It is."

"Are you from Richmond?"

"No—rather, I was once, but . . ." He cast a glance toward the entrance. Several other young men had come in. They were clustered near the door, their combined gaze on the hall down which Mrs. Forsythe must soon walk.

"Are you not from Richmond anymore?" Diana inquired.

"I will be," he flushed. "I was born here," he amplified, "but I have been living in Canada."

"Canada?" she repeated interestedly. "That is a very long way from here."

"Yes, a long way," he said rather absently, his eyes on the door.

Diana followed his gaze. More people were coming in—and from the door leading to the stage Mr. Hornby, still in his makeup as Sebastian, the friend of the marquess, had entered. Diana had an admiring glance at him. To her mind, he was twice as elegant as Mr. Gifford, and a better actor too.

She said, "Do you miss Canada?"

It was an effort that her companion shifted his gaze from the doorway. "I do, a bit," he acknowledged. "I have been away only two months and most of that time was spent in traveling."

"Canada must be very different from England."

"It is."

"I have often thought it would be pleasant to tour Canada. Do they have many theaters there?"

"There were none where I was . . . and a great deal of the country is very wild. Probably you and your troupe would be better received in Philadelphia or Charleston now that the hostilities are at an end. The only theater in Canada is, I believe, in Quebec, where they would necessarily perform in the French tongue."

"I speak French," Diana told him. "I should like to perform the works of Corneille or Molière. I could also see myself as Phèdre. I do admire Racine, do you not?" She fixed her compelling green gaze on his face and managed to bite down a threatening smile. He was becoming edgy. More people were in the green room, and a burst of applause had just signified the entrance of her mama. However, Mr. Mallory, if uncouth in appearance, was obviously a gentleman and therefore compelled to answer politely as he now did, "I am not acquainted with Racine's works."

"Are you not? A pity. Racine is easily the equal of Euripides. To my mind, Corneille is the French Sophocles—I am speaking about Pierre, not Thomas—and Molière is Aristophanes, the comedian. But Racine's *Phèdre* is my favorite. It is a magnificent play. It is such a pity he gave up writing for the stage after it was so ill-received; he should have realized it was the work of his enemies. Everyone pretended to praise Jacques Pradon's *Phèdre*, which was produced at the same time, but that was inferior and it is now completely forgotten. That is always the way. So many connected with the stage are so petty, do you not agree?"

"I have not had the opportunity of meeting anyone connected with the stage save yourself."

"I am the first, then?" Diana asked.

"You are," he acknowledged, and stiffened as someone said pleadingly, "But you are not leaving already, Mrs. Forsythe?"

"I am sorry—but I must," came her answer, delivered in a soft pleasant voice.

Mr. Mallory paled and rose, but Diana guessed, as she looked in the direction of her departing parent, that he had had little more than a glimpse of Mrs. Forsythe's golden curls and the back of her cloak, the former quickly shrouded in her hood as she prepared to brave the chill December air.

"Miss Diana." Moira, unnoticed by her, had come to her side and was now regarding her with her grimmest watchdog expression.

"Oh, I must go." Diana rose swiftly. "I fear I have

kept you from meeting Mrs. Forsythe, but she will be performing again, the day after tomorrow.'' With little or, rather, no compunction, Diana visited a bright smile on her erstwhile companion's set face and followed Moira from the room.

"Who was that country bumpkin with whom you were conversing?'' Mrs. Forsythe demanded as Diana joined her in their hired post chaise.

"Oh, someone who must be very angry.'' Two dimples showed at the corners of Diana's mouth. "His name is Sabin Mallory and he is from Canada—or has been there and is now returned to Richmond.''

"Canada?'' Her parent rolled speaking azure eyes. "That accounts for his, er, costume.''

"And why is he angry?'' Moira demanded brusquely. Before Diana could answer, the abigail added, "And why were you speaking with him?''

Again before Diana could frame a response, Mrs. Forsythe said, "A very good question, Moira, my dear. Why were you conversing with him, Diana? Sure you know better than to encourage the young men who come to the green room.''

"Rascals, the lot of 'em,'' Moira muttered, unconsciously adding more fuel to Diana's theories concerning her father.

"He was interested only in you, Mama,'' she said defensively "And I know he is most disappointed that you left so early.'' A touch of anxiety crept into her tones. "And sure it is most unlike you not to spend at least an hour in the green room.''

"I could not face *them*.'' Flavia Florsythe leaned back against the squabs of her carriage. "I am weary. I could wish, indeed, that we were not in Richmond until Monday next. I had not remembered that the Yorkshire climate was so uncommonly chill.''

Diana regarded her mother with considerable surprise and concern. It was very seldom that she admitted to being tired. Generally she was exhilarated after a performance and could remain for at least an hour and sometimes even two in the green room, receiving the plaudits of the admirers who came flocking back. Some of these were actually known to follow her from town to town, though, to do her credit, she never encouraged them. No, Diana thought bitterly, she only encouraged Mr. Gifford, but much to her relief, not even he was with her tonight. Of course, she thought resignedly, he might easily be waiting for them at their lodgings.

A short time later, coming into the suite of rooms she was sharing with her mother, Diana said, "Will Mr. Gifford be joining us, Mama?"

"No, I could not even face dear George, which, I am sure, hurt him."

Diana, in the act of divesting herself of her cloak, visited a narrow look upon her mother's face. Mrs. Forsythe had a pensive expression that brought to mind Diana's earlier suspicions. However, she contented herself with saying merely, "He must be tired, too."

"He, never," Mrs. Forsythe exclaimed. "He has the strength of ten!"

"Because his heart is pure?" Diana could not resist inquiring.

"Because he neither drinks nor smokes save when these actions are required on the stage—a marvel for a man in his position," Mrs. Forsythe said admiringly.

"That is amazing." Diana concealed a sigh. "I think," she added, "that I am a little tired myself."

"You should be, my love." Mrs. Forsythe turned anxious eyes on her daughter. "You should not have waited all those hours. This is your one chance to rest this week and you did look peaked when you arrived."

"I have told you it was only the traveling, Mama. Richmond is a goodly way from London. They—the Marchants treat me very well, as I have often told you."

"Still, I will be pleased when this apprenticeship, as it were, is at an end and you in your own school. And while

I am thinking about it, what did you find to say to that young man with whom you were conversing so earnestly?''

Amazed but not surprised by her mother's rapid change of subject, Diana merely laughed. "Oh, we talked of you. He is one of your ardent admirers, Mama, and I am sure he is not at all pleased that I kept him from joining the rest of them.''

"I am glad that you did, my love.''

"Tell Moira, then, I beg you. She is primed to give me a tongue-lashing. She seems to forget that I am of age.''

Mrs. Forsythe said merely, "Dearest Moira, do not be angry with her. She has your best interest at heart, as you are quite aware.''

"That,'' Diana groaned, "must be the sugar that sweetens the elixir, but enough. I will bid you good night, Mama.''

"Good night, my dearest.'' Mrs. Forsythe put her arms around her tall daughter and held her close. "It is lovely to have you here with me for these few days. I wish . . . But I will not be selfish. You have your way to make.''

"I wish I could have been an actress,'' Diana said pointedly.

"Be thankful, my angel, that you did not possess the requisite talent.''

"I can be very convincing when I choose,'' Diana retorted. "There's not one of the girls I knew at school had any inkling that my mama was a famous actress or, indeed, any sort of an actress at all.''

"As I have so often told you, my love, acting requires considerably more than the ability to fabricate a tale.'' There was a sudden flash of anger in Mrs. Forsythe's eyes. "And now, as I have told you, I am tired and I must go to sleep.''

"I know you must and you do look tired. I should not have kept you talking so long,'' Diana said contritely. She kissed her mother good night and went to her own chamber.

Having undressed and performed her ablutions, Diana slipped between the sheets of her little bed, glad of the hot

brick the chambermaid had deposited there. The bed was
very hard, as many of those she had occupied during their
peripatetic existence. It was an existence that, to all intents
and purposes, was now behind her, had been for the last
nine years save on the holidays or in the summer when she
left school to join her mother; there had been times when,
Flavia being in Scotland or Cornwall, she had been forced
to remain at school or, on occasion, to go home with one
or another friend. Indeed, the theater was becoming more
and more foreign to her. She had not been telling the
absolute truth when she had expressed a desire to follow in
her mother's footsteps.

"I wish," she murmured, and thought of the Marchant
mansion and of their estate in the country: miles and miles
of woodland where one could ride for the better part of the
day and never even see the boundaries of that vast prop-
erty. It would be lovely to live in the luxury that Lady
Aurora, for one, took for granted.

Diana made a little face. She did not like Lady Aurora,
a sentiment heartily reciprocated by the possessor of that
name. Diana had the distinct feeling that Lady Aurora
deeply resented her presence in the household. However,
when she had protested, she had been opposed by the Earl
of Marchant, by his widowed mother, and most of all, by
Lady Aurora's two younger sisters, Rosalie and Eustacia.
They, as it happened, were directly responsible for Diana's
employment.

"We cannot exist at that horrid school if you are not
there, Diana," had been Rosalie's impassioned protest a
few months before the end of Diana's sojourn at the
academy.

"No," Eustacia had echoed. "We will run away and I
have told that to Rob and Mama."

Evidently concerned over these threats, Rob—who was
Robert Gresham, fifth Earl of Marchant—and Mama had
taken the sisters quite seriously; on a subsequent visit, they
had tendered the position Diana currently held as instructor

or, her preferred word, "pedagogue" to the two younger girls. Rosalie was sixteen and Eustacia, fifteen.

"But I shall not be there above two years, Mama," Diana had assured her protesting parent. "And then I shall return to Bath, Miss Prentiss is totally in agreement. She feels that it would be a very good experience for me to live in London."

"I do not want you to be a mere governess." Flavia had frowned. "I wish to buy into that school and—"

"But it is agreed that I shall not be in the least 'mere,' Mama," Diana had interrupted.

She uttered a short mirthless laugh. Her mother had known whereof she spoke. Granted that she did have privileges a mere governess could not expect, including a bed and sitting room adjoining those of Rosalie and on the second as opposed to the third floor. She was not required to use the backstairs and she had her meals with the family when guests were not present. She was also invited—in fact, expected—to attend the balls and routs that took place in the house. Furthermore, she had a full instead of a half-day to herself, and her salary was munificent, compared to that which most governesses commanded; but at the same time there was Lady Aurora's marked enmity and her habit of treating Diana as an inferior when there were none present to mark her attitude.

"Do hem this gown for me, my dear," she had said on one occasion, appearing at Diana's door very late in the evening. "It was torn badly, and Mary, my abigail, is so clumsy with the needle, alas. My sisters have informed me that you make most of your garments—and very well, too, I have seen. So do be a dear. It is one of my favorites."

Given her privileges, Diana, awakened out of a deep sleep, could not display her indignation. Fortunately, this exchange had been overheard by Rosalie, who had stayed up to quiz Aurora about the ball. She had reported the exchange to her mother and the countess had reprimanded Lady Aurora, reminding her that Miss Forsythe was not there to do her bidding unless she chose to do so. It was that softening clause that had put Diana in the position of saying, "Of course, I shall be glad to do it, Lady Aurora," a statement they both knew to be false.

Lady Aurora had refrained from asking for other "favors," but at the same time Diana was aware of suspicious looks directed at her by her friends, and when she appeared at a ball and danced every dance with a number of admiring young men, those glances had been hard as diamonds. It was well, she thought, that she had, at the most, another year there. She had never been one to enjoy being subservient, particularly when she felt herself the equal of anyone in Marchant House! And if the truth were to be known, she considered herself far superior to Lady Aurora, who was vain, empty-headed, and frivolous, and who, moreover, had the pink-and-white looks and the bright-yellow hair of a china doll—but unlike the doll, these would fade, and in a very few years. However, even that thought failed to console her for the slights she had and would continue to receive from Lady Aurora. Once more she thought of her unknown and, possibly, noble father. Yet, even were he an earl or a marquess, there would be the bar sinister emblazoned on her escutcheon. Diana sighed. It was terrible to be poor as a church mouse—well, not quite that poor—and as proud as a duchess and, moreover, much as she preferred to deny it, a glorified governess!

On this demeaning thought, Diana composed herself for slumber and achieved it more quickly than she had anticipated.

2

It was a clear cold morning. Diana, coming out of the inn, pulled her hood forward but at the same time gratefully breathed in the chill air. It was very fresh and extremely welcome after the various odors of the inn, cooking drifting up from the kitchens and stale beer from the taproom. She took a second breath and let it out in a sigh of relief because Moira, who used to sleep like the proverbial cat, with one eye open and both ears as well, alert to the slightest sound, even with her door closed, had not stirred as she tiptoed across the floor. Evidently she had not heard the squeak of unoiled hinges either as Diana opened the door to the hall. Moira, Diana thought, was getting old, and her claws were blunted, as well as her perceptions. That reflection failed to cause her the pain it might have induced in her mother. Moira had never been particularly kind to the child she had been, nor had she scrupled to divulge the source of her all-too-evident prejudices.

"She be like 'im . . . the spit'n image," she had heard the old woman remark to Flavia on more than one occasion. Generally her mother hushed and reprimanded her.

"She's not anything like . . . How can you say so, Moira?"

" 'As 'is colorin'n 'is temper, too. She be both willful 'n stubborn."

"She's only a little girl. You're far too hard on her, Moira."

"As the twig is bent so grows the tree," Moira had been wont to growl.

Diana shook her head and breathed in more chill air. Moira's estimate of her had not changed. It was only too obvious that she still regarded her with suspicion and distrust directed, she was positive, as much at her father as at herself. Yet, no amount of artful questioning had ever persuaded the old witch to reveal his name . . . Why was she dwelling on Moira again? Because, of course, had she been awake, she would have sternly prevented Diana from faring forth from the inn without a companion. Furthermore, since that companion must needs have been herself, she would have insisted on coming with her and would have groaned over her rheumatics every step of the way— and it would not have been a long way. Nothing could ever have persuaded Moira to venture as far as Richmond Castle!

Since she was standing on a slight rise of ground, Diana could see the great stretch of ruins quite well. High broken walls were still intact, and so was the square tower beyond them. Diana, clutching her sketching pad, thought of extracting her charcoal from her reticule but changed her mind. It would be better to get as far away from the inn as possible. There was always the chance that Moira would awaken and find her missing.

As she started down the hill, she smiled in anticipation of her excursion. She had always loved castles. She had seen many in their travels—mainly rising in the distance, bringing to mind other times when knights sallied forth to fight dragons and when captive maidens peered from arrow slits in the high towers.

Diana could laugh at these fancies now, but she still loved castles or, rather, their histories. In addition to sketching it, she could make use of Richmond Castle to quiz her two pupils on its history. She followed the path to a town already abuzz with morning activity. She was glad of the protection afforded by her hood. She did not want to invite the sort of advances that made it impossible for a female to venture abroad in London. In London, she had Betsy, who was Rosalie's abigail, to accompany her. The girl had wanted to come to Richmond with her and it had been necessary to invent an elaborate reason as to why she could not, the which, due to the acting ability her mama had said she did not possess, had seemed entirely plausible.

She was passing Trinity Church now. She smiled as she remembered her mother mentioning that there were shops inside, among them a pork butcher and a tobacconist! In another few moments, she had skirted the marketplace and found the narrow little street described by her mother, who had visited the castle in the company of Mr. Gifford when they had first arrived.

"This road," Flavia had said, "leads right around the castle cliffs." In a few more moments, Diana had reached it. She started up the walk that led past the ancient walls. It seemed amazing that bricks and mortar could hold up so well through seven hundred years, but she reminded herself, she had heard of the Acropolis and the pyramids, both of which had been standing for thousands of years. Diana sighed. She would love to see both these ancient wonders and all the far lands she had read about, but she did not anticipate a time when she would be vouchsafed a sight of them. She would probably live her whole life in England, and what manner of life would that be?

Her mother had already determined that. It was her dearest wish that Diana become the head of a school—an academy similar to that owned by Miss Prentiss. However, she could not even contemplate such a position until she had served her apprenticeship at Marchant House and later in Bath under the firm hand of Miss Prentiss. That would take years, she had no doubt, and perhaps when she was very old—say, forty—she might have the opportunity to travel to Paris with a flock of other teachers, as had Miss Prentiss when she was a very young student-teacher. She had never forgotten that journey, not surprising when it was the only time she had ever set foot on the Continent.

"It was when poor dear Queen Marie Antoinette was still alive. It was 1784, and she was but twenty-nine, such a beautiful creature. I glimpsed her when she rode in a procession—the royal coach, all covered with gold, it was—and such fine white horses to draw it—eight. Alas, who would have thought . . .'' She was wont to sigh when describing this experience to her class and invariably she invoked a shudder in her pupils as they contemplated the sad demise of the queen.

"Such a terrible occurrence could never take place in England," Miss Prentiss always added.

"But it happened to King Charles the First," some pupil was always eager to point out.

"Not to a *woman*," was Miss Prentiss's proud response.

Miss Prentiss: pale, nervous, fluttering, and self-effacing when faced with the noble or wealthy parents of her pupils; stern and considerably less fluttering with those same pupils; and downright harsh to her teaching staff. She had visited some of that harshness upon Diana, whom she fully expected to train. She had been, however, delighted when Diana had gone to Marchant House.

"You will do very well, my dear, and it will be a wonderful credit—employed by an earl."

Diana made a face. In another year she would be back at Miss Prentiss's academy as an underpaid, put-upon teacher, and when her mother thought her ready or, rather, seasoned, as she was fond of saying, she would follow the path designated for her.

And would she never marry?

It was unlikely. On the whole, schoolteachers tended to be spinsters, and actually, Diana could honestly admit that she had never met a young man who attracted her. Of course, she had not met very many young men, save those with whom she had danced or chatted briefly at Marchant House. Some of them had been attractive enough, and one or two had seemed interested in her, but on meeting them at subsequent balls or routs, she had found them patently disinterested and had no doubt that Lady Aurora had been quick to inform them of her status in the house. It was just as well, for even if Lady Aurora had not been so obliging, they must have found out sooner or later. She had, she reminded herself, also met several actors who were very pleasant-spoken, but every time she had fallen into conversation with one or another of them, her mother or Moira had intervened and had later told her, in no uncertain terms, that she was not to become friendly with them. Indeed, her only real friend in the company was Silas Hornby, who, though handsome, elegant, charming, and obviously a gentleman, was also purported to have been madly in love with one who had rejected his suit, which accounted for his air of settled melancholy.

A gust of wind suddenly sent Diana's cloak flying, and remembering where she was, she started walking again, her eyes on the crumbling walls. She was just rounding a bend in the road when she suddenly stepped into a hole she had not seen. Her ankle twisted and she fell heavily, barking her knees on the pebbly ground and bruising her hands, which she had unconsciously flung out to save herself.

For a moment, Diana lay where she had tumbled, the wind knocked out of her and various portions of her body smarting or aching. Then, she pulled herself to a sitting position and, looking down at the offending hole, used words that she had heard at various times around the theater and that had no place in a female's vocabulary. Then, staring about her, she saw her sketchbook lying a few feet away. Her reticule was, of course, still attached to her wrist. Her palm smarted, and upon examining it, she saw the indentations of pebbles on the flesh and also a few drops of blood. At the same time she felt a dull ache in the vicinity of her ankle, which, she decided, she must have bruised when she had stepped into the hole. Shaking her head and mentally castigating herself for being so deep in thought that she had failed to watch where she was going, Diana started to get up, but as she put her weight on her left foot, a most agonizing pain shot through her ankle. Sinking back down, she stared at it and uttered a little cry of amazement. Her ankle had swelled to twice its size!

"Oh, dear," she murmured, and casting a glance behind

her, she found that she could not even see the town. Wrapped in her thoughts, she had gone farther than she had realized; she would have quite a distance to cover before she reached the inn. A quavering sigh escaped her. She was very near to tears but these would not serve to alleviate the pain. She must concentrate on finding her way down the hill. She glanced at her ankle again and groaned. It appeared to have swelled even larger, and the idea of trying to stand on it must needs be abandoned. Then, would she have to crawl down the hill on hands and knees or, perhaps, roll? Neither plan appealed to her. She could use the wall . . . But how?

"If only . . ." Diana said, and emitted a mirthless laugh as she remembered all the if-onlys she and the other pupils at Miss Prentiss's School for Young Ladies had been wont to sigh: If only it were vacation time. If only we did not have to return . . . If only I could meet a handsome noble or a soldier . . . If only, if only . . .

"If only I had told Mama I wanted to visit the castle," she muttered to herself, and groaned, remembering her foolish pleasure at having escaped Moira's vigilant eyes and ears. Now no one knew where she was, and she suddenly discovered, it was getting very cold. She would have to find a way down. She suddenly tensed as she heard a whistle. It was a tune she recognized. Mentally, she furnished the words.

> Of all the girls that are so smart,
> There's none like pretty Sally.
> She is the darling of my heart,
> And she lives in our back alley.

In a minute, the whistler had come around the bend, and Diana, looking up, flushed deeply as she recognized her mother's disappointed pursuer Mr. Mallory.

He stopped midwhistle and looked down at her in a consternation that was followed by a slight frown, the reason for which she knew only too well. "You!" he exclaimed.

"Mr. Mallory," she said, and felt her cheeks grow warm. "G-good morning."

"Why are you . . ." he began, and paused, staring down at her leg.

Following his look, she blushed, realizing that she had pulled the skirt of her gown almost to her knee. She started to ease it down, only to have him kneel and stop her.

"You've hurt your ankle."

She nodded. "I stepped into a hole. I do not imagine it is much . . . Please, you mustn't," she protested as he quickly removed her shoe.

"It is a sprain, and a bad one, I think. I hope you've not tried to walk upon it," he said concernedly now.

"It just happened a short time ago," she explained. "I did try to stand, but—"

"You should not have tried," he interrupted. "I have had a similar injury, and rest is what is needed. Where are you staying?"

"We . . . I am at the King's Head Inn."

"I will take you back," he said. He shook his head. "You will need to stay off this for several weeks. I do not believe you will be able to act."

Diana felt her cheeks grow even warmer. "Oh, can I not?" she questioned, trying to sound disappointed.

"No. You'll need a crutch for a month or so—else it will only grow worse." He picked up her sketchbook. "I imagine this belongs to you?"

"Yes, I had hoped to sketch the castle. It is very beautiful."

"It is," he agreed, "but you certainly should not have come up here alone, a young girl like you."

"I am over eighteen," she flashed.

He smiled. "That is not precisely ancient, but no matter, I must get you back to the inn. You will need to send for a physician." He handed her the sketchbook. "You carry this and I will carry you." Without further ado, he scooped her up in his arms.

"I fear I am too heavy for you," Diana said contritely as Mr. Mallory carried her down the hill.

"Not in the least," he assured her. "I cannot imagine, however, why you would climb up there alone. Sure you must have known better."

"I told you why," she said patiently. "I wanted to sketch the castle. I did not expect to fall."

"Falling is the very least of what might have happened to you." He gave her a stern and, at the same time, searching glance. "I should think that one who has traveled as much as yourself would know better than to court such dangers, unless, of course, you were meeting someone." He stared down at her suspiciously.

"I was not," she flared. "I wanted to sketch the castle so that I might be able to show my—" She paused, flushing. She had very nearly said "pupils." "I had wanted to show my colleagues my sketches," she finished.

The sternness had not left his tones as he remarked, "I am sure you are a gifted artist, but it was the height of folly for you to walk up that hill. Do you not have a female companion besides that old woman I saw last night? She—" He paused, for they had reached the steps going up into the town. "The King's Head is, I believe, a few yards from Trinity Church?"

"Yes," Diana said weakly. Her ankle was beginning to throb and pains were shooting up her leg. The jouncing, unavoidable because he was carrying her, was making her feel ill.

"You are very pale," he said concernedly. "I am glad that your lodgings are close by. The sooner you get to bed, the better it will be."

"Yes." Diana nodded. She flushed, thinking of Moira and her mother. She hoped devoutly that neither would be stirring. It was still early and Flavia had been very weary when she retired. She might very well sleep the morning away, and Moira as well. It would be a mercy not to find either woman up and fretting over her absence. She had not taken that into consideration when she had decided to walk to the castle. She had been concerned only with the exigencies attendant upon getting away as quietly as possible. And now . . . A little shudder coursed through her as she thought of Moira.

"You are cold," he said concernedly again. "But look, we are almost there."

Diana raised her head slightly and smiled her relief as she saw the battered old sign that hung before the front entrance of the inn. "I am grateful to you," she said. "It was uncommon kind of you to bring me all this way, especially after—"

"It was the least I could do." His interruption had kept Diana from explaining that she was sorry she had prevented him from speaking to Mrs. Forsythe the previous night. He continued, "I hope that you will be better soon and that you will regard your accident as a lesson."

"I shall," she said meekly. She added, "You can leave me in the common room. I am sure the landlord will find someone to bear me to my chamber."

"I will take you there," he said insistently. "You must retire at once. And—" He paused as he pushed open the door.

As they entered the dark interior of the inn, there was a loud cry, which brought Mr. Mallory to a standstill and filled Diana with trepidation.

In another moment Moira had bounced into view. "Ach, an' what have we here?" She glared at Diana. "You've hurt yourself, then?" she continued. "An' where were you at this hour of the morning?" Before Diana could respond, Moira yelled, "Mrs. Forsythe, my love, 'tis back she is an' wi' an ankle which is swole all out of proportion!" With arms akimbo, she stared up at Mr. Mallory. "An' who might you be?"

Diana, raising her eyes, saw confusion written large across her rescuer's countenance. She choked down an interior groan. "Moira's my mother's abigail. She—"

"Your mother?" he interrupted, looking even more confused.

"My love." Flavia Forsythe hurried in. She paled as she looked at her daughter. "But what has happened?"

"I fell, Mama," Diana sighed. "My ankle . . . I wanted to see Richmond Castle and I stumbled on the path. This gentleman was kind enough to bring me back."

"You went to the castle alone!" Moira demanded in ascending accents. *"Alone?"*

"I thought only to sketch . . . but my ankle—"

"Oh, my dearest, it *is* swollen, and we must get you to your bed," Flavia cried. She turned to Mr. Mallory. "But please . . ." She pushed forward a chair. "You must put her down. You must be sorely fatigued. It was a long way for you to come."

"She is not heavy, ma'am," he assured her. "I would be glad to carry her to her chamber."

"No, no, we can see to it," Mrs. Forsythe said quickly. "Here, you may put her in this chair," she said a second time.

"Very well." He gently deposited Diana in the proffered place, saying quickly, "You must keep that foot up for the nonce. I have been similarly discommoded as I explained—"

"Here be a footstool, sir." The landlord hurried forward.

Taking it from him, Mr. Mallory put it down and gently eased Diana's foot onto it. "There, that should suffice." He nodded at the landlord, and then, turning to Mrs. Forsythe, he continued, "You ought to call a physician and have her ankle bound up."

"Oh, I will," Mrs. Forsythe bestowed one of her brilliant smiles upon him. "I cannot tell you how very grateful I am."

"It is nothing, Mrs. Forsythe. I am glad that I found her."

"As am I," she said with a rueful look at him. There was a touch of anger in her tone as she continued. "Ever since she was a child, Diana has wanted to do as she chooses and never mind the consequences. Perhaps this accident will provide her with a lesson she'll not soon forget."

Mr. Mallory had a penetrating look for Diana. "I hope so," he said. He added, "I hope you will soon feel more the thing, Miss Forsythe."

"I am sure I shall," Diana sighed. "And again, I do thank you."

"As do we all," her mother said.

Several hours later, Diana, aroused from an uneasy slumber by the throbbing of her ankle, thought of the chagrined expression on Mr. Mallory's face as he absorbed the information that the golden beauty who had won his admiration and, possibly, his heart on the previous evening was her mother!

She sighed. He had been ill-rewarded for his pains, and he was so nice—kind, too. It occurred to her that despite his ill-fitting garments, he was no "country bumpkin" as her mother had termed it last night. His speech and his courtesy, as well as his handsome features and well-proportioned body, suggested refinement and good schooling. What were his origins? But he had told her he had been born here in Richmond and had gone, later, to Canada. Why Canada? She would have liked some answers to those questions. In fact, she would like to see him again. Perhaps he would come to inquire about her ankle, but more probably, he would not, not after all the lies she had told him. Besides, he was not interested in her. He had been attracted by her mother's golden loveliness.

"Oh, dear," Diana murmured. "I wish . . ." But she was not quite certain what she did wish, and anyway, there was very little likelihood that she would ever see him again.

3

The back parlor at Marchant House was located on the first floor and looked out over a garden, now buried under the snow that had fallen earlier that morning. There was a fire burning on the hearth, and an oval mirror hanging over the mantelpiece reflected a sofa, a round table piled high with books and papers, a bookcase, and another table and chair. Not captured by the mirror was a blackboard, pushed to one side and near to the small desk where Diana, in her role as pedagogue, usually sat.

Now, however, she was ensconced on the sofa, with her books and papers on the floor at her side. Perched on the far end of the sofa was Eustacia Gresham, a small, slim girl with quantities of flyaway fair hair and big blue eyes set in a pale oval face. Her features were delicate, but unfortunately her mouth was small and her nose had a bump in the middle, depriving her of the beauty possessed in such abundance by her older sister, Aurora, and by Rosalie, the middle sister. Though the latter did not resemble the exquisite Aurora, it was believed by her brother and her mama that she was quite as lovely. They also agreed that she was a throwback to the Portuguese girl who had been brought home as bride by Sir Basil Gresham, who had wooed and won a maid-of-honor to Her Majesty Catherine of Braganza, wife of King Charles II. Rosalie's eyes were dark brown, her hair blue-black, and her skin olive, a combination that had moved her sister Aurora to dub her "the nut-brown maid," in accents more insulting than teasing. Still, despite their lack of conventional beauty,

Diana thought both girls far more attractive than one of the subjects of their present conversation—which were Lady Aurora and the gentleman, nameless for the moment, who had made his appearance at the ball given by the earl for Aurora's eighteenth birthday.

"It was bright-blue satin, the coat, I mean." Eustacia wrinkled what Lady Aurora had called her "unfortunate" nose.

"And he wore a gold brocade vest and yellow satin knee breeches. There were immense clocks on his stockings. These were white, the stockings not the clocks, which were black." Rosalie giggled. "I do wish you had been present, Diana."

"Indeed." Eustacia also giggled. "Everybody was looking at him. He was such a figure of fun!"

"Perhaps he will come again and Diana can see him." Rosalie had a commiserating glance for Diana's ankle. Most of the swelling had gone down, but she could not yet dance and consequently had not put in an appearance at the ball.

"Who is he?' Diana asked.

"We are not sure," Rosalie answered. "He is a friend of Rob's, that is all we know. Aurora has begged him not to invite the 'creature,' as she calls him, again. Rob was very angry. He told her that clothes do not make the man, and then they went on it hammer and tongs, as usual. I do wish we could have stayed to watch him go down the country dance with Aurora, but it took place too late in the evening and Betsy insisted that we leave at ten, as usual, Fancy, he trod on Aurora's foot. Is that not lovely?''

Diana bit back words of agreement. "I am sure it was not lovely for your poor sister."

"Oh, Diana," Eustacia said disgustedly. "I do loathe it when you become sententious. And we are both fully aware that you dislike her as much as we do."

Once more, Diana was minded to speak the truth, but again, in the interests of diplomacy, she said, "She *is* your sister."

"*We* did not choose her," Eustacia retorted. "It is a great pity that she was born at all. She is really so dreadfully horrid!"

"We had better stop discussing her. It is making Diana uncomfortable," Rosalie reproved. "She must be loyal, you understand. Oh, dear, I wish we were back at school."

"You don't," Eustacia exclaimed. "You hated it just as much as I did."

"That is true, but at least we could say what we really meant. You cannot possibly *like* Aurora, Diana."

"Of course she does not," Eustacia said loyally. "No one could."

"Well," Diana capitulated, "I must say that I do not—but she is very popular."

"That is only because she is so beautiful and also because no one outside of us knows what she is really like." Eustacia scowled.

"She is fiendishly clever at hiding her feelings," Rosalie admitted. "A real wolf in sheep's clothing."

"She certainly is," Eustacia sighed. "She is forever trying to get someone in trouble—mainly myself. Look what happened this morning."

"You should not have said—" Rosalie began.

"I know," Eustacia interrupted. "But how did I know she was in the hall? And I did not speak very loudly. She has ears like a fox! Would it not be lovely if someone offered for her and took her far, far away—to Land's End, for instance?"

"That is in Cornwall and it is not nearly far enough," Rosalie commented. "I would prefer to see her in Saint Helena with Napoleon."

"I would rather see her in Esfahan," Eustacia declared.

"Which is farther—Esfahan or Saint Helena?" Diana asked.

Both girls regarded her, wide-eyed. "Do you not know?" Rosalie demanded.

Diana laughed. "I know—but do you?"

"Esfahan, is it not?" Eustacia hazarded, and then glared at Rosalie, who laughed.

"No," she said. "Esfahan is in Persia and Saint Helena is off the coast of Africa. And now our dearest Diana will command you to study your geography. Is that not what you had in mind, Diana?"

"I ought to." Diana nodded. "And you should, Eustacia."

Eustacia rolled her eyes. "Well, I did know that it was far, far away, and that is where I should like to see Aurora or, better yet, in New South Wales, where they send the convicts."

"Or best of all, married to that man in blue satin. It would serve Aurora right if he offered for her and Rob accepted." Rosalie grinned.

"It really would," Eustacia agreed. "I heard someone say that if the Beau had been present to see him, he would have swooned."

Had they but known it, the gentleman under discussion was seated in his suite at Stephen's Hotel in Bond Street, pondering upon the vision of beauty he had seen the night before.

"Aurora . . . Aurora . . . Aurora . . ." he murmured ecstatically. Occupying his inner vision was an image of the lady, all white and gold with huge blue eyes, porcelain white skin, and masses of red-gold hair. She was very slim, yet well-proportioned, an exquisite figure, almost too perfect to be real, he thought.

"Aurora, goddess of the dawn! She is, indeed, well-named. And she does not, cannot have a daughter who is eighteen or even older." Sir Sabin Mallory winced, re-membering the sad disappointment he had suffered upon viewing Mrs. Flavia Forsythe by the cruel light of day.

She *was* beautiful, but the stagelights were far kinder to her than the sun's rays pouring through the window of the inn. By his calculations, the actress had to be thirty-five at the very least! As for that green-eyed chit, her daughter— far from being annoyed at her as he had been on the evening they had met in the green room, he really owed her a debt of gratitude for keeping him unwillingly at her side while the object of his brief passion departed from the theater. And . . . But he did not wish to dwell any further upon the Forsythes, mother and daughter, not when he had the incredibly beautiful image of Lady Aurora Gresham engraved upon his mind and heart! No one in this world had ever made so telling an impression upon him. Not only did she conform to his ideal of feminine beauty, but it was obvious that no manner of artifice had been employed.

The color on that lovely cheek owed nothing to the rouge pot, and the gold of her hair reminded him of Bassanio's praise for Portia in *The Merchant of Venice*. He repeated those lines to himself—those lines to which, if Shakespeare had seen Lady Aurora, he must have added even more encomiums.

Her sunny locks hang on her temples like a golden
    fleece,
Which makes her seat of Belmont, Colchos' stround.
And many Jasons come in quest of her.

How many Jasons?
Sir Sabin groaned, remembering the cotillions, waltzes, and country dances Lady Aurora had graced, and each with a different partner, himself being one of them. He groaned a second time, remembering that he had not only stumbled over his own feet twice, he had also stepped on her tiny foot, eliciting a slight gasp from her—but followed by a most bewitching smile and an assurance that he had not lamed her.

"If it had been Canada . . ." He sighed as he recalled the wild dances in certain forts, with half-breed maidens and himself comfortable in buckskin garments worn for hunting and trapping or, at a later date, in his uniform at Fort William. There were country dances at the fort, too, but none of them had been so elegant as those he had seen last night, and also there was something the matter with his attire!

Rob had given a slight start of surprise when he came in and his gaze had flickered. He had not immediately understood the meaning behind that glance until he had noticed that very few of the gentlemen present were garbed in what the little tailor in Fort William had described as "the very latest, my good sir." Rob had been in sober black and white, and many other men had been similarly clad. True, there had been several young men in bright satins, but their garments had been of a far different cut then his own—similar, in fact, to those he had seen upon the residents of this hotel when leaving of an evening.

Then, he had been quite unable to converse with Lady Aurora or anyone else for that matter. While they were waiting for the music to begin, she had casually mentioned someone called Lord Byron, who, despite his title, appeared to write poetry. Despite what she described as his wild ways, she appeared to prefer him above all other poets, saving only Walter Scott, with whose work he was also unacquainted. Though he was tolerably well-educated in the classics, mathematics, and the sciences and was acquainted with the works of Shakespeare, Milton, and John Donne, the last being a favorite of his father, there had been scant opportunity to keep abreast of the newer masters of literature. He had been equally ignorant of matters important to those who dwell in this city. He had heard bits of conversation regarding politics and the Prince Regent's mania for building, but these had held no meaning for him, either, since he was so newly arrived in this city and upon this island.

"Oh, God," Sir Sabin groaned, and buried his face in his hands, cursing his late uncle Sir Hubert Mallory anew. It was due to his profligate ways that he—with his brother, Richard, and their father, Mr. Clarence Mallory—had been forced to set sail for Canada seventeen years ago. They had been bound for Clarence Mallory's Canadian holdings, these deeded to him by his late father. Until the latter's death, Clarence had managed the family estate outside

Richmond, while his brother, Hubert, enjoyed himself in London in ways that had been near to wrecking his health.

Richard and Sabin had been very happy in those years, but their happiness had come to an end with the death of their grandfather and that of their mother, which had followed fast upon it. Then, Hubert, succeeding to the title, had come home and pronounced himself furious over Clarence's Canadian bequest. He had accused his brother of influencing a dying old man and he had ordered him to take his sons and leave. A seven-year-old Sabin had overheard some of that heated conversation.

"I'll not have you staying here. I do not care how well you have managed the estate. I expect that our father would have left that to you, also, had he not died beforehand. Since you've stolen the Canadian acreage from me, have it for your home. It is almost worth it not to see you here looking down your damned long nose at me. I intend to live as I choose, and may I never need to look upon your ugly face again!"

To live as his uncle had chosen was with one doxy after another and, finally, a late marriage contracted with the intent of keeping his hated brother from inheriting. The plan had gone awry. The bride and the son she had borne Sir Hubert died within a day of each other, and the baronet had returned to his profligate existence. Meanwhile, Clarence had tried to make something of his lands and, failing that, had sold them and turned to the fur trade, where he did prosper until slain by a drunken French trapper.

Richard and Sabin had inherited a goodly pile of gold, which they too had helped to accumulate before they joined the army amassing to fight the Americans. Sir Hubert, meanwhile, died of apoplexy just one month after Richard was felled in the Battle of New Orleans. At that time, Sabin Mallory had been a prisoner of war in Louisiana and half out of his mind with fever. It had been in what passed for a prison hospital that he had made friends with Captain Lord Marchant, also recovering from fever.

Three months later, cured and released, he had returned

to Fort William to find a letter from his third cousin Ralph Mallory, informing him of his inheritance. He had had little joy in that news, not with Dick dead. He missed him still and it was manifestly unfair that he should have died. Dick would not have had his problems. He had always had an innate elegance. He would have been at ease in any setting and, in fact, had often reproved Sabin for the half-wild life he had led among the trappers.

"You will be returning to England one day and will need to take your place in society," Dick had said.

"You will, Dick, not I," had been his invariable response.

"I shall want you with me," his brother had insisted. "And you cannot be sure which one of us will inherit."

"You are the next in line."

"Father was the next in line," Dick had responded meaningfully.

Had he had some inkling of his early demise? Sabin wondered.

"Did you, Dick?" he muttered to the tall, smiling young man in scarlet who yet dwelt in the back of his mind—with the father he had loved only a shade less than his brother. The loneliness that was never far from him claimed him once more. For the thousandth time, he wondered if he ought to have left London. He had not acted upon Ralph's letter immediately—he had not returned until the fall of 1815. And though he had been in England six months, he doubted that he would ever feel comfortable here. Yet, he must make the effort. He owed it to his father, who had loved Mallory Manor deeply and had never felt at home anywhere else. He also owed it to Dick, and soon he would take control of the estates. He had spent November, December, and January at the manor, but a fortnight ago he had left it in the capable hands of his cousin Ralph. He had had no particular plan when he had done that; he had wanted only to see London. Now, however, he did have a plan. He wanted to marry and bring his bride home to the lovely Palladian house where he had been born and where he wanted his children to be

born. He would name his first son Richard—if Aurora had
no objections.

He laughed a little at this particular fancy. Then, his
laughter died on his lips, for to think of her was to
experience a whole new series of sensations: to grow hot
and cold, to perspire or shiver. The "fever of love" so
often mentioned by poets was no longer a mystery to him.
He wanted to be with her. He wanted to bask in the glory
of her smile. He could now understand better the tales of
knights-errant that had thrilled him as a lad because of
their deeds of derring-do. The clash of steel on steel, the
snorting of horses, and the groans of felled ogres or other
villains had excited him then. However, the idea of a
captive maiden had left him unmoved. But all that had
changed now. He could almost wish that the beautiful
Aurora, goddess of the dawn, were in peril that he might
ride forth with her garter fastened to his lance . . . He
rather thought it was a garter, but perhaps it was a scarf.
Either must have sufficed, but alas, the days of chivalry
were at an end and all he could do was send her flowers or
a rich jewel? No, that would not be permissible, but he
would send flowers and then, tomorrow, he would call
upon Rob or perhaps meet him at his club and quiz him
about his sister. He sighed deeply as he thought of the
hours that must intervene before he could put that plan into
effect.

"*He* was here again today," Rosalie said to Diana,
"and *more* flowers arrived for Aurora. Can you imagine?"

Diana nodded. By now she had learned the identity of
Lady Aurora's impassioned suitor, and she could also
understand why Sir Sabin (Sir as opposed to plain Mister)
Mallory was so taken with the girl. Lady Aurora's hair
might be a shade redder, but by and large she had the
coloring of her mother, though, in her estimation, she did
not have one-tenth Flavia Forsythe's charm and beauty.
No, that was not entirely true. She did have beauty—there
was no denying that. However, Lady Aurora was lacking
in charm, though Diana was also fair enough to admit that

she might have charms aplenty for those who did not know her. It was well, however, that Sir Sabin Mallory could not hear her comments concerning him and the expensive floral offerings that arrived each day and that she parceled out to her various friends and even to her abigail.

Lady Aurora did admit that he was handsome, a conclusion with which her sisters and Diana also concurred. She herself felt very sorry for him, but she thought, she would feel even sorrier were he to conquer the heart of Lady Aurora, provided, of course, that she possessed a heart that was used for purposes other than the merely physical. Concurrent with that feeling was the ardent wish that he would soon be discouraged by Lady Aurora's continued coldness.

Selfishly speaking, it would be disastrous were they to meet and he to reveal her background to Lord Marchant. Though the earl seemed to like her well enough and his mother appeared to be of that same opinion, neither would be happy to learn that the young woman who was instructing Rosalie and Eustacia had theatrical connections. However, since she was usually in the back parlor, she could reassure herself with the fact that such a meeting would not take place. Still, she must needs to continue avoiding the routs and balls that were given at Marchant House, something that would undoubtedly delight Lady Aurora. Diana grimaced. She was such an unpleasant girl, she thought—truly the bad apple on this particular family tree.

"Diana . . . Diana, dear," Eustacia said.

Diana looked up startled. "Yes?"

"Where are you?" Rosalie asked.

Diana blushed. "I am sorry, I was thinking."

"About your lover?" Eustacia probed with a giggle.

Diana laughed. "I do not have a lover."

"And if she did, it would be no concern of yours, Eussie," Rosalie reproved. She turned wide eyes on Diana. "Though you should, you know."

"You must tell that to your sister Aurora and perhaps

she will be kind enough to provide me with one of her cast-offs,'' Diana said sarcastically.

"I am sure she would love to give you Sir Sabin Mallory." Rosalie giggled.

"No, she would not," Eustacia said sagely. "Aurora was furious when Lord Ryland started pursuing Olivia Drake last year after she gave him that cruel set-down."

"That's right." Rosalie nodded. "And Aurora did not give a fig for Lord Ryland."

"She is a dog in the manager," Eustacia said.

"I would call her a cat," Rosalie commented.

"A bat," Eustacia countered with a giggle.

"Girls—we are talking a great deal of nonsense," Diana reproved. "Now, Eustacia, perhaps you can turn your mind to something practical and give me the pluperfect tense of the verb '*être*.' "

Finally it was Tuesday, her full day, and Diana had resolved to visit Montague House again. It was the home of the British Museum and she dearly loved the collection of Egyptian antiquities and the artifacts from Greece and Rome. Betsy, unfortunately, was not well and could not accompany her, but the museum was not far away and she could take a hackney in both directions. There were always plenty she could hire on this street.

Dressed in a new green coat and a close-fitting bonnet, she hurried down the stairs and, coming out of the front door, had gone down the three steps to the brick walk when she heard the front door open agan and close behind her. She cast a glance over her shoulder and tensed as she saw the all-too-familiar visage of Sir Sabin Mallory. Any hope that he had not recognized her faded in seconds as he caught up with her, saying as he reached her side, "Miss Forsythe."

Coming to a stop, Diana flushed and said, "Good morning, sir."

"But what are you doing here?" he demanded amazedly. "Are—are you perchance a friend of Lady Aurora's?"

A lie trembled on her lips but she swallowed it. Anything but the truth would only lead to impossible complications. "No." She cast a nervous glance over her shoulder, glad now that Betsy had not accompanied her and hoping devoutly that the butler, who must have opened the door for Sir Sabin, had not seen him greet her. "Please," she added urgently, "will you follow me to the corner? I must speak to you, but not here, I beg you."

He looked surprised, as well he might, but after an infinitesimal pause he said, "Very well, Miss Forsythe, I will join you at the corner."

"I thank you," she murmured, and hastily let herself out of the wrought-iron gate that fronted the walk. In another few minutes, she had reached the corner, which was fortunately a good distance from the house. Coming to a stop, she looked back and found Sir Sabin a few paces behind her.

Reaching her side, he said, "I am indeed pleased to see that you have recovered the use of your ankle."

She was surprised and also pleased by that observation, especially in view of all the questions he must be longing to put to her. "I do not expect that I would have recovered so quickly had you not carried me all the way to the inn, Sir Sabin," she responded, and was immediately annoyed with herself. She never should have addressed him as *Sir* Sabin. Her use of his title would probably confuse him even more.

Fortunately, it seemed he was sufficiently surprised by their unexpected encounter not to notice her form of address. He said merely, "I was glad to have been of help, but please, will you not shed some light upon my ignorance? Why are you here? Are you a friend of Lady Aurora Gresham?"

He seemed to have forgotten that he had already asked that question, and the worshipful way in which he had pronounced her name brought a wry smile to Diana's lips, which she managed to suppress quickly. "I am acquainted with Lady Aurora, but I am not her friend. I am employed as a pedagogue—or governess, I suppose you would term it—for her two younger sisters?''

"I see," he said. "Have you held this position long?''

"Over a year." She flushed. "I was at school with them in Bath and afterward, their mother, learning that I planned to become a teacher, offered me this position. So you see, I—I am not an actress.''

"But I think you are," he responded with a slight smile. "At least you were able to convince me of that.''

"My mother would never agree with you," she said lightly. "But," she continued hastily, "I beg that you, as a friend of the family, will not tell them that I—or rather, my mother is an actress. It would not set well with them, I can assure you.''

He regarded her gravely. "You may trust me, Miss Forsythe. I would never betray you.''

"I do thank you," she said feelingly. "I would not blame you if you did, especially in view of my prevarications. I do hope you will forgive me for—for teasing you.''

"Of course I do," he assured her. He added wistfully, "I expect you must see Lady Aurora quite often.''

"Every day," Diana responded. "I take my meals, most of them, with the family. My position in the household is a bit ambiguous in that I was a friend of Rosalie and Eustacia at Miss Prentiss's academy and it was at their urging that Lord Marchant and his mother decided to hire me. Originally, I had intended to remain at school as a student teacher.''

"I see," he said. "I do not imagine that Lady Aurora has ever mentioned me?''

There was a wistful expression in his eyes that touched Diana's heart and at the same time made her very angry with Lady Aurora. She had a strong desire to tell him just what Lady Aurora had said about him, and also how she had treated all his bouquets—but that would be too cruel. That he was in love with her was only too obvious. She said kindly, "She has mentioned you," and stifled a sigh as she saw the hope in his eyes.

"Has—has she said much?" he asked eagerly.

"Not much, at least not in my hearing," she said carefully. "She does have several suitors, you know."

"I do know," he groaned. "How could she not? And all of them, I am positive, are far more up to snuff than myself. It would not take much for them to be, I fear."

Diana regarded him with no little surprise. She had not expected him to be so sensitive to his failings. "Well," she temporized, "she does feel that you are a bit lacking in town polish."

His face clouded. "More than a bit, I am sure," he sighed. "Miss Forsythe, I am not a dunce. I have eyes, you know, and I can see that I am considered a complete outsider, not to say country bumpkin, and I am sure that is how I must appear to her."

Diana heard worship in his tone and read it in his eyes as well. She felt very sorry for him. "It is not difficult to acquire town polish, you know," she said comfortingly.

"I do not know," he cried. "It is well-nigh impossible for me, I'm thinking. I have lived the life of a veritable savage in Canada, among the fur trappers and later as a soldier, and neither occupation has prepared me for society."

"But you have the will to learn, I think," she said.

"Oh, I do, but sure it will take years."

"It should not. Not for you," she insisted.

"Miss Forsythe," he said eagerly, "I should like—I mean, where are you bound at this particular moment? Do they expect you back at any given time?"

She shook her head. "This is my free day, sir, and I am going to Montague House."

"Is that the home of a friend?"

"No, it is a museum. It is where the Elgin Marbles are kept and also many Egyptian antiquities."

"The Elgin marbles?"

"They were brought from Greece, sir, by Lord Elgin and are taken, in part, from the Acropolis."

"You see how ignorant I am?" he sighed. "Might I accompany you there? I must talk to you."

"I do not believe we should converse there. We are like to meet one or another of the family. It would not be seemly."

"I do understand. Where might we converse? I would be most grateful if you could give me your candid opinion on what I must do to improve myself in the eyes of society."

Meeting his pleading gaze, Diana felt herself quite unable to give him the refusal she ought to have done, considering her present circumstances. After all, she reasoned, she did owe him a debt of gratitude for having carried her back to the inn on that day she had hurt her ankle. In her mind, she ran over a list of places where they would not be likely to encounter any members of Lady Aurora's rather wide circle of friends and acquaintances. "I think we might go to the museum, after all," she said finally. "We will not linger on the upper floors but rather seek the basement, where the scientific specimens are kept. I cannot think we would be disturbed there. It is not nearly so fashionable as the marbles. However we must contrive to go there one at a time, and I will let you know if it is safe to converse."

There was a gleam of amusement in his eyes. "I think, Miss Forsythe, that if you were not a pedagogue, you would make an excellent spy."

"I must be careful," she said defensively.

"I quite understand. May I at least escort you to the museum?"

"I had planned to go by hackney and perhaps—"

"Of course." Before she could protest, he had stepped into the street and hailed one. "I must let you give the direction," he said as he helped her inside.

"I will," she said, and obliged. Her heart was close to her throat but a look out of the window convinced her that there were no familiar faces on the street and, consequently, no one to report her to her employers. And, she reminded herself, she would not be making a practice of this—she would give him as much information as she considered tactful and there would be an end to it.

4

Montague House, a mansion built in the seventeenth century, had been the home of the British Museum since 1759, but as Diana had often observed, there was a distressing lack of order in the exhibits. While the first room, just off the entrance hall, did contain mainly Egyptian and Etruscan artifacts, there were two mummies acquired in Saqqara, Egypt, which with their caskets were to be discovered among Mexican curiosities in Room Three, which also contained a cabinet displaying the miniatures of such distinguished people as Marie Antoinette and Napoleon. Diana passed through these swiftly and also through the room containing artifacts brought back from his travels to the South Seas by that intrepid and ill-fated explorer Captain Cook.

Among these were some particularly horrendous idols that to Diana's mind were even uglier than the twenty-three-foot crocodile that stretched along the balustrade of the stairs leading to the basement, an area that did not boast as many candles as those on the higher floor and was necessarily without any sunshine. However, the resulting dimness did not disturb her as much as a clearer view of the serpents, fish, and assorted reptiles floating in glass jars and tanks might have done.

As she had anticipated, this room was free of visitors. Standing in the semidarkness opposite a jar containing a late fish with spiny appendages that rendered it highly unattractive, Diana looked nervously toward the entrance. Her nervousness increased as she heard footsteps descending the stairs. Her common sense informed her that these sounds were probably being made by Sir Sabin Mallory, but belatedly she had remembered that some governesses might be wont to bring their charges here, or possibly, a father or an uncle, looking for some instructive way to entertain a child, might perform that same service and recognize her.

That would indeed be disastrous, for they could only regard her presence here as clandestine—or would, when Sir Sabin joined her. She rolled her eyes in the direction of heaven and whispered a prayer that the visitor would be Sir Sabin. Despite her pity for him, she must not meet him again, but she reassured herself hastily, that would not be necessary. In fact, if the truth were to be told, there was no real need for this present meeting; she ought not to have consented, especially in view of her opinions about Lady Aurora. She threw another glance at the entranceway. Sir Sabin, if it were he upon the stairs, was taking his time in joining her. It would be better were she to leave, but at that moment he entered.

"A most amazing saurian on the balustrade," he remarked as he joined her. "I am glad I did not come face to face with him in real life. And what have we here?" He gazed at another fish-inhabited jar. "Really, the ocean has a most curious population, but I expect if these could speak, they might have similar comments about us."

Diana said hurriedly, "No doubt, but I beg you will not examine them further, sir. Our time is necessarily limited."

"Indeed, I know that to be true," he said apologetically. "I must beg your pardon for the digression." He hesitated and then said, "I—I sought your opinion on myself, mainly, but—" He swallowed and added in a low unhappy tone of voice, "Dare I even aspire to the hand of the Lady Aurora?"

So might a humble Greek shepherd have spoken of Artemis, goddess of the moon, Diana thought and smothered a giggle as she contemplated the several answers she could give him and those the lady's sisters would have provided. However, she said merely, "I am sure that you could, were you to be more like the gentlemen she knows, sartorially speaking, mainly."

"I have recently heard the name of Beau Brummell. Rob, er, Lord Marchant mentioned him to me. I was asking about a tailor and he told me that someone named Weston designed the garments worn by the Beau."

"I would think it was the other way around," Diana mused. "Beau Brummell is an arbiter of fashion, the king of dandies, a veritable god of the wardrobe. He does patronize Weston in Old Bond Street. However, it is the Beau made Weston, not the other way around. His dictum is simplicity, cleanliness, and neatness. It was he who first wore black and white for evening and who first insisted that the cravat be starched. He also brought the stockingnette trousers into fashion. He's known to spend five hours a morning at his toilet and he takes three baths a day—one in cologne, it is said." She paused as she saw that Sir Sabin was regarding her with an amazement tinged with horror. "Is there something that does not please you?" she asked.

"Miss Forsythe, I am all admiration for your knowledge, but sure I am not to scent myself like some popinjay and to—"

"No, of course not," she interposed swiftly. "I was only telling you about the Beau, who, according to Mr. Hornby, who was my informant in these matters, carries everything to extremes. I do not say you must emulate him, Sir Sabin, but a good tailor *is* a necessity. I suggest that you patronize a tailor such as Weston. It will not be easy to get an appointment and you might find him very dear, but if you are determined to become elegant, clothes are important. Fortunately, you are handsome and well, uh, formed, and—"

"You are very kind," he cut in. "But—"

"I am not being kind, Sir Sabin. I am merely telling you what I see. Your garments, as you have already said, are the antithesis of elegant. Now, as to boots, I have been told that Hoby is the best maker. His shop is at the corner

of Piccadilly and St. James's Street, and Luce is where
you buy your hats. I do suggest that you hire a valet. As it
happens, I know of one who is seeking a position, his
master having been killed in a duel. Betsy, the abigail I
share with Rosalie, was talking about him the other day.
He will be able to advise you much better than myself.
Failing that, I know of an actor who might be even more
informative. Indeed, I have mentioned him already. His
name is Silas Hornby, and I have reason to believe he
comes from a good family.'' She paused and then said
thoughtfully, ''Actually, it would be far better to have him
instruct you in dress, for sure Weston, Hoby, and the rest
are in business and it is their business to sell as much as
possible.''

''I am sure you are right.'' He gave her a grateful look.
''And I will be happy to wait upon Mr. Hornby, but
clothes, Miss Forsythe, though they are certainly important, are not my only problem. Oh, I do wish Dick had
lived,'' he sighed.

''Dick?'' she questioned.

''My brother. He was at ease in any situation. He did
not stand silent as a dunce in a crowd, I can tell you. He
was a downy bird, was Dick.'' Another long sigh escaped
him. ''Lady Aurora would have fallen in love with him at
first sight. I never thought . . . But there it is,'' he loosed
another sigh. ''I pray you'll forgive me for digressing,
Miss Forsythe.''

''I am sorry about your brother,'' she said gently. ''The
war?''

''Yes. But no matter, I do apologize for wasting your
time. This is your day away and you should not need to
expend it on my concerns.''

''I am glad to be of help, Sir Sabin. I do not know what
I would have done without your help that day last January.''

He smiled. ''You would have found a way, Miss Forsythe. I consider you a young lady of infinite resource.''
His dark gaze dwelt on her face for an instant and then he

continued. "But enough! What else must I know? Rather, what, for instance, is a betting book?"

"It is used at clubs like White's, Watier's, Brooks, Boodles, and other hells to enter bets. Some are monstrously silly—such as how fast can a turkey cross a road or whether Lady Such-and-such will give birth to twins or . . . I heard of one gentleman who bet that his mother would die at a certain hour."

He looked shocked. "You'll never tell me that!"

"But I do," she assured him. "And I am happy to tell you that he lost a tidy sum, for she lingered another hour just to spite him."

"I hope he lost a fortune!"

"I believe he is yet in debtor's prison."

"It serves him right." He leaned forward, frowning now. "Miss Forsythe, am I expected to attend bearbaitings and dogfights." His face darkened. "I can tell you that while I do enjoy a mill, I cannot bear to see dumb beasts wantonly tortured in the name of sport. I have hunted in my day and trapped animals for their pelts, but to hurt them unnecessarily . . ."

"You need not," she said quickly. "It is not required of a gentleman, nor does it make him more manly to attend a bull or bearbaiting. It is a pursuit that one might say with Hamlet, 'is more honored in the breach than the observance.' "

His relief was visible. "I am glad of that." He smiled. "I am fond of *Hamlet*, fond of Shakespeare, a wonderful companion in the wilds, Miss Forsythe. If I had such speech extempore, I would feel at home in any society."

She laughed. "But not in present-day London, where sentiments are hardly so lofty and where the cut of a jacket or the turn of a cuff will gain you entrance to polite circles more easily than the most admirably framed sentence."

"In other words, Miss Forsythe, clothes make the man."

"As I have tried to point out, they are a most necessary adjunct. Then, you might shoot at Manton's and box at

Gentleman Jackson's Parlor, where, I am told, one learns the art of self-defense."

He grinned. "That is one art that I have mastered. By the way, Miss Forsythe, what is a Charley? I heard someone at my hotel say that one of them had furnished rare sport."

"A Charley is a nightwatchman, and some of our young bucks think it highly pleasurable to knock down their boxes. It will gain you entrance to some circles, but they are not necessarily polite."

He said disgustedly, "I thought the day of the Mohawk was dead."

"These are not Mohawks. They do not maim or kill their victims—they just pummel them a bit."

"I begin to think London is not unlike Fort William . . . but I fear we digress. I have heard mention of Almack's. Rob said it was very difficult to get a voucher for their dances. He gave me to understand that Lady Aurora is often there."

"She is. It is considered a rare privilege, the *ne plus ultra* of the polite world. Mama says that even the air is different at Almack's. Countesses, duchesses, marchionesses, throng its halls and there are, of course, earls, dukes, and marquesses to accompany them—also baronets. However, it is necessary to pass the scrutiny of its four patronesses. They are Lady Jersey, Mrs. Drummond Burrell, Lady Cowper, and the Countess Lieven. They have subscription dances on Wednesday evenings and—"

"Say no more," he begged. "I can already hear the doors being slammed against me."

"Not necessarily. Lord Marchant might be able to obtain a voucher for you."

"I would not dream of asking him until . . ." he sighed. "Oh, Miss Forsythe, I feel as if I am John Cabot searching for the Northwest Passage to Asia."

She laughed. "Unlike the explorer, I think you stand a better chance of finding your passage, Sir Sabin."

He shook his head. "I do feel lost here, among these

people who talk of places I have never seen and activities . . . It seems to grow more complicated with each passing minute."

"You must meet Mr. Hornby. He is in town—on leave from the company, I understand. I will seek him out and see that you meet him next week on this same day, if that is agreeable to you."

"It is entirely agreeable and I will be in your debt forever." He paused and then added, "Shall we use this same place again?"

Diana sent a look around the room. It had remained undisturbed, she realized, since their arrival. "Yes, I think that would be agreeable. I will meet you here and bring Mr. Hornby with me."

"No," he said firmly. "I shall escort you here. You must not think of coming by yourself."

"But I often have," she said.

"You are uncommon brave, Miss Forsythe, not to say foolhardy. I might be a greenhorn in many ways, but I know better than to put you at unnecessary risk." Almost sternly, he added, "You are, in your own way, very beautiful."

"You are kind to say so, sir."

"I am not being kind. I am merely stating a fact. Now, were you minded to remain in the museum or had you another destination in view?"

"I had thought to walk in the park, sir."

"Let us choose a distant park and I will accompany you."

"But that is unnecessary, sir," she began, but seeing the set look of his mouth, she recognized a chivalry that most of the young men of the *ton* did not extend to governesses and their ilk. That such women were thought not to merit the protection afforded to their more sheltered sisters was another lesson he had yet to learn. She said, "Perhaps you might care to view those sights of London where we are not likely to be recognized. I am talking about the Tower or the Temple."

"The Tower . . ." he began eagerly, and then added hastily, "it is kind of you, but if you would prefer a park . . ."

"Either would suffice, and there's much that is parklike about the Tower and its grounds."

"Then"—he smiled—"let us leave our finny friends at once."

"Very well." She smiled back at him. "Though I warn you it is not in the least educational."

"I must differ from you there. It will be most educational for one who left his native country at the age of seven and to whom, in those tender years, London remained as distant as, say, Nova Scotia to you."

Diana gazed at him wide-eyed. "You do not know this city at all?"

"I am beginning to know a little of it, but as a child, I did not. We may have passed through it on our way to our port of call, but I have no recollection of that. So, you see, I am very much in need of your guidance."

"I shall give you as much as I am able," she said impulsively, "but again, Mr. Hornby must provide the broader view."

He gave her a quizzical look. "I begin to believe that your Mr. Hornby must be a virtual paragon."

"Actually," she said thoughtfully, "he might be, and certainly he is an enigma. All the company's agreed on that. You see it is not difficult to tell the true from the false when it comes to background—that is, if you have a nose for it, and my mother has, right enough. But with Mr. Hornby, she counts herself totally puzzled. You will soon meet him and see for yourself."

"I am quite looking forward to it," he responded. "But come, again we speak when we ought to be on our way."

"Oh, yes," she said quickly, thinking that it was all too easy to fall into conversation with him. "We must go."

Again he hailed a hackney, and a short time later they were at the great drawbridge to the Tower. They passed along a walk bristling with cannon, which, Diana was able to tell her companion, numbered seventy-three and were fired on such occasions as the king's birthday or a great victory. "There was such a blast after Trafalgar and again after Vitoria," she explained.

"But none for *us*," he remarked ruefully.

"Where did you fight?"

"The American conflict," he said.

"Oh," she had a commiserating look for him. "I have been given to understand that the American soldiers fight in ways that are totally foreign to our troops."

"Of a truth, they do. They fired down upon us from trees and they move through the forests like savages. We were outguessed and outmaneuvered time and time again, as you probably know."

"It does not seem as though they fought fairly."

"By their standards, they were fair enough," he assured her. "And we burned Washington City. Think how we should feel if they had come over here and set fire to London?"

Her eyes widened. "We should have been very angry."

"Ergo, sauce for the goose." He smiled and looked up at the square brick building confronting him. "This is . . ."

"The White Tower," she identified.

"I count more than *one* tower. And the facade is not quite even."

"It is very old."

"I know. It was built in 1056, was it not?"

"It was."

"Then, I have a passing grade?"

"If all your other answers are equally satisfactory."

"I am depending on you—or rather your, er, pedagogues—to make them so."

"You are teasing me," she chided. "But 'pedagogue' does sound more dignified than 'governess.' "

"More accurate, too, I am sure." He favored her with a slight bow. "What does the White Tower contain?"

"Arms, sir. All manner of them, including enough for

ten thousand seamen, and there are all manner of warlike implements . . . instruments of death.'' She shuddered slightly. ''They are all monstrously unpleasant-looking, but if you would like to see them . . .''

''I would not,'' he said quickly. ''I have had enough of that.''

''I am sorry,'' she spoke as quickly. ''I was forgetting—''

''You must not be sorry,'' he interrupted. ''It was a natural question and a natural place for them to be found—in these buildings with their bloody history, their tortures, and murders.'' He was walking as he spoke and he stopped suddenly. ''But what is this Tower?''

''It is called the Lion Tower and houses the Royal Menagerie.''

''Have you seen it?''

''No. On the day I was here, there were some rowdy young men . . .'' She paused, biting her lip. ''I mean . . .''

He nodded. ''You mean, Miss Forsythe, that they failed to recognize the fact that you were a sober pedagogue and instead had it in mind that you were a beautiful girl of eighteen and fair game for such as themselves. I hope you did not suffer from the experience.''

''No. I was able to elude them,'' she said in a small voice. ''There was a guard helped me.''

''But learned nothing from it, if today is any criterion.''

''I did have Betsy with me, the abigail I share with my pupils.''

''Two babes in the woods rather than one,'' he said caustically. ''But enough!'' He smiled at her. ''If you've not visited the menagerie, shall we?''

''I should like to see it,'' she admitted.

''And so should I, even though I fear it will not add to my enlightenment in the slightest.''

''You cannot be sure,'' she said.

''You have a dimple when you smile,'' he observed, and flushed slightly. ''But pardon me, I fear I grow too familiar.''

Two dimples were in evidence as Diana looked up at

him. "You do, sir, but it is forgiven." She quickly smoothed out her smile. "We enter through this gate."

The price of admission proved to be a shilling, and inside they found a number of cages, housing several lions, tigers, and wolves. There were also raccoons and a leopard. A short, husky man grinned at them as they entered. "Would ye like me to show ye around?" he demanded.

"That would be most helpful," Sir Sabin said cordially. "You'd be a keeper, I trust?"

"I am that." The man nodded.

"Gracious," Diana said. "That leopard looks fierce, and the lion also."

"They're not." Their guide moved to a tiger cage. "This 'ere's 'Arry'n 'e's as sweet as a kitten. Been wi' us twenty-three years, 'e 'as." He moved to a cage containing a lion and lioness, lying at their ease on the gravel. "An' this 'ere's Young 'Ector'n Miss Jenny, 'is wife. They was presented to the king on March sixth, 1801. Lord Broome 'ad 'em brought from Persia. They 'ad a daughter an' she be over there." He pointed to another lion. " 'Er name's Miss Fanny 'Owe, 'n them two leopards down there? They're both females. Miss Maria 'n Miss Nancy's wot they're called. They come from the Coast of Malabar . . . an' over 'ere be Dunco. Lord Anson presented 'im to 'is Majesty. You ever see a better-tempered lion?"

Receiving an interrogative glance from their guide, Diana said, "I cannot tell."

"Well, I can tell you." The keeper nodded. "This 'ere animal's got a better disposition 'n my wife. 'Twasn't more'n couple years back that 'is cage needed fixin' an' so they sent for a carpenter, bleedin' coward 'e was, 'fraid to go in the cage until I said as 'ow I'd keep old Dunco entertained at the back while 'e worked on the front o' the cage. Well, 'e were shakin' in every limb, but 'e obliged'n meanwhile I sat back there wi' old Dunco'n 'e was gettin' sleepy an' so were I . . . an' so we took a snooze'n the next thing I 'ear's that carpenter squallin' away'n announcin' to all'n sundry that I'm *dead*. I tell you, it woke us both up, me'n Dunco'n the carpenter, 'e brings a guard in 'ere'n Dunco yawns'n puts 'is paw on my chest'n the carpenter yells out that 'e's about to tear me 'eart outa my body. 'Bout scared old Dunco to death, 'e did. So I reaches out'n shakes 'ands wi' Dunco'n 'e yawns an' goes back to sleep'n I takes that poor fool o' a carpenter out'n 'e ain't been back since.''

Sir Sabin laughed. ''That's a delightful story,'' he said when he could speak again. He tipped the keeper, who touched his forelock.

''Mighty obliged to you, sir.''

Coming out of the menagerie a few minutes later, Sir Sabin had sobered. ''Poor beasts,'' he said to Diana. ''I suppose it would take the heart out of anyone to be pent up so long in those small cages.''

''I expect it would,'' she agreed, liking him for his sympathy.

''In fact,'' he mused, ''I'd not be surprised if it was like an unhappy marriage.''

''An unhappy marriage?'' she questioned, giving him a startled glance.

He was not looking at her. He was staring into space. ''Where one might lose one's heart out of disappointment and inertia and in the end not care what happened.''

Her surprise increased. ''I expect that could happen,'' she said meaningfully. ''And that is why one must choose one's partner in life with particular care.''

''Yes, and that is why I am in favor of a love match, Miss Forsythe. A man, also a woman, ought to be able to choose their bride or groom, rather than having the decision forced upon them by a parent or near relation, do you not agree?''

''I do,'' she said, wondering what had prompted his comment. Unable to down her curiosity, she added, ''Have you known someone who suffered the consequences of such a decision?''

''I have. My brother married at my father's command.

It was shortly before his death, again I speak of my father. I expect he thought it a good match. She was well-connected, the daughter of Lord Scargill, who is a power in the Hudson Bay Company. Dick was in love with someone else. My father did not believe her worthy to bear our name, and Dick, being an obedient son, finally acceded to his wishes and wed Louise. He was little more than twenty; she was five years older. From the first it was a misery.'' He sighed. ''But I must weary you with this tale.''

''You do not,'' she hastened to assure him. ''Is your brother's wife still living?''

He grimaced. ''She is that, and wed again. She was very angry that she had no son to inherit the title.''

''It was a mercy that she did not,'' Diana cried impulsively.

''You are very kind, very understanding, Miss Forsythe.''

''I am not being kind, sir. I am being honest. From the little I have seen of you, I am quite sure that you deserve your inheritance.''

''I thank you, Miss Forsythe, but you might not have thought so had you met Dick. Still, enough of that. Shall we visit the chapel?''

She hesitated and then said decisively, ''I would rather not. I find it depressing when I think of the bodies that lie beneath its floor. Lady Jane Grey, the nine-day queen, for one. Can you believe that she did not live to see her seventeenth year, poor child?''

''Those were hard cruel times,'' he said soberly. ''Shall we agree that we have seen enough of the Tower, then?''

''You have seen very little of it, sir. You must not let my sentiments discourage you.''

He gave her a long look. ''I have similar sentiments, Miss Forsythe. I find that, after all, I have little desire to remain in an edifice dedicated to confinement and cruelty.''

''Oh!'' Diana clasped her hands. ''I do hope you will not change too much, sir.'' She blushed, as she met his wondering glance. ''I mean . . .''

"What do you mean?" he pursued.

"I . . . Well, it is difficult to avoid cruelty in one form or another if you are determined to become fashionable. And no doubt you will laugh at me now when I tell you that it is *de rigueur* to excel at blood sports. The most popular of these is, of course, hunting in some wooded country estate where the beaters go before you and frighten the sitting birds so they fly up to be shot. But equally exciting is riding to hounds and chasing foxes so that they may be mangled by the dogs. Oh, I know that foxes have 'blood' sports of their own. They kill chickens, but only because they are hungry; they do not do it for sport, and if they must be taken, let it be with a single shot, not being 'happily' pursued by hunters and hounds in full cry." Tears stood in her eyes. "When I was little, we lived briefly in the country and someone gave me a fox cub. It escaped me and . . . Oh, dear, I am being foolish. It was all a very long time ago and I did not mean to wax so passionate upon—"

"I beg you will not apologize," he interrupted. "I have trapped animals most of my life and have yet to conceive a liking for the pursuit. It was how we earned our livelihood in Canada, the three of us. I am glad it is over now, Miss Forsythe, believe me."

"I do," she said. Impulsively she continued, "Again I beg you not to change too much. I am sure that Lady Aurora would appreciate much about you as you are now."

"I will change only what needs changing, Miss Forsythe," he promised. "And now, where shall we go?"

"There is the Monument. It is an easy distance from here and of interest mainly to visitors from the country."

"The very place," he assented eagerly. "For sure, I am from at least two countries." His laughter rang out, and two or three people turned to look at him. Seeing a pair of elderly ladies smiling at them indulgently, Diana guessed that they had misread the situation and saw before them a pair of lovers. She smoothed away a derisive smile of her own, wondering what they would think, were they to be told that here was an overage pupil with his governess. It was a very strange role for her to play.

"You've grown thoughtful, Miss Forsythe," Sir Sabin commented. "May I offer a penny for them?"

"A farthing would be too much," she returned lightly. "On to the Monument, then?"

"At once," he assented. "And one day I should like to see Whitehall and the Houses of Parliament."

"You will have to depend on Mr. Hornby for that," she said quickly.

He looked disappointed. "You may not go?"

"Let us say that I should not go. There are acquaintances of Lady Aurora's family who are numbered among the members of Parliament. I must be circumspect, and so must you, sir."

"Of course," he agreed hastily. "And again, let me say how very grateful I am for your help."

"No more grateful than I on that cold day in January last, when you were kind enough to carry me all the way back to the inn," Diana said softly. "And I, at least, do not need to carry you, sir."

"But in a sense, that is exactly what you are doing," he replied earnestly. "You are helping a veritable numbskull to learn the ways of society."

"It is a far lighter burden then myself."

"I disagree, but before we fall into an argument, let us go." He offered his arm.

"You do look weary, Diana, you must have done a great deal of walking yesterday," Rosalie commented as she joined her in the back parlor.

A memory of the Tower flashed in and out of Diana's mind.

"I did, and it was very instructive, too."

"Instructive, how?" Eustacia demanded.

"I visited historical sites, the Monument and the Tower of London."

"I thought you'd seen them before," Rosalie said.

"I have, but one cannot see them too often. There is always something new." Diana was heartily glad that neither of her pupils could see into her mind and witness the young man pictured there as he looked at the old stones with such interest, his comments making them new again.

"You are blushing," Rosalie commented.

"Am I?" Diana managed to look surprised. "I cannot think why."

"Maybe," Rosalie murmured, "You had an adventure yesterday."

"And maybe," Diana commented tartly, "you have been reading effusions from the Minerva Press again! We—or rather, I am here to instruct you, not to indulge in silly conversations." She was uncomfortably aware of long looks from the sisters and she was also aware that Sir Sabin Mallory was still occupying far too large a portion of her thoughts. She blamed that not so much on the day they had spent together, as on the fact that she had dreamed about him last night. She could not remember the dream in its entirety, save that it had been exceptionally silly. It was even more silly to look forward to the following Tuesday and to wish that the intervening days would speed by on Mercury's winged feet.

"You are a convenience only," Diana told herself sternly. "You must remember that and not anything else."

"Do you not think my accent is improving, Diana?" Eustacia asked.

"Very much so," Diana said hastily, not having heard a word of her recitation. "Now, let us read from Madame de Sévigné, if you please." She fixed her attention on her pupils and was more than a little confused at the amount of effort it cost her to do so.

5

"My dear Diana," Silas Hornby had written in his fine copperplate hand.

Your letter was forwarded to my current habitation, and though I would, of course, have been delighted to undertake such instruction as I am capable of providing your pupil, I am currently in the midst of an engagement which, at this present time, precludes my presence in London. Meanwhile, I recommend Mr. Abel Bryans, whom you know. You will find him expert in guiding your pupil through the hells of the town and explaining to him the difference between sharps and flats, the which, as you no doubt know, have nothing to do with the art of music. Mr. Bryans understands deep play and the shoals awaiting the unwary. He is admirably equipped to steer Sir Sabin "straight," as it were.

You will find him awaiting your response at the Old Friar's Inn in Chelsea.

Again, I thank you for your flattering recommendation and hope to be at your service before much time has passed.

I remain, yours etc.
Silas Hornby

"I, of course, will be unable to accompany you to those places," Diana explained as Sir Sabin finished reading Mr. Hornby's letter. "I will, however, go with you to the Swan with Two Necks, which I designated as our meeting place. You will need to recognize Mr. Bryans and I cannot think that a mere description will suffice, especially in such a turmoil. The Swan is, as I think you might know, a coaching station."

"I do know," he told her. "I took the stagecoach from Richmond."

"So far by public conveyance?" she asked in some surprise.

His eyes glinted. "I have put up with such hardships before, Miss Forsythe. My inheritance is of recent vintage, as I think you know. And I decided to purchase such vehicles as I need here in London—my horses as well. I do know something about cattle and the name 'Tattersall's' was often mentioned by my father."

"Ah," Diana said in some relief, "I am happy you'll not need advice from me in that quarter. There I am quite at a loss and you could advise me were I ever to need such information—an unlikely prospect at best."

"I disagree. I would imagine that one day you might have them and a town residence as well."

She laughed. "A governess, sir?"

"I cannot believe that you will remain a, er, pedagogue forever," he said earnestly.

She smiled at him, amused and even a little touched by his deliberate use of her alternate title. "No, Sir Sabin, one day I will head my own school somewhere outside of Bath or even Brighton. It is my mother's ambition. She has money put aside to help me achieve it."

"And is it your ambition, too?"

She was conscious of surprise. It occurred to her that she had never really agreed with her mother concerning that particular destiny. She had merely accepted it as inevitable because, despite her longing to act, she had a suspicion she was not really gifted. Yet, to be a teacher all her life—was that the only alternative? A swift recapitulation of the opportunities available to a young woman in her circumstances, the daughter of an actress, a profession despised by all who were not connected with it, moved her to respond lightly, "I think it must be."

He gave her a speculative glance. "If that is what you want, I'll not argue with it, but if you have other ambitions—and I do not see why you should not—I hope that these rather than those of your mother will be gratified. It would be a shame, at least in my opinion, to see you toiling in some classroom."

Again she was startled by his concern and sympathy. However, she said merely, "The pupils will be toiling. I shall be walking up and down the aisles with a long ruler."

He shook his head. "Alas, Miss Forsythe, it is an image that eludes me utterly. I can rather see you with your own coach and four and with a crest on its panel."

Her laughter bubbled up. "Surely you are teasing me, sir."

She received no answering laugh. He said gravely, "No, Miss Forsythe, I am not. I have not been abroad in society much, as I hardly need reiterate, but I have not seen many young women who possess your intelligence, your beauty, and your air of distinction."

He had spoken so dispassionately that Diana could not call his remarks ardent. In those circumstances, there was absolutely no reason why she should feel her face grow warm and experience a pounding in her throat. Fortunately there was no quaver to the tone in which she responded, "You are very kind to tell me so. I do thank you." She added quickly, "I think we must be on our way to the inn."

If the Swan with Two Necks was an inconspicuous place to meet, it was also extremely congested, and while they were unlikely to encounter any members of the *ton*, it was difficult to forge a way through groups of people going in every conceivable direction and often in states of confusion, fear, and anger.

Children wailed for parents suddenly parted from them. Frantic mothers screamed for lost children. Delighted greetings were loudly exchanged. Boisterous apprentices from the shops, from the stables, and from a hundred other activities strode through the courtyard. Wheedling or whining beggars clutched at the jackets of passengers disembarking from newly arrived stagecoaches. Women selling seasonal fruits and flowers pushed their way through the crowds by means of sharp elbows. Piemen screamed their wares and sneak thieves and pickpockets artfully plied their trades. In addition, there was the usual complement of confused young girls fresh from the country seeking employment as abigails or shop assistants in London. These were often interrogated by mild-looking old ladies, who offered advice and were actually procuresses in search of innocents attractive enough to snatch. Diana knew this particular sisterhood by sight and wished she might warn off their prey, but in addition to being unsuccessful, she would have created a disturbance the likes of which her companion might not be able to handle.

"Stay close to me, Miss Forsythe," Sir Sabin yelled as he took her arm.

She nodded. An answer was unnecessary and, in this din, would have proved inaudible. Mr. Bryans was to be located by the ticket office, and it was in that direction that they endeavored to make their way. They were only a few feet from their destination when Diana, jostled by a couple evidently bound on reaching the office before herself, felt her arm seized in a hard, hurtful grip.

"Eh, but yer a pretty piece. All alone, I see."

Diana, looking up in angry surprise, was startled to find herself clutched and held by an immense man with a soiled kerchief wound around his thick neck and garments greasy with dirt. A most unpleasant odor assailed her nostrils, and even more unpleasant was the look in his narrowed eyes. She cast a glance over her shoulder but did not see Sir Sabin. Yet, he could not be far distant, at least so she hoped. She was not quite a stranger to such situations. She and her mother had taken many a stagecoach in their years on the road. Lifting her chin, she said freezingly, "Will you kindly release me, sir? I do not appreciate such familiarity, nor, I think will you discover, does my husband."

Rather than obeying her, her captor threw back his head

and laughed loudly. "An' wot would you say, lovey, if I was to tell ye I don't believe ye 'ave a 'usband?"

She was both released and spared the necessity of further conversation with the rogue as he went staggering back with a hand to his bleeding mouth. With a roar of anger, he rushed at his assailant, only to be floored again while a chorus of complaints arose from those whose limbs or stomachs had come in contact with his plummeting body. In another second, Sir Sabin had pulled Diana out of the melee. Rather breathlessly, he said, "A thousand pardons, Miss Forsythe. We were separated in the crowds. I pray you will excuse the familarity"—he put his arm around her—"but I cannot risk your being put in so untenable a position again."

Before she could respond, another man stepped forward. "Miss Forsythe," he exclaimed, "I 'ope you were not 'urt."

It took a second before Diana recognized Mr. Bryans. He was a blond, handsome young man, dressed a bit too ostentatiously for her taste and certainly no pattern for Sir Sabin to follow. Fortunately his lessons would have nothing to do with apparel. She was pleased to see him, since his arrival signified their immediate departure.

"Well-met, Mr. Bryans," she said cordially. "This is Sir Sabin Mallory."

"Delighted," bawled Mr. Bryans, his trained voice cutting through the noise about them. "Good Lord, you did gi' 'im a facer, right enough, er, the blow to the face was expertly delivered, sir." Mr. Bryans blushed. "You 'ave a punishin' right."

"It was developed during my days in the wilderness," Sir Sabin yelled back. "I expect you are Mr. Bryans?"

"I am that. Yer from the country, eh?"

"From Canada," Diana amplified, wishing that Mr. Hornby had not suggested Mr. Bryans, whose speech, she now recollected, reflected that which he must have learned during a childhood spent in the noisome purlieus of Covent Garden, from whence he had somehow made his way to the stage. However, she assured herself quickly, it was that same atmosphere that gave him his knowledge of the gambling fraternity. Still, she did wish Mr. Hornby were with them and wondered how long his engagement would last and why he had taken one outside the company. Once they were a comfortable distance away from the cacophonous sounds of the coaching inn, she put that question to Mr. Bryans and was surprised to see a knowledgeable and not altogether pleasant grin spread across his face.

"Bless you, Miss Forsythe, 'tisn't no h'engagement that's detainin' 'is 'ighness. 'E be in debtor's prison, 'im bein' temporarily h'embarrassed, uh, embarrassed," he corrected himself again.

The evident pleasure that he took in imparting this information both surprised and annoyed Diana, especially since Mr. Bryans was by way of being a protégé of the other actor. However, she guessed that in common with other members of the company, the young man resented Mr. Hornby's cultivated speech and elegance, attributes that obviously came naturally to him. She did not even acquit Mr. Gifford of this envy. She said coldly, "Where is he lodged, then?"

"Whitecross Street," Mr. Bryans said with a self-righteous complacency that irritated her even more.

"Oh, dear, poor Mr. Hornby," she murmured.

"But," her informant said hastily, "I beg you'll not divulge this h'information to yer . . . your Mama, Miss Forsythe. 'E wouldn't want 'er to know, nor 'im, neither. Mr. Gifford, I mean."

Diana gave him a side glance and surprised a smile that she had no difficulty interpreting. Contrary to what he had just averred, she was positive that Mr. Bryans wanted both manager and manageress to be informed of the actor's circumstances in the hopes, no doubt, that they would see cracks in his perfection, as it were. Her dislike of the man increased.

"Did I hear that Mr. Hornby is in Whitecross Prison?" Sir Sabin inquired.

She gave him a startled glance. Her colloquy with Mr. Bryans had been in a low voice and she was not aware that he had been listening—being, she had imagined, more intrigued with the sights about him.

"He is that." Mr. Bryans nodded.

"It is a debtor's prison, is it not?" Sir Sabin questioned, further surprising Diana.

"It is, poor man," she said. "How would you know that, sir?"

"My father was lodged there—before we left for Canada." Sir Sabin frowned. "I told you I did not know London well, but I knew that place. My uncle had him arrested for debt in the hopes that he would turn over an inheritance he had received, but a kind friend rescued him. My brother and I were with him. I was but seven at the time, but I remember it very clearly."

"Nasty spot," Mr. Bryans said.

"Has he been there long?" Sir Sabin asked.

"Upwards of two weeks, sir."

"And none to lend the money that would free him?" Sir Sabin pursued.

"Not to my knowledge," Mr. Bryans said indifferently. " 'E's in over 'is 'ead—head." He produced a sheepish grin.

"Then, I think he must be pulled from that pond." Sir Sabin spoke determinedly. He gave Mr. Bryans a long look. "I would appreciate it if you said nothing about this."

"Mum as the grave, that's me." Mr. Bryans grinned. "An' now I've been told you'd like to visit some 'ells, there be plenty o' them around Covent Garden an' o' course there's Brooks and—"

Sir Sabin said quickly, "I think we must attend to the needs of Mr. Hornby first and put off the other for some time in the future." He added quickly, "But I am sure that you must have put yourself out to meet us and must have

some recompense for your pains.'' He brought out a small
leather purse and produced a guinea. ''Would that be
enough, sir?''

Mr. Bryans appeared highly gratified. ''Oh, yes, quite
enough, sir. Thank you. Per'aps another time. There ain't
an 'ell I don't know.''

''Another time, yes.'' Sir Sabin nodded.

''Then, I'll be takin' my leave. Good day to you, Miss
Forsythe, 'n to you, sir.'' Without waiting for any further
response, he walked hastily away, whistling a lively tune
from *The Maid of the Mill*, an operetta in which he had
recently appeared.

Sir Sabin turned to Diana, saying apologetically, ''I
hope you did not mind my dismissing him, but I found I
could not abide his all-too-patent pleasure over this misfor-
tune of his fellow actor. And surely the relations between
pupil and master must be amicable.''

''Of course they must, and I certainly did not mind,''
Diana returned warmly. ''I am delighted to see the last of
him. Undoubtedly he is jealous of Mr. Hornby, and well
he might be, since *he* is his superior in every aspect of his
profession and certainly in his character.''

''I am most eager to meet him. However, I regret to tell
you that it must be without your companionship, Miss
Forsythe.''

''I understand,'' she said hastily. ''Mr. Hornby would
be most embarrassed were I to see him in such circumstances.''

''I am sure he would be, but that was not my main
reason in suggesting that you do not accompany me. It is
hardly a proper milieu for one as gently bred as yourself.
You did say you had other plans today.''

''I have.'' She nodded. ''But I might tell you that I am
not unfamiliar with the interiors of more than one debt-
or's prison.''

''As a visitor, I hope.'' He frowned.

She shook her head. ''My mama and I have had some
hard times—mainly when I was little, sir. And since there

was none with whom she might leave me, I shared her quarters."

His frown deepened. "I am sorry to hear that, Miss Forsythe. From my memories of Whitecross Prison, those places are not conducive to the presence of a little girl."

"Nor were they to a little boy, sir. But, as you, too, might remember, many children were, at all times, present. I can remember that I shed many tears at several departures because I was leaving so many young friends behind. You are looking extremely disapproving, sir," she said quickly, "but I can assure you my mother had no alternatives. She did not want to leave me with some elderly lodging-housekeeper, and furthermore, the experience has left no lasting mark on me."

"On the contrary"—he gave her a long grave look—"it has left you with memories you should not have needed to entertain. And let me assure you, Miss Forsythe, that I disapprove only of the law that allows young mothers with children to be incarcerated in such a place. I hope there will be a time when I may be among those who initiate changes in some of the existing statutes."

She was touched by his words but managed to say lightly enough, "Do I ascertain, sir, that you are contemplating a career in politics?"

He was silent a moment. "I am not indifferent to the idea of a political career. I have often thought that when I marry . . ." He paused. "But now, I think, is not the time to discuss that, not with your Mr. Hornby languishing in Whitecross Prison."

"I expect not," Diana agreed, not entirely unhappy to be spared Sir Sabin's rhapsodies on the subject of his, hopefully, future bride. "I will take leave of you, then."

"And where are you going?" he demanded quickly.

"I am bound for the reading room of the British Museum, sir. There are some admirable periodicals from France among its collections, and I might be able to find some anecdotes with which to entertain my pupils as well as improve their French vocabulary. I often do that on a day when the museum is open.''

''You must permit me to drive you there and call for you at such time as you wish to leave.''

''But it is out of your way, Sir Sabin, and I can easily summon a hackney.''

''I will summon the hackney and accompany you to the museum,'' he emphasized.

''But''—Diana looked him in the eye, saying steadily—''I am quite able to—''

''I beg you'll not argue with me,'' he interrupted. ''Good God, how have you survived so long in this city without more experiences of the nature we encountered at the Swan? You are far too lovely to set foot on a London street unaccompanied. I marvel that your employers countenance it.''

''They do not countenance it, sir. I am supposed to have Betsy with me. However, since that would have proved awkward for your purposes, I gave her leave to do as she chose today.''

Sir Sabin loosed a long sigh. ''So the blame must be laid at my door. I am sorry for that.''

''You should not be, sir,'' she said quickly. ''When I am with you, I have no need for a protective abigail.''

He laughed. ''See that you remember you told me that, Miss Forsythe, and I beg you'll cease to cavil at my strictures, since you have finally admitted that I am responsible for your safety.''

''I did not mean . . .'' She suddenly laughed. ''I see that I am hoised by my own petard.''

''Quite so,'' Sir Sabin agreed, and stepping into the street, he hailed a passing hackney.

Whitecross Prison was, as Sir Sabin regretfully remembered, a dim, dirty building with small miserable rooms for its inmates—rooms for which they were forced to pay a ''garnish'' to the jailers. There was an odor about the place of mustiness, unwashed bodies, and general decay.

The atmosphere depressed him, the more so since, young as he had been, he could still recall his father's misery at their plight, for which he blamed himself. He had never ceased to bless the name of the man who had rescued them. Judging from what Mr Bryans had implied, no such kind friend would be forthcoming to ransom Mr. Hornby. He would remain there indefinitely—or would have, Sir Sabin decided with some relief, had not the odious Mr. Bryans betrayed his confidence.

A jailer having been dispatched to summon the man, in a short time Sir Sabin was confronting a slender gentleman in garments conspicuous for their elegance and, alas, for their age. There was a sheen to his coat that would have been absent in the years when the garment was new, and there were carefully mended portions visible in the trousers so tightly strapped beneath his shining boots. His linen, amazingly enough, was spotless, his cravat intricately tied. In fact, Sir Sabin was willing to admit that despite his situation, Mr. Silas Hornby outshone him in every aspect save cleanliness, where, despite his incarceration, he was at least his equal.

Furthermore, all Miss Forsythe had said regarding his general air also proved accurate. Here was a gentleman—this last quality taking the form of a general insouciance that rendered their encounter casual rather than fraught with the embarrassment that a less self-confident man might have displayed. There was no denying that Mr. Hornby had an air as well as a goodly amount of nature's endowments, being slender but broad-shouldered, with fine gray eyes set in a handsome, aristocratic countenance, topped by dark hair seamed with a few threads of gray and dressed à la Brutus with a perfection that suggested an excellent barber. Indeed, meeting Mr. Hornby's quizzical glance, Sir Sabin was aware of a pride that almost precluded what he had come to tell him. Instead of making the bald announcement that he was ready to pay his debts, he would have to frame his message in a way that must maintain the latter's pride. In answer to Mr. Hornby's look of polite interrogation, he said, "You do not know me, sir, but I am Sabin Mallory."

"Ah, yes." Mr. Hornby nodded. "The gentleman I am to instruct." There remained a natural question in his eyes.

"No doubt, you will wonder why I am here," Sir Sabin said, and without giving Mr. Hornby a chance to reply, he doggedly continued. "Inadvertently Mr. Bryans told me where you were. I myself having had experience with this establishment as a child when I was incarcerated here with my father and brother . . ." He paused. "But that is aside from the point, I think. I am much in need of the instruction Miss Forsythe mentioned in her communication. Consequently I would like to relieve you of your financial embarrassment and free you. I am in hopes that you will allow me to help you."

There was a moment before Mr. Hornby replied. "I thank you, sir," he said finally. "And I do recognize your good intent, but I cannot be indebted to a stranger."

"But you will not be indebted to me, sir. I intend to exact payment from you in the form of the lessons Miss Forsythe has mentioned and which I had fully intended to be remunerative." As he was watching Mr. Hornby closely, Sir Sabin saw his chest rise and fall in an inadvertent breath of relief.

"In those circumstances, I am at your service, Sir Sabin," Mr. Hornby said. There was a touch of huskiness to the beautiful speaking voice, which, more than anything else, reflected the suffering he must have been enduring— the suffering and the hopelessness.

"I am much in your debt, sir," Sir Sabin said gratefully. "In partaking of such instruction as Mr. Bryans would have provided, I would be, in a sense, putting the cart before the horse, as I think you can understand, having seen me." He ran a hand down his coat.

"The cut of a gentleman is not determined by his garments, Sir Sabin," Mr. Hornby returned. "But come, I will introduce you to the authorities to whom you must speak."

6

On an afternoon some six weeks after Sir Sabin secured himself the services of Mr. Hornby, Diana, sitting in the back parlor and waiting for her pupils to join her for the afternoon session, received a note, which Betsy, in delivering it, said, "It was brought to you by 'and, miss."

The abigail looked at her, wide-eyed, and Diana had no difficulty in interpreting her thoughts. She scented a romance, and seeing a direction on the back of the envelope that she immediately recognized, Diana found her heart pounding quite as if the missive in question was what Betsy believed it to be. She was immediately annoyed with herself for this feeling and even more annoyed because her voice was not quite steady as she said, "Thank you, Betsy." Accepting the letter, she put it into her notebook for later perusal.

Between its arrival and the reading of it loomed at least two hours, and to say that her attention span was troubled by the communication went without saying. She had been devoting much more time to thinking about Sir Sabin's progress than she even liked to admit to herself and, indeed, had been somewhat exercised by his failure to be in touch with her for a full month and a half.

Unfortunately, Rosalie and Eustacia were less interested in the lesson than the forthcoming ball given by their brother to celebrate his engagement to Lady Charlotte Frizell, a young woman they could not like, being, as they both agreed, even more horrid than Aurora.

Having met Lady Charlotte—or Charlie, as Lord Marchant

curiously called her—Diana was not in agreement. Fair-haired and quite pretty, Lady Charlotte was merely quiet and extremely self-contained, qualities that the sisters construed as snobbishness but that Diana attributed to an all-abiding shyness. That the ball in question would not be given until the middle of April did not matter to her pupils, who spoke of it as if it were to take place the day after tomorrow. Try as she did, Diana could not persuade them to turn their attention to their French conversation until the matter had been thoroughly discussed, or rather, worried to the bone. Consequently, it was a good two and a half hours before Diana could hurry to her room and read what Sir Sabin had written:

My dear Miss Forsythe:

   I pray you will pardon my not having communicated with you, but this business of being an ornament—or if not precisely an ornament, but an apprentice to being an ornament—to society has taken rather longer than I anticipated and has consumed the better part of each day, encompassing, as it has, not only the buying and fitting of garments but also those visits to Watier's and White's and other less-known gambling establishments, known to Mr. Hornby, who, I am glad to say, has decided to superintend my entire education with one exception, which I shall presently explain.

   At present, I do feel more the "crack," as it were, and I am delighted with Mr. Hornby's instruction. I could only wish that I could find some way of repaying him in kind—but more about that when I see you. Meanwhile, I have been invited to the Marchant ball and here, I need you. Would it be possible for you to devote your next precious Tuesday to a meeting with me? I should like it to be as early as nine in the morning so that I may take you to a place where we are extremely unlikely to encounter any of your acquaintances or mine.

I await your reply with impatience. You may dis-
patch it to my hotel.

I remain yours with gratitude,
Sabin Mallory

In view of his lengthy silence, Diana was inclined to toss
into the fire a letter that, between its lines, she interpreted
as demanding rather than supplicating. However, that was
hardly the reaction she ought to have, she told herself in a
spate of more lucid second thoughts. There was no reason
why he should have been in touch with her. She had
fulfilled her obligation to him, had secured him the services
of Mr. Hornby, and that was that. The only trouble about
this particular line of reasoning was that *that* was not that.
She had missed him, and much as she had a mind to
punish him for his sins of omission by telling him that her
next five or, rather, ten Tuesdays were fully occupied, she
was quite unable to restrain her curiosity concerning some
of the points mentioned in his letter. With that in mind,
she wrote an immediate reply and expending a shilling in
dispatching Joseph, one of the footmen, to deliver it to his
hotel.

A March wind that had evidently not been told about the
lamblike properties it ought to assume some ten days into
the month, was blowing as Diana came out of the house
early enough on Tuesday morning to have easily dispensed
with Betsy's services before any of the family was astir to
question her on the subject. She gathered that Sir Sabin, in
electing to meet her at this hour, had had that in mind. She
also wondered where he would take her, but these speculations were put to flight as she saw the post chaise at the
end of the street. Dark green in color and obviously new,
it was drawn by four grays that fully bore out Sir Sabin's
contention that he knew horseflesh. There was a smartly
dressed young footman standing by its door, and as she
approached, a tall, young gallant, garbed in what Diana
did not hesitate to describe as the very "glass of fashion,"
sprang from the vehicle and, taking a curly-brimmed bea-

ver hat from his well-coiffed head, bowed deeply and then carried her hand to his lips.

"Miss Forsythe," he murmured as he released her hand.

"Sir Sabin!" she breathed. "I hardly recognized you!"

He grinned. "I have had that same difficulty myself. Fine feathers, Miss Forsythe, but come, lest you be observed entering this carriage with a stranger."

Diana, with precisely that same thought in mind, wasted no time in obeying him.

As she settled back against squabs that, in common with the seat, were covered in green velvet and very comfortable, he took his seat beside her, the horses sprang forward and Diana exhaled a breath she hardly realized she had been holding. Turning to her companion, she was once more amazed at the change his "plumage" had made in him. No one, not even the derisive and discerning Lady Aurora, could have faulted the cut of his garments now. Obviously they had been turned out by an expert, even an inspired tailor, and they showed off his muscular body to perfection. Nothing could have been brighter than the shine on his Hessian boots, unless it was the bright gold of the tassels. It was also possible to see that his waist was as slim as his shoulders were broad. She had already noted that rather than the gold fobs sported by so many young sprigs of fashion, his were of plain leather and his long fingers were innocent of rings. His cravat was intricately tied, his shirt collar impeccably starched. His coat was of a golden brown, eminently flattering to his dark coloring. That he was wearing buckskin breeches suggested that they might be bound for the country, though, of course, such attire was perfectly correct in the city as well. She noticed something else about him. There was an ease about his bearing that had been absent before. She wondered if that were the result of his lessons with Mr. Hornby or because he now felt more comfortable in this society into which he had been so suddenly and summarily thrust.

"Am I allowed to hope that you approve the change, Miss Forsythe?"

She looked up quickly and felt her cheeks grown warm as she met his intent gaze and realized that she had been looking at him just as intently. However, she said calmly, "I must assure you that I do."

"Ah, it wanted only that assurance." He smiled.

"I cannot think that you needed my assurance in particular, not with Mr. Hornby acting as your mentor, Sir Sabin."

"But I did," he responded. "I had been holding my breath until you provided what I hoped would be your sanction."

"I think you must be funning me, sir," Diana reproved.

He bent a grave gaze upon her. "Never, and I hope you are not trying to flatter me when you speak of my improvement. I am sure that there is much that is still wanting."

"Nothing that I can see."

"Ah, then half the battle is won, but before I can claim a victory, Miss Forsythe, I need your aid."

"Mine?" She regarded him in surprise and received a pleading glance in return.

"As helpful as Mr. Hornby has been in every way, he cannot dance with me, and though he has taken me to places where I can tread a measure with one or another young lady, I, alas, have difficulties. I have learned not to stride through rooms as if I were on an all-day march, as he is pleased to put it—or to look warily about me, giving the impression that I expect to find a savage behind the draperies. However, I cannot school my feet to either lead or follow the patterns of the dance. I require a partner, one who is aware of my deficiencies and also of my intentions regarding Lady Aurora, so that my attentions may not be misunderstood and my attentiveness taken to be what it is not. That is why I dare to ask you, who are cognizant of my situation, if you will give me that instruction that must complete my tardy education."

As she heard his words and met the pleading stare that accompanied them, Diana's emotions were sadly mixed. Uppermost among them was a pleasure in seeing him again that remained undimmed even by his statement concerning his "situation." Conversely, however, there was a feeling of anger that he had wrought this most felicitous change in himself because of his love for the undeserving, frivolous, and empty-headed Lady Aurora. In a sense, she was doing him an unkindness to continue preparing him for his "debut," as it were, as the lady's suitor. If he were as intelligent as she believed him to be, he might even be angry when he came to understand the true nature of the chimera he was currently pursuing. She wished she might reveal to him all she knew of the lady's nature, but as her mother had often told her, gentlemen did not appreciate ladies who criticized the objects of their devotion, and Sir Sabin did believe himself in love with Lady Aurora. Consequently, he would be particularly resentful of any attempt to open his eyes to her deficiencies. He would, she thought regretfully, have to find that out for himself, and it was quite possible that he would not discover his mistake until it was too late.

Lady Aurora had recently quarreled with Lord Grosmount, who, rather than attempting to make amends, was happily pursuing another female. According to her sisters, it had been a bitter blow to her vanity if not her heart. Consequently, seeing Sir Sabin in this new guise, she did not doubt that Lady Aurora would appreciate him as fully as she did herself, but Diana realized unhappily, she had appreciated him even before Mr. Hornby had taken him in hand. In fact . . . But she could not dwell on that—not now, with Sir Sabin waiting for an answer she was most reluctant to give.

"You are very silent," he commented.

"I was thinking," Diana responded. Rather lamely, she added, "Those lessons must needs take place at night and in spots where none of the *ton* is likely to go."

"Mr. Hornby has suggested that we go to various assembly rooms. There are some in Hampstead and Islington. Naturally, you would be chaperoned. He mentioned a Miss Martin, whom he met at your home in Chelsea. A retired actress, I believe.''

"Oh, yes, she is." Diana smiled. "She is a good friend . . . and a good suggestion, for she can be very closemouthed.''

"May I hope that you will help me? I cannot think that we will need to go often. I—I am, as Mr. Hornby has told me, 'a quick study.' ''

Hearing this theatrical expression, Diana could not contain her laughter. She said finally, "That, sir, is entirely true. I expect that since I have not been very explicit about my family, I could invent an aunt or a grandmother, lately arrived in town, who might demand my presence at a dinner party and who might follow that up with other invitations.''

"Ah." He actually clapped his hands. "The very thing. You do agree to come with me, then?''

"I do," she said.

He caught her hand and bore it to his lips again. "Miss Forsythe, once more I bless the day I met you." Before she could respond, he added, "I expect you are wondering where I am taking you?''

"It had crossed my mind," she said, and felt her cheeks grow warm. She had not even considered their destination. The mind she had just mentioned had been fully occupied with the man beside her and the regretful realization that she was suffering from that well-known disorder that novelists from the Minerva Press described as "the pangs of unrequited love.''

"I thought we would drive to Islington.''

"To the assembly rooms?" she asked in some surprise.

"No, not today. I thought we might walk about a bit and have our repast at the Queen's Head.''

"Oh, that would be lovely," Diana said, meaning it and not meaning it. It would prepare her for the exquisite pain of two or more Tuesday evenings spent in his company; at least she hoped it might, but stealing a glance at his handsome profile, she was not very sanguine upon that matter.

"Years ago my mother performed at the Wells," Diana said breaking the small silence that had fallen between them after having passed the turnpike and come into the village of Islington. "She said they were a better audience than you could find in a London theater."

"I am sure that is true," Sir Sabin said. "Mr. Hornby tells me that Islington was once renowned for its gardens. He talked of merry times at Bagnigge Wells but says that it is no longer so felicitous a spot."

"So I have heard, and the same is certainly true of Sadler's Wells."

"However"—Sir Sabin grinned—"this place does have a certain sentimental attachment for me. My father, down from Oxford, used to go with a lot of friends to Garrick Gardens. He was wont to frighten Dick and myself with his description of the Bees on Horseback."

"The bees on horseback?" Diana questioned.

"Did your mother never tell you about them?" As Diana shook her head, he continued, "It was a trick performed by a certain equestrian named Daniel Wildman. He put his horse through all manner of tricks, firing pistols and the like, while his face was masked with live bees."

"Good gracious! Didn't they sting him?"

"My father never found out. He had a strong stomach, God knows, but he left midact and did not return."

"I cannot say I blame him." Diana shuddered.

"Sir Walter Raleigh came here, too, as a young man," Sir Sabin continued, "as did the Earl of Essex. He owned a house here, which is now an inn."

"Poor Essex," Diana sighed.

"It is late to mourn him."

"Oh, I know, and foolish too, but one hates to think of him dying so young."

Sir Sabin frowned. "Others in London die younger, of poverty, dirt, and disease. Their demise is less romantic, but who knows what they might have achieved had they a choice and a chance?''

'' 'Many a flower's born to blush unseen and waste its sweetness on the desert air,' '' Diana quoted. ''It is true.''

''But ought not to be.'' He sighed.

''I believe you are admirably suited for public life, Sir Sabin,'' she remarked thoughtfully.

He regarded her rather ruefully. ''I thank you, but at the same time I must ask your pardon for spoiling this day with my comments.''

''You do not spoil it for me, sir,'' she responded quickly. ''Nor do you need to protect me, a female, from the knowledge that observation must bring to us all, however we may choose to ignore it.'' She was thinking of Lady Aurora with increased regret. If her Ladyship was attracted to Sir Sabin and eventually granted him the wish of his heart, he would have precious little time to expend upon the problems of London's poor. Not in her wildest imaginings could she see Lady Aurora as the wife of a political leader. She bit down a sigh as she thought of the ball for which she must prepare him. Lady Aurora could not fail to note the change in him, and undoubtedly this time she would be attracted to him, especially in the light of his wholehearted admiration for her!

''You know,'' Sir Sabin said musingly, ''thinking about the poor reminds me of Mr. Hornby. He seemed in dire straits when I met him at Whitecross Prison.''

''He often is, from all accounts,'' Diana said. ''He is by nature generous and I think he has difficulty keeping such monies as he earns.''

''I saw him only once onstage, but I seem to remember that he's a good actor.''

''Excellent,'' Diana said warmly. ''But we all wonder about him. Mama has often remarked on his difference from the rest of the company.''

''And no one knows his origins?''

''None of us, save that he had acting experience in smaller companies . . . provincial theaters.''

"It seems to me . . ." He paused.

"To all of us," she said, and blushed. "If you are talking about the fact that he is out of place in our company for all he is so accomplished an actor."

"Yes, it is obvious that he comes of no common stock."

"But," she pursued, "he has revealed nothing to you, either?"

"Nothing. I made so bold as to ask him where he was born."

"He did not answer?"

"His attention seemed momentarily deflected. And when he did answer, it was to say only, 'I did not hear your query. Would you have the goodness to repeat it?' "

"Which," she laughed, "you did not."

"I said that I had forgotten what I had asked."

"And consequently he remains a puzzle that none of us can solve. Not even Georgiana Pemberton knows anything about him."

"Georgiana Pemberton?"

"She plays second leads and comedy parts. She worships Mr. Hornby. He has chosen to be kind to her. However, I am positive that she knows no more about him than anyone else among us. However, we are fortunate to have him. Mr. Gifford cannot play every leading role."

Sir Sabin bent a searching look on her face. "I do not believe that you like Mr. Gifford."

"He is well enough." Diana shrugged.

"I agree, but he is not the equal of your mother. The one time I saw them I could not help noticing that he was inclined to rant and rave while she was all subtlety."

"That is true," she responded with an edge of surprise to her tone. Once again, he had startled her with his incisive comments.

"And she is certainly beautiful," he continued.

"I'll not deny that either, thank you."

He scarcely heard her comment, intent as he was on pursuing his own thoughts. "And she is extremely well-spoken. In common with Mr. Hornby, she appears to be the role she plays, and I find no difference offstage either.''

"There's no mystery about my mother, sir," Diana said coolly. "She is the daughter of an actress and a nobleman who did not find it necessary to bestow his name upon his mistress or to acknowledge his child. I imagine my antecedents are similar, though Mama is extremely closemouthed on the subject.''

"Ah, so there is a mystery." He cocked an eye at her. "You do not know the identity of your father.''

She shook her head. "I do not, sir. However, I feel I must resemble him since, as you have observed, there is little likeness between me and Mother.'' She caught a look of sympathy on his face and wondered what on earth had prompted her to be so utterly frank. She had no answer for that.

He said, "Your father must have been very handsome, Miss Forsythe.''

She refused to accept that subtle compliment. Matter-of-factly she responded, "I suppose he might have been and succeeded in turning my mother's head, no easy task, I can assure you.''

"I need no assurances on that count, Miss Forsythe. Your mother gives the impression of possessing a most lively intelligence. I find her a remarkable woman.''

"Yes, indeed, she is," Diana said softly. "If only . . .''

"If only what?''

"Nothing," she sighed, conscious of already having said too much, beguiled by the fact that it could not matter what she told this man, who knew her background already and who loved another. On second thoughts, she was not sorry she had told him. It was a relief to speak her mind to someone who had no interest in repeating her confidences. Unless . . . She tensed as she belatedly remembered his friendship with the Earl of Marchant. She raised her eyes to him. "What I have told you, Sir Sabin—" she began.

"Will not be repeated to anyone by me, Miss Forsythe," he said gently. "I do understand your position.''

He slipped an arm around her shoulders and drew her against him for a moment. "I am your true friend, you know."

"I do know that, sir," she said a little gruffly. "And I—I thank you."

Reaching her chamber that night, Diana looked over a day spent walking through some of the surviving pleasure gardens of Islington until the high March winds drove them inside but to a delightful dinner at the Queen's Head Inn, which turned out to be that selfsame inn that had once served as the summer house for the Earl of Essex. The inn had been charming, but though she had walked through it and admired artifacts said to date from Essex's day, she could not remember a one of them. She could remember only that moment when Sir Sabin had held her against him and pronounced himself her friend.

However, being a sensible young woman, she was able to remind herself that even if he had been attracted to her, which he patently was not, her background must needs have precluded a serious attachment. Consequently, there was absolutely no reason why she was so long a time stemming the tears that dampened her pillow once she had retired for the night. Once she had managed to fall asleep, she had truly silly dreams that embarrassed her greatly when she awoke and made her seriously consider sending Sir Sabin a note telling him that she must find another to instruct him in the art of dancing.

Yet, even in the act of lifting her pen, she recalled that, at the most, she would only see him on three more Tuesdays; after all, she had given him her promise that she would help him. She was reasonably sure that she would not see him after the ball. Resolutely, she put her note-paper away and went down to give Rosalie and Eustacia a most grueling test in French verbs.

7

Standing in front of the long mirror in the bedchamber of Miss Euphemia Martin's Chelsea house, Diana regarded her image with a mixture of excitement and regret. The excitement had arisen out of the fact that she was going to taste of forbidden fruit this night. At Miss Martin's suggestion, Sir Sabin had procured a box at the Opera House Masquerade. It was a spectacle that Diana had long wished to view and that her mother had forbidden her ever to attend. "No one who values her reputation should ever be seen there," Mrs. Forsythe had said, her mobile features expressing the disgust she herself had felt during her first and last appearance at that dubious entertainment. Because of the domino and half-mask that lay on the chair behind her, no one would see her there, Diana assured herself, and because much of the evening would be devoted to dancing, it would also be an excellent opportunity for Sir Sabin to perfect the steps he had learned over the last two weeks. She had a reminiscent smile at his chagrin on that first Tuesday when they had gone to the assembly rooms in Hampstead.

"I'll be hanged if I can understand what I am supposed to do, Miss Forsythe," he had complained after a waltz in which, despite some earlier training from Mr. Hornby, he had hopped rather than glided. His gratitude had been immense when, in the course of their next three waltzes, Diana had softly counted "One two three, one two three . . ." as she had once seen a ballet mistress do during a rehearsal at Covent Garden.

After one or two fruitless attempts, he had suddenly caught on and improved amazingly the third time around, even though she had seen his lips moving as he too counted. Last week, at the assembly rooms in Islington, he had managed not to count after the second waltz, but before he could savor the triumph to its fullest, he had become hopelessly confused in a quadrille. Still, by the evening's end, he had mastered not only the quadrille but the country dance. Tonight, he hoped to gain ascendancy over the cotillion. She had no doubt that he would. Though, she hardly liked to admit it to herself, she must perforce believe that love had rendered him uncommonly precocious. Hence, the regret that tinged her excitement. She was sure that by the time they had left the masquerade, her pupil would have completed his education.

"My dearest Diana, are you ready, then?" Miss Martin, a small, plump woman in her late fifties, bustled in. Her eyes, still a vivid blue, were bright with anticipation. She was already swathed in a pink satin domino purchased, she had told Diana, years ago when she used to attend such festivities more frequently.

"Masquerades ain't for everyone, lovey," she had said frankly, "but they are ever so exciting, an' as long as we 'ave a box, we will be safe." That comment had added a touch of spice to the projected outing, even though Diana was uncomfortably positive that it might not be without its perils, particularly since she would not be remaining in the box. Still, she could not repine, for this was a night when she was prepared to throw caution to the winds and enjoy herself as much as she might, given the unfortunate state of her heart.

"I am quite ready," she told Miss Martin.

"It is a lovely gown, my dear."

"Lovely?" Diana echoed. "I have worn it the last two times. Do you not recognize it?"

"Hmmm, it don't look the same." Miss Martin eyed the garment in question speculatively. "It didn't 'ave green ribbons, that's it. They do make a difference. They're just the color of your eyes, lovey. I am sure he'll agree.''

"I am sure he will not notice," Diana retorted brusquely now. She continued, "I have explained the purpose of these expeditions."

"You 'ave that, my love, but 'e does look so eager. I could almost believe—"

"He is eager to perfect his dancing," Diana interrupted. She added dampeningly, "For that he needs a partner. Out of friendship, I have agreed, and that is all there is to it."

"No doubt you are right, my love," Miss Martin murmured, but to Diana's annoyance, she still looked unconvinced. In Miss Martin's lexicon, a young gallant took his lady dancing for one reason only, no matter what his purported excuse might be, and she was sure it was with that in mind that the lady added, "Do smile, my dear."

The April night was chill and Diana was glad of the black domino that she had wound around her.

Sir Sabin was also in black and his spirits were high. "I have never been to a masquerade," he said. "I am looking forward to it, though I understand from Rob that they can be rowdy. You must never stir from my side, Miss Forsythe."

"Not even during the dances?" she inquired with a laugh.

"I am sure you took my meaning," he responded. "And you must stay beside me, too, Miss Martin."

"Oh, sir," she giggled. "It is ever so gallant of you, but bless you, I'll not need protection. It is the young things they'll be after."

"I'd not count on that. You look most fetching in that domino."

"Oh, la." She slapped him on the arm with her fan. "If you ain't a charmer."

"I am telling you no more than the truth," he insisted. "Indeed, I think I shall be much envied tonight with two such lovely ladies to escort."

The opera house was brightly lighted and the stage as

well as portions of the floor was full of dancers in every conceivable costume: nuns, harlequins, clowns, sailors, pirates, ballad singers, orange girls, kings, peasants, monks, beggars, queens. It was a dizzying spectacle and Diana needed no second invitation to stay close to Sir Sabin as they made their way across the crowded floor in the direction of the boxes.

"Good gracious," she exclaimed. "They are playing a waltz across the floor and a country dance is in progress onstage, and no one seems to have any trouble following the patterns of the dances."

"I will have trouble," Sir Sabin protested.

"And I say you will not," Diana contradicted.

"Well, perhaps, if I count."

"You'll not need to count, dearie." Miss Martin put a hand on his sleeve. "You was grace itself last week."

"You are too kind, Miss Martin. And . . ." He broke off as a man in pirate costume with a ferocious black mustache pasted to his upper lip and a bright-red kerchief tied about his head lurched against them and righted himself by seizing Diana's arm.

"An' wot do we 'ave 'ere under this domino?" He grinned and then groaned as Sir Sabin thrust him away with a well-aimed elbow to the ribs. For a moment, it appeared that he would retaliate, but he was a small man, and muttering under his breath, he slunk away.

"Did he hurt your arm?" Sir Sabin asked concernedly.

"Not in the least," Diana responded quickly.

"I begin to wonder if I should have brought you here, Miss Forsythe."

"I have always wanted to come and I am very pleased to be here. It will be an adventure." And, she thought to herself, it will be a memory to cherish—no matter what happens. She smiled up at him and received an answering smile.

"You are game, Miss Forsythe. How will I ever repay you for all you've done for me?"

"Must I remind you yet again of that cold January

day?" she questioned lightly. "I might not have been able to dance had you not carried me home."

"I beg you will not keep mentioning that. It is a drop in the bucket compared to . . ." He paused as someone else careened into them. "We had best get off the floor and to our box." He frowned.

The box in question was on the second tier, and having settled down in their chairs, they could easily see the vast house and at the same time wonder at the crowds. The auditorium had been stripped of its seats and two orchestras had been set up: one on the stage and one at the back of the house. It was a marvel, Diana thought, that with the music of the waltz vying against that played for a country dance, the dancers could acquit themselves so well. Sir Sabin, however, looked concerned, she noted.

"I am wondering if I should take you back down there. Some of those couples are badly foxed."

"We can avoid them," Diana said positively. "We have come here to dance and I would love to waltz."

"Would you . . . honestly?"

"Honestly and truly." She smiled. She pushed back her domino. "It is passing warm in here."

"But you must not take it off, for . . ." He looked down. "Green ribbons!" he exclaimed. "They are a match for your eyes."

"That is what I told her," Miss Martin said. "She ought to wear more green."

"I agree. A gown of that hue would be most becoming." He nodded. "And . . ." He paused as a shriek of laughter reached them.

Looking down, they saw a lightly clad lady running across the floor, pursued by a gentleman dressed as a devil. He was carrying a most realistic pitchfork.

Sir Sabin shook his head. "Are you sure you'd not rather go home, Miss Forsythe."

"We came to dance," Diana reminded him.

"Very well." He rose and turned to Miss Martin. "Would you excuse us?"

"I should say I would, my dear. Go along with you now."

"Remember," Sir Sabin adjured as they descended to the floor again, "you are not to leave my side."

"Then, we must needs concentrate on the waltz."

"It is my favorite," he said. "One need not be separated from one's partners by the patterns of the dance."

"True," she agreed, wishing that she had not received an instant vision of Sir Sabin waltzing with Lady Aurora, an image, she was sure, that must be drifting through his mind as well.

"Then, come," he said, taking her hand. "Let us waltz."

Despite the crowded condition of the floor, as observed from on high, it was easier than Diana had imagined to find enough space to dance. She could wish, however, that Sir Sabin's touch did not bring with it sensations to which she had been a stranger until meeting him. Despite his half-mask, he was looking very handsome tonight. As his domino swung back, she saw he was wearing one of his new suits of clothing—an understated black. Nothing could have been whiter than his shirt, its starched points grazing his cheeks. Earlier that evening she had seen and pronounced judgment on his cravat, which Ericson, his new valet, had tied in what he called "the ballroom style." It was becoming, though, being longer in the neck, it did keep his chin at a rather unnatural height. However, part of Mr. Hornby's tutelage included the wearing as well as the choosing of the garments, and obviously Sir Sabin had been an apt and discerning pupil. He looked extremely elegant, and out of the corner of her eye Diana saw more than one young woman directing a languishing look at him.

Some of these ladies had not troubled to don a domino over gowns that aped styles popular some years back when females from all walks of life wore gossamer-thin silks or muslins, artfully dampened so that a slender or even a voluptuous form might be blatantly revealed. Yet, to do him justice Sir Sabin hardly glanced at them. He was wholly intent on the music and, seemingly, upon herself, though of course she knew better than that.

At his insistence, they remained in that area for several dances before going back to the boxes.

"Well," he said as they started toward the stairs. "What do you think?"

She pushed up her mask, and gazing into his eager and, at the same time, apprehensive face, she said, "Can you not answer that question for yourself, Sir Sabin? I would say that were you taking this course at, say, Oxford, you must have been given a degree with honors."

He came to a stop. "Now you are pleased to make sport of me," he accused.

"You must be making sport of *me*, if you say such a thing," she countered. "Is it possible that you do not know that you have become an excellent dancer? Lady Aurora cannot possibly find any fault with your performance upon the floor, I am sure." She greatly regretted the necessity of mentioning that name, and regretted even more the eagerness she discerned in his eyes as he said, "Do you really think so?"

"I am positive of it," she said staunchly.

"If that is true, then I am in your debt forever, Miss Forsythe. You have taken a sow's ear and done the impossible."

"Nonsense," she said tartly. "Why will you continually underestimate yourself, Sir Sabin? You were never a sow's ear. You were a silk purse with a few threads loosened."

He laughed merrily. "Oh, Miss Forsythe, I do admire your turn of phrase, even if it is undeserved and . . ." He suddenly pulled her aside, and seizing her in his arms, he pressed a long kiss on her lips. Shocked and angry, she began to struggle but ceased as he muttered, "My apologies, but please let us go down this way, else we'll both be in the basket." Lifting his head, he wound his arm around her and pulled her away from the stairs, saying, "Come, my dearest Clarissa, where we can be more private." With a loud, slightly drunken laugh, he pulled her into a narrow passageway. A few seconds later he released her quickly, saying, "I am deeply sorry, my dear, but I saw some friends of Lord Marchant, whom I have met at his house. Will you forgive me?"

"Of course," Diana said breathlessly. "You'd best leave me here and fetch Miss Martin. It would be better if we left immediately."

"I would not think of leaving you for a minute in this maelstrom," he said. "Only slip your mask back on, please."

"Oh, dear, I forgot I had pushed it back," she said contritely. "That was stupid of me."

"You could never be stupid, Miss Forsythe." His smile bordered on tender as he continued, "You only wanted to look me in the eye and assure me of your honesty, is that not true?"

"Quite true, Sir Sabin." She laughed. "But we had best go, do you not agree?"

"I do, for both our sakes, and again, do let me apologize for taking such a liberty."

"You are entirely forgiven," she managed to say lightly. "I accept it in the spirit in which it was proffered."

"You are quite unique, Diana," he said warmly, but added quickly, "Miss Forsythe. I apologize for yet another solecism."

"And are forgiven again," she said lightly.

"You are very kind. Do you know, I wish I might do something for you in exchange for all you've done for me."

"You will not," Diana spoke firmly. "We are even."

"We will never be even!" He stared at her for a long moment. "Those green ribbons . . . Might I not have a gown made for you in that same hue, so you might wear it to the ball?"

"No," she protested quickly. "You must not even consider it, sir. It would hardly be proper."

"Proper or not. You can tell your employers that it is a present from your mother."

"No, I beg you, please. I have told you once and will tell you again—what you did for me that day last January was far and away enough."

"It was not enough—not nearly enough to compensate for these lessons or for the introduction to Mr. Hornby."

"If you wish to dispense rewards, Sir Sabin, Mr. Hornby should be your target, and I am sure you have been more than generous there. Now I do think we must fetch Miss Martin and leave before your friends catch sight of you."

"Yes, there you are right," he agreed with a shade of regret in his tone. "You are sure that I will pass muster?"

"If I were your commanding officer, you'd be promoted from lieutenant to major in an instant!" Diana gave him a mock salute.

"I thank you, my general," he said solemnly. Looking about him, he added, "I think it would be best if I escorted you to the carriage and then returned for Miss Martin."

"I agree." She nodded.

Sitting alone in the darkness of the coach, Diana took several long breaths and tried to blink away the threatening tears. She was extremely glad of the near contretemps that had resulted in these few moments alone. By the time Sir Sabin would have returned with Miss Martin, she must have regained an equilibrium that had been sadly shattered by his unexpected and not unpassionate embrace. That it was merely a ploy against discovery had not made it any the less startling and, much as she preferred to deny it, thrilling. That it was ridiculous to feel such an emotion went without saying. It was even more ridiculous to wish that he had experienced sensations similar to her own. However, obviously he had not. He had been merely playing a part. She wondered dolefully if Mr. Hornby had, in addition to his other instructions, given Sir Sabin some acting lessons? She also wondered if he had been aware of the fact that, at the very first, she had not struggled. She

doubted it. Her reactions meant less than nothing to him.
She was sure of that and glad of it, too—or was she?

Her common sense reasserted itself. It was ridiculous to
moon over a man who was in love with another, no matter
how unworthy that other love might be. Consequently, by
the time Sir Sabin returned with Miss Martin, she was
smiling quite naturally. Still, she was pleased that Miss
Martin, who had been informed of the reasons for their
abrupt departure, kept up a steady stream of chatter regarding their narrow escape in particular and the masquerade in
general all the way back to Chelsea. If she had not, Diana,
realizing that this was the last time she would ever see Sir
Sabin alone, might have been hard put to keep from
displaying a regret that would have been as embarrassing
to him as it was to her.

The ballroom was being readied for the long-anticipated
evening, now only a day and a night distant. Lord Marchant,
having instigated the proceedings, had cravenly withdrawn
from a house full of scurrying servants, a distracted housekeeper, not to mention his mother, who was oversee-
ing the housekeeper as she oversaw the ballroom. Front
and side doors were constantly assailed by tradesmen and
by footmen bearing late acceptances or later rejections. In
common with her brother, Lady Aurora, too, had withdrawn to her mantua maker for some last-minute alter-
ations to her recently finished gown. Rosalie and Eustacia,
being still in the schoolroom, were describing the creation
for Diana's edification. As usual, both sisters alternated
between frank envy and equally frank contempt of their
older sibling.

"It is new," Rosalie said discontentedly, "her gown
. . . I do not see why she must have a new gown. Her
armoire is stuffed with gowns she has yet to wear!"

"It is white lace over white crepe," Eustacia said.
"Aurora is always at her best in white, and she has had
new slippers made, kid, of course."

"And," Rosalie added, "she will be wearing Great-grandmother Lucia's pearls, the small circlet."

"I expect those will go to Lady Charlotte once she weds Rob," Eustacia said in a pleased voice.

"I do not believe they will," Rosalie told her. "I think those were willed Aurora by Cousin Helen, who inherited them from our great-grandmother, if you will remember."

"Oh, dear"—Eustacia pouted—"I wonder what moved Great-grandmother to be so generous."

"You should wonder what moved your Cousin Helen to be so generous," Diana said.

"She's a great silly, that's why." Eustacia grimaced. A half-second later, she brightened and managed to surprise both Rosalie and Diana, by adding, "She will look beautiful." She softened the impact of this remark by quickly saying, "Let us hope that someone at the ball falls madly in love with her and takes her far, far away."

"To the ends of the earth," Rosalie amplified.

"Farther," Eustacia giggled.

"Ladies," Diana felt it incumbent upon her to protest. All she received were giggles plus the combined and unwanted attention of her two pupils.

"What will you be wearing, Diana?" Rosalie inquired.

"My white muslin," Diana said without interest.

"Whatever is the matter?" Rosalie pursued.

"Matter?" Diana repressed a sigh and opened her eyes wide. "Why ever should you think anything's the matter?"

"Because ever since you came back from your visit to your aunt last week, you have been drenched in gloom," Rosalie said frankly. "Today seems to be no exception."

"My aunt is gravely ill, as I think I explained." Diana kept her eyes on a pillow inexpertly covered with a needlepoint rendering of a possible dog, executed by Aurora at the age of ten.

"We never knew you had an aunt," Eustacia commented.

"Everyone has aunts," Diana responded coolly. "And why all this untoward interest in me? Should you not be thinking of the ball?"

"Only if it succeeds in its designs and deprives us of Aurora before it is our turn to come out," said the irrepressible Rosalie. "It is certainly time and past that someone offered for her."

"But this ball is to celebrate your brother's engagement," Diana reminded them.

"It is to kill two birds with one stone," Eustacia giggled.

Thinking of the stone that would, very possibly, bring down Aurora, Diana sighed and again took refuge in her role of pedagogue. "Enough talk," she said crisply, and forthwith launched into a French dictation concerning a balloon ascent that both sisters pronounced incredibly dull.

Upon finishing the afternoon's instruction, Diana, tiredly ascending the stairs, was thinking of rest and possibly even sleep, which would hopefully obliterate the thoughts that had been plaguing her ever since her night at the Opera House Masquerade. A moment later, she decided that she did not want to sleep because, in her dreams, she would be wafted back to that moment when Sir Sabin had clutched her in his arms and kissed her.

After tomorrow night, Sir Sabin's kisses would be placed on Lady Aurora's lovely hand, then cheek, then mouth, as familiarity grew and if it remained untinged by contempt. His toward her, of course. That would be highly unlikely, she knew. Tomorrow night Sir Sabin would astound Lady Aurora with his appearance and with his prowess upon the dance floor. She would melt into his arms and he would be beside himself with joy. No, there would be no contempt on either of their parts!

Armed with this knowledge, she could easily have relieved the combined fears of the Ladies Rosalie and Eustacia. Their sister would not be queening it over them for yet another Season. In fact, she could envision their joy at what she was positive would be Lady Aurora's unimpeded progress from ball to bridal chamber. The painting of Lady Marchant, soon to be the Dowager Lady Marchant, that hung at the top of the stairs blurred, and Diana, wiping away her tears with an impatient hand, whispered, "One would think that in six days, I would have forgotten that night." Unfortunately, she knew full well that she would not forget Sir Sabin's embrace in a year—or even ten. Once Rosalie and Eustacia were launched in society, which would happen as early as next October, she would be back at school and then . . .

"Oh, Miss Diana," Betsy called from the top of the stairs, "you've a present from your aunt."

Diana came to a sudden stop, two steps from the second-floor landing. She felt her face burn but managed to respond calmly enough, "When did it arrive, Betsy?"

"An hour since, Miss Diana. I put it in your chamber. It is from Madame Hortense." Betsy pronounced the name of a famous and fashionable mantua maker with awe.

Though her mother had often derided her acting ability, Diana was sure that Mrs. Forsythe would have been both surprised and pleased at her daughter's even calmer "Oh, really? My aunt did say she might be sending me a gown for the ball. I tried to discourage her, but she insisted," a statement that admirably concealed her churning speculations.

"Might—might I 'elp you unpack it, Miss Diana?" Betsy asked eagerly.

"If you so desire, Betsy," Diana returned casually. However, as they came into her chamber and she saw the large box on the bed, she wished that she had not been so generous with her permission. If Sir Sabin had enclosed a card, it might be very difficult to provide an explanation, but she recalled, Betsy had mentioned her aunt. Consequently, she said merely, "Did my aunt enclose a letter?"

Betsy shook her head. "The person who brought it said it were from 'er." Almost reverently, the abigail undid the ribbons, and lifting the lid of the box, she gently extracted the gown from the layers of tissue paper that protected it.

"Ooooh, miss," the girl exclaimed, her words fortunately covering Diana's own shocked exclamation as she beheld the gown or, rather, the creation.

It was green and white—grass green, a popular shade,

according to *La Belle Assemblée*. However, none of the plates in that fashionable monthly magazine could equal the lines of a gown that seemed simplicity itself. It had a low square-cut neck and big puffed sleeves that were of a green-and-white-striped satin to match the brief bodice, and a front panel extending from bodice to the bottom of a white satin skirt. It was quite the loveliest gown Diana had ever seen, something to treasure—but to wear?

After Betsy had reverently placed the gown in the armoire and left the room, Diana ran to look at it, tears rolling unchecked down her cheeks and her thoughts in chaos.

"I cannot . . ." she whispered. "I can never appear at the ball in this, but if I do not, he will be hurt. I could say I have the headache and not go at all, but then I will never see him again. But if I do see him, it will be with Lady Aurora, and will she not wonder where I acquired so fine a gown? And, again, if I do not appear, he will be hurt. He might even think his taste is at fault. I do not want to make him unsure of himself. Yet . . . Oh, what shall I do?"

Diana stared at the door resentfully, but of course, she was not seeing the door; she was seeing an image of Sir Sabin Mallory, the same that had troubled her dreams and haunted her waking hours as well, transforming her from a levelheaded and intelligent young woman to a "maiden all forlorn"—she did not remember from whence that quotation came but certainly it was apt. The situation was not without its ironies, she reasoned dolefully. In providing lessons for him, she had learned one herself, a most unwelcome bit of knowledge, too. Yet, the idea of the dress still concerned her. No gentleman should provide a lady with apparel unless . . .

Diana flushed at the thought of that "unless." It was a word that implied a connection with the painted sisterhood that bespoke some of the very best boxes at Drury Lane, Covent Garden, and the Italian Opera, and also occupied some of the most resplendent carriages at Hyde Park Corner every evening at five.

Harriette Wilson was a name that came to mind, unblushing Harriette, who had often come backstage to chat with one or another of her friends, much to Flavia Forsythe's disgust. Diana suspected that her mother repented the sins of a youth which gave her a reluctant kinship to the flamboyant courtesan. Uncomfortably, she thought of her father. Who had he been? And what had he done that caused her mother's lips to tighten and her eyes to darken whenever a younger Diana had tried to coax some information concerning him from her.

"I forbid you to mention him," had been her chill response on any and all occasions.

Had he promised marriage and had a younger Flavia been foolish enough to believe he meant it? That was Diana's hypothesis now that she knew more of the world. Yet, at the same time it surprised her. Flavia Forsythe was a most determined woman in all her dealings. Had she learned that determination from her experience with the man who had sired her only child? Diana emitted a sharp little sigh. These matters had very little to do with her present situation, or rather, they had everything to do with it! She owed it to her mother to behave in a manner that reflected the care with which she had been raised. Despite her profession, Flavia Forsythe was a veritable paragon of virtue, and had been throughout her daughter's life. She had set an example that obviously she wanted Diana to emulate—and emulate it she must if she were to succeed in her chosen profession or, rather, the choice that, at her mother's bidding, she had accepted.

A pedagogue, one who eventually aspired to be headmistress of a select school for young ladies, must avoid the slightest hint of scandal. She shuddered. If anyone were ever to find out about the lessons, she, to use Sir Sabin's term, would certainly be "in the basket," a very tall hamper from which she would never be able to escape. But the dress was so beautiful. Still, all the same, she must send it back to her "aunt" at his hotel in Bond Street, and the sooner the better. She paused in her thinking at a knock on the door and, going to open it, found her pupils outside.

"Diana," Rosalie said eagerly, "do let us see the gown your aunt sent you. Betsy says it is a creation."

"Please," Eustacia added.

Diana hesitated, realizing that she had no excuse for not showing it. In fact, it would look very strange, even suspicious were she to refuse. In that moment, her mind was made up. Matters had been taken out of her hands. She had no excuse not to show it, less even to wear it. "Come in," she invited, and hoped she did not sound as nervous as she felt.

8

The ballroom at Marchant House was decorated with hothouse roses set in baskets on either side of it. These were reflected into infinity by the facing mirrors, which also appeared to increase the number of guests and the giant crystal chandelier brought from Austria by Lord Marchant's great-grandfather.

Diana, dancing with a young man whose name escaped her, saw herself reflected with the chandelier into infinity and, for once, was not intrigued with the effect. She was beginning to be weary, but she was actually more dispirited than tired. She had danced once with Sir Sabin, a waltz, during which she had managed to thank him for his gift and to hear his gratified whisper that he had known that the gown would suit her. He had been so pleased over the success of his selection that she had not been able to chide him for his deliberate flouting of her wishes. Others among the male guests, not excluding Lord Marchant, had been equally complimentary, and the cool or sharp glances of many a female guest had been, in a sense, equally flattering.

"You look utterly beautiful, Diana," had been the combined opinion of the Ladies Rosalie and Eustacia, and if she were to be perfectly honest with herself, she must needs agree with them. She did look beautiful. Betsy had managed miracles with her hair, and the gown not only displayed her lovely shape but made her green eyes appear even greener.

Donning it the first time, she had wondered by what

legerdemain, Sir Sabin had managed to guess her measurements, for the gown had been an absolutely perfect fit. However, it had not been magic, she knew, but rather the cooperation of Miss Martin, who had some of her gowns in her Chelsea house. Diana sighed. It would have been far better had Miss Martin discouraged rather than encouraged Sir Sabin. She wished she could rid herself of the feeling of unease that was currently possessing her. Occasionally these feelings arose in her mind and invariably they presaged some uncomfortable happening. She remembered Miss Fanny Stephens, an actress friend of her mother's, telling her that these unusual perceptions arose from the fact that she had been November-born under the sign of Scorpio.

"It is a sign to be found in the horoscopes of many fortune-tellers," Miss Stephens had said.

Flavia Forsythe had laughed at her friend, saying lightly that no one could see into the future. Miss Stephens had also laughed as she replied, "But you, my dear, are April-born, an Aries, and consequently hardheaded. You would never believe in anything you could not see."

The music came to an end and Diana's partner, murmuring his thanks, escorted her to the edge of the floor. Standing waiting for her next partner, she had forgotten his name, Diana looked across the ballroom and saw the flaming hair of Sir Sabin's "goddess of the dawn." Lady Aurora was in dazzling white and she did look her very best. She was standing beside Sir Sabin and smiling up at him. With a pang, Diana saw that he appeared bedazzled. She looked away from him hastily and, in so doing, met the appraising stare of Lady Julia Derwent, a particular friend of Lady Aurora's, and guessed that she was wondering about the gown. Lady Aurora had not admired it, she remembered, and as her sisters had said, it was not to be expected that she would.

"Miss Forsythe . . ."

Diana looked up quickly and met another admiring glance, that of young Sir Henry Barrington, her partner for the quadrille. She smiled at him and saw him blush. He was as fair as she was dark and very handsome in his way—but, alas, she could think only of the man who had, it was obvious, finally won the attention of Lady Aurora Gresham. The lessons had been successful, so successful that Diana could hardly wait until the evening was at an end and she alone in her chamber and able to shed the tears that were currently threatening to spill out of her eyes. However, she reminded herself tartly, she was not an actress's daughter for nothing! The smile she managed to bestow upon Sir Henry brought a deeper blush to his cheeks and an answering gleam in his blue eyes as he led her onto the floor.

Much to Diana's regret, the conversation that occupied Rosalie and Eustacia on the morning following the ball was neither French nor pertinent to their lessons. The ball, at which they had made the briefest possible appearances, was their subject, and worse yet, they were concentrating on Lady Aurora's unusual preoccupation with Sir Sabin Mallory.

"Did you see him last night?" they had asked Diana, and upon her admission that she had, they had both marveled at his amazing transformation. On the one hand, she was glad that he had been such a success, and on the other she was heartsick to hear of Lady Aurora's newly awakened interest in him and her opinion that she never would have known that it was the same person. As to Lady Charlotte, she might not have been at the ball last night, for all the attention she received.

"Only Rob noticed that she was present," Rosalie said.

"That is not entirely true. There was the announcement of the engagement," Eustacia reminded her.

"But everyone just clapped politely and toasted them. It was Aurora who was, as usual, the center of attention. She was in good looks last night, do you not agree, Diana?"

"Why should she agree?" Eustacia said before Diana had a chance to reply. "Diana outshone her."

"Nonsense!" Diana said hastily.

"It's not nonsense," Eustacia contradicted. "You did outshine her. That gown was so becoming. All the ladies were looking daggers at you and all the gentlemen were soliciting dances, even Sir Sabin Mallory. What did *you* think of him, Diana? He is greatly changed, is he not? I wonder how it came about. Someone must have put a flea in his ear."

"Ugh, what an expression!" Rosalie made a face.

"Aurora has accepted an invitation to ride in the park with him," Eustacia said. "Rob and Charley will be with them, of course, but no doubt he will soon be taking her up in his curricle." She exchanged a delighted look with her sister. "She'll be gone before next October, do you not think so, Diana?"

"I think it possible." Diana nodded.

"Oh, that will be lovely." Rosalie paused at a knock on the door, which was subsequently thrust open by a rather flushed Betsy, who bobbed a curtsy and, giving Diana a wide-eyed stare, said, "Beggin' yer pardon, Miss Forsythe, but ye'll be wanted in the second drawing room."

"I?" Diana regarded her with considerable surprise. "Why?"

"It's 'er Ladyship, er, Lady Marchant 'oo 'as requested that I hask you to come at once."

"At once?" Eustacia and Rosalie chorused. "Why, Betsy? Has anything untoward happened?"

"I wouldn't be knowin'," Betsy responded nervously. "But 'er Ladyship said as you should 'urry, Miss Diana."

"Of course, I will come with you immediately," Diana responded, a pulse beginning to beat in her throat. Her feelings of unease were back, and she wondered if they had ever completely left her. She was not sure. She had had an unusually restless night—or what had been left of the night—and she had awakened after only four hours of sleep. She turned to the sisters. "I suppose I need not hope that you will study your verbs during my absence?"

"Never, Diana, dearest," Rosalie giggled. "I do wonder what Mama can want? It is the first time she has ever interrupted one of your lessons.''

"You must hurry back and tell us,". Eustacia prompted.

"We will see." Diana produced a nervous smile and followed Betsy out of the room.

Several chambers intervened between the back parlor and the second drawing room. Diana, walking with Betsy, found her nervousness increasing with every step, particularly since the abigail, questioned again, retained what was for her a most unusually noncommittal silence. Since this was accompanied or, rather, augmented by several surreptitious side glances, Diana was positive that Betsy had more than an inkling of why she had been summoned. Evidently Lady Marchant was upset about something. Had it to do with her teaching methods? Was she unhappy with her pupils' progress? No, it had to be something else. She never would have interrupted a lesson to discuss that.

They had arrived at the drawing-room door, which was closed. As James, one of the footmen, opened it, Diana surprised an odd smile on his usually impassive countenance. What had amused him? Her speculations changed to shock as she walked inside to find Lady Aurora, Lady Julia Derwent, and Lady Marchant occupying two chairs and a sofa. Lying over the top of another chair was her green-and-white ballgown. When she saw the garment, her shock was replaced by amazement and a touch of anger. What was it doing here? Had Lady Marchant deemed it unsuitable for a governess to wear, even a governess who had been accepted as "one of the family?"

"Miss Forsythe." Lady Marchant rose from the sofa, and regarding Diana with a coldness she had never seen before, at least not directed at herself, she said in tones as chill as her gaze, "We are much in need of an explanation. I am in hopes that you will be able to provide one that will prove satisfactory."

"An explanation, Lady Marchant?" A pulse was throbbing in Diana's throat and questions were speeding through her mind. They centered about the gown that lay draped across the chair. Before Lady Marchant could respond, she added, "Why is my gown here?"

"You cannot guess?" Lady Aurora demanded sharply.

"Aurora," her mother said. "I will do the questioning and provide such answers as I may." Her cold eyes dwelt once more on Diana's face. "I had been told that the garment in question was a gift from your aunt. Is that true, Miss Forsythe?"

The pulse was beating harder than ever. More questions surged through Diana's mind. They revolved around Sir Sabin. Could he have *told* Lady Aurora of his lessons and the reward he had given to one of his mentors? No, he could not have done such a thing, but meanwhile, Lady Marchant had asked a question and she must be given an answer. "Yes, from my aunt. Betsy unpacked it for me. She can tell you that the messenger who brought it said it came from my aunt."

"Betsy has already vouchsafed that information," Lady Marchant said. "However, we have reason to believe that one or both of you is in error."

"I fear I do not understand, Lady Marchant," Diana responded in tones that she managed to keep steady.

"Perhaps I can clarify the matter for you, Miss Forsythe." Lady Julia rose and fastened icy gray eyes on Diana's face. These were large and set very far apart on a face with blunt features that, to Diana's mind, resembled the pen-and-ink drawing of a grasshopper she had once seen in the science department at school. The memory brought an unexpected twitch to her lips, which she quickly smoothed away—but not quickly enough. Lady Julia's eyes widened. "You are amused, perhaps, Miss Forsythe. I, for one, do not find this situation, or your part in it, at all amusing."

"I fear I do not understand you, Lady Julia," Diana replied. "And I was not smiling."

The cold eyes rested on her face for an unsettling moment before Lady Julia continued, "Be that as it may,

Miss Forsythe. You say that this gown you wore to the ball last night was a present from your aunt. Then, how was it that I, in one of Madame Hortense's fitting rooms, heard a gentleman telling Madame's assistant to send that gown to Marchant House? I am an old customer of Madame Hortense, and naturally, after the gentleman departed, I came out and, seeing the gown, was able to ask her the identity of the sender. She told me that it was Sir Sabin Mallory. Naturally, I was surprised and I further questioned her as to how she happened to be sending the garment in question to Marchant House? I could not imagine that it was destined for either Lady Aurora or her mother.

"Madame Hortense pretended ignorance on that count, but pressed by me, she finally admitted that the gown was a gift for Miss Forsythe. I asked if Sir Sabin had brought the lady into the premises for a fitting and she told me he had not, but had provided her with the said young lady's measurements. At the time, I was rather confused, for I did not remember that a Miss Forsythe resided at Marchant House." She directed an even colder glance at Diana. "But, of course, directly I saw her wearing it, I remembered that Miss Forsythe was employed as governess to my dear friend Lady Aurora's two young sisters."

"What have you to say to this, Miss Forsythe?" Lady Marchant demanded.

Before Diana could respond, Lady Aurora said in tones even colder than those of her dear friend Lady Julia, "What answer can she give?"

Once more Sir Sabin's remark concerning "baskets" returned to Diana's mind. She was in the hamper of her imagination and its lid was tied down tightly with strong wire-reinforced hemp. She said, "I do not believe that I am required to answer these questions, and furthermore, no matter what I say, I can see that your mind or, rather, minds are made up. I will leave this afternoon."

"A wise decision, Miss Forsythe," Lady Marchant said coolly. "I hardly need add that I am both surprised and deeply disappointed in you. I think I must tell you that it will be useless for you to try to obtain another position in this profession. I cannot believe that you are fit to instruct young ladies and I believe it my duty to lodge this information with the various agencies dedicated to the hiring of governesses. I also feel that I must write to your teachers at the academy and state my reasons for this action as well as conveying to them my deep disappointment and shock at these unwholesome revelations.''

"No doubt," Lady Aurora said with something very like a sneer, "Miss Forsythe will find other more felicitous occupations open to her."

"I am sure that I will," Diana responded out of a churning anger.

"Doxy!" Lady Julia exclaimed. "You ought to be whipped at cart's tail like any common whore!"

"Lady Julia," Lady Marchant said distastefully, "I believe that enough has been said on this subject. Namecalling is beneath you."

Diana gave Lady Julia a long look. "Had I been a whore, Lady Julia, I am sure that I should have been a most uncommon one." Ignoring three outraged exclamations, she moved forward and, lifting her gown from the chair, left the room.

Two hours later, her possessions packed in her portmanteau, she bade farewell to a weeping Rosalie and Eustacia, who, having learned the whole story from Betsy, had followed Diana out of the house and down the street to the corner, assuring her at every step of the way that neither of them believed Lady Julia's allegations and that they knew she had been unfairly treated and that they loved her as much as ever.

Tears sparkled in her eyes, but holding herself erect, Diana bade them a gentle farewell and hailed a passing hackney. She gave Miss Martin's address to the coachman. She did not look back at Marchant House, but neither did she look forward. The way was familiar and there was nothing to see that she had not seen before. The thought went through her that it took very little to ruin a life. That was, she decided, a most important lesson—something she could tell her pupils—but then, she remembered that she had no pupils. She would need to find another position, but what it might be was a matter which, at the present time, eluded her.

In some measure, it might have comforted Diana to know that on the day following her dismissal, Sir Sabin, arriving for his promised ride with Lady Aurora, was greeted by an embarrassed Lord Robert Marchant, who looked everywhere but directly into his friend's eyes.

"My mother and my sister want to see you. Some, er, matter has come to their attention. I cannot believe . . . But you will find them in the drawing room." The earl gave him a brief smile and directed him toward the chamber in question.

Sir Sabin's surprise at Marchant's manner was augmented by the fact that he had not been in riding clothes. Evidently, he thought disappointedly, the plans had been changed and Lady Aurora wished to give him an explanation. This theory was, he believed, substantiated when he came in to find mother and daughter occupying a single sofa in the huge room and looking extremely . . . glum was the first description that occurred to him. Disappointed was the second. A minute later, he was not so sure of his beloved Lady Aurora's state of mind.

He had received a side glance that suggested anger rather than disappointment, an anger that was, for some odd reason, directed at him. He hoped he had been mistaken. He also thought that that particular emotion did not become her. It quite transformed her lovely countenance, causing him to wonder uneasily if she did not have more than a bit of a temper. Much to his further surprise, he was regretfully reminded of the girl who had married his brother. He banished this thought hastily. Louise could have nothing in common with the beautiful Aurora, and then all speculations ended as Lady Marchant said coldly, "Sir

Sabin, it has come to our attention that you have been acquainted with Miss Diana Forsythe.''

To say that he was surprised by her question was to minimize the shock that went through him. So many disjointed conjectures raced through his mind that he was unable to distinguish between them. He said merely, ''I do know her, yes. I danced with her at your ball.''

''Surely,'' Lady Aurora said in cold, accusing tones, ''that was not the first time you had seen her.''

''Aurora, please,'' Lady Marchant said. ''Leave this matter to me.''

''Er, matter, Lady Marchant,'' Sir Sabin's confusion increased. ''Is . . .'' He paused as something else suddenly occurred to him. ''Has something happened to Di, er, Miss Forsythe?''

Lady Aurora sniffed and her mother rose, drawing herself up to her full, if not very considerable height. ''Miss Forsythe, Sir Sabin, has been dismissed.''

''Dismissed?'' he repeated blankly. As the full impact of her statement hit him, shock was added to his initial confusion. ''For God's sake, why?'' he demanded, and then he flushed. ''I mean—''

''Not for God's sake, Sir Sabin, but for the sake of my young daughters, who were her pupils.'' Lady Marchant's tone was even colder and her gaze accusing. ''It has come to our attention that you and Miss Forsythe enjoy a friendship of a nature that cannot be tolerated in one employed here.''

His confusion increasing, Sir Sabin looked from Lady Marchant to Lady Aurora, noting that the latter's expression bordered on the petulant, again bringing him unwelcome memories of his late brother's bride. ''I have some small acquaintance with Miss Forsythe, yes—'' he began, only to be interrupted by Lady Marchant.

''I would say that this acquaintance, you mention, is rather larger than you would have us believe, Sir Sabin, since you—''

''Bought her a gown!'' Lady Aurora shrilled.

He paled. "Miss Forsythe told you that?"

"Indeed, she did not," Lady Aurora snapped. "She lied to us, the little wretch. It so happens that my very dearest friend, Lady Julia Derwent, was present in the mantua maker's shop when you were ordering it—"

"My dear," her mother broke in.

"Do not interrupt me, Mama. I think he should have the entire account." She fastened her angry eyes on Sir Sabin. "As I was saying, Lady Julia heard the whole transaction. Was it your idea that she tell us that the gift was from her aunt? Oh, I do feel so demeaned. I had the impression last night, Sir Sabin, that you had changed, and for the better— but I see I was mistaken. You—you and my sister's governess! Oh, it is too, too lowering!"

Sir Sabin's eyes widened and then narrowed. He said, "Just what are you suggesting, Lady Aurora?"

"My daughter is not suggesting anything, Sir Sabin," Lady Marchant said freezingly. "She is stating what we believe to be a fact. Will you deny that you and that young woman were on more than friendly terms?"

He barely heard the question. He was thinking of what Lady Aurora had just told him. He stared at her. "Am I to understand," he said slowly, "that you have dismissed Miss Forsythe because you believe her to be my mistress?"

"Sir Sabin!" Lady Marchant favored him with an icy stare. "How dare you mention such matters in the presence of my young daughter?"

He was silent a moment, looking from one of his accusers to the other. "I am sure," he said finally, "that the term I have used is not unfamiliar to Lady Aurora, since she has already, in so many words, implied such a relationship. However, she is completely in error and I find myself appalled that Diana Forsythe has been blamed for something about which she knew nothing."

"Indeed?" Lady Aurora said sarcastically. "As it happens, Sir Sabin, *she* did not even trouble to deny it."

"That was probably because she was as shocked as I myself," he responded. "I see that I have been guilty of a very great error. Miss Forsythe has been very helpful to me, and knowing that she was attending the ball, I wanted to show my gratitude in a way that I hoped would please her. And—''

''I am sure that it must have,'' Lady Aurora hissed.

His eyes rested on her face for another silent moment. He said concernedly, ''I cannot think that it could have, since it has resulted in her dismissal.'' He shifted his gaze to Lady Marchant's chill countenance. ''Have you given her references?'' he demanded.

''References?'' Lady Marchant repeated. ''Can you imagine—'' she began.

''No,'' he interrupted. ''I cannot imagine that you did. And if I tell you that there was nothing between us, nothing at all, would you let her return or, failing that, give her those recommendations she would need in order to obtain another position?''

''I am unable to do that,'' Lady Marchant said.

''Because you do not believe me?'' he demanded.

''In the very hour of her dismissal, I dispatched letters to her school and to all agencies that hire governesses explaining my reason for letting her go. I cannot call them back.''

''Or will not?'' he inquired with a coldness that matched her own.

''The young women who instruct our children must be, in common with Caesar's wife, above suspicion,'' Lady Marchant responded.

''That young woman, I can tell you, *is* above suspicion, above reproach,'' he said furiously. He looked from one implacable countenance to the other. ''What will happen to her now that you have closed all the doors in London to her?''

''I was sorry to do that, Sir Sabin, sorrier, however, that I had been in error regarding my original estimate of her character. My younger daughters were fond of her, the school praised her scholarship. I did not inquire into her character. And—''

"Enough!" he exclaimed. He took a turn around the room and came back to stare from mother to daughter again. "I cannot think what Lady Julia divined from her session in the mantua maker's salon, but if she suggested that there was anything between myself and Miss Forsythe, she was grossly in error. I have the utmost respect for Miss Forsythe and I owe her a great deal more than I can tell you."

"I think, Sir Sabin"—Lady Aurora stood up—"that you need not refine upon that any more than you have already. We both understand the nature of your connection." Turning on her heel and holding her head high, she went swiftly out of the room.

Shocked to his very core, Sir Sabin did not so much as glance in the direction of his once-adored Aurora. He said evenly, "I am sure you will excuse me, Lady Marchant."

"I will excuse you, Sir Sabin," she responded. "And though I cannot speak for my son, I hope that if you wish to continue seeing him, you will meet him at his club. I do not wish you to enter this house again."

"And I, Lady Marchant, have absolutely no desire to enter this house again. I will bid you good morning." With a perfunctory bow, Sir Sabin wheeled and strode out of the room. In a matter of minutes he was also out of the house, and receiving his horse from a groom, he rode swiftly away without so much as a backward glance at what he had, earlier that morning, characterized as the "temple containing the beautiful goddess of the dawn, the Incomparable Lady Aurora."

9

"H'intolerable . . ."

"*In*—intolerable."

"*In*-tolerable. You shall find that h'I'll 'ave . . ."

"Enough." Diana put down the book with which she
had been following the lines of *The Jealous Wife*, a play
for which she was preparing Miss Georgiana Pemberton,
the young actress who would understudy the role her
mother was currently acting. She said impatiently, "Miss
Pemberton, we do not put the letter *h* before i, nor do we
extract it from the word 'have.' It is not h'I 'ave. It is
I—I—I, Miss Pemberton. I ha-ve—I ha-ave."

"I ha-ave," muttered Miss Pemberton.

"Not ha-ave. I am stressing the 'ha' for your benefit,
but the word is simply have, have, have . . . had hired,
he, hat, help, Miss Pemberton. Have you practiced them at
home as I have begged you to do?"

Georgiana Pemberton directed a furious look at Diana.
"H'I'm damned if I'll take this." She flung the book
down. "H'I'll be talkin' wi' Mr. Gifford'n 'e'll gi' you
what for." She flounced out of the row of seats in the
darkened theater and went up on stage and thence to the
small room where the other actors were running through
lines. Diana could hear her calling, "Mr. Gifford! Mr.
Giffffforddddd!"

She was not worried about Mr. Gifford's reaction to
Georgiana's complaints. He would listen patiently to them
and then explain that she, Diana Forsythe, a renowed
pedagogue, had been hired to rid Miss Pemberton and

114

other actors and actresses of the accents they had learned
at their mother's knee. Diana had been told that Georgiana's
mother came from Covent Garden. Her informant, Mr.
Bryans, had known her and told Diana that before her
death she had been plying a flourishing trade on the streets
while leaving her little girl with a friend, who worked at the
theater.

"Shere 'angin' about when she were this 'igh." He had
held his hand a foot from the floor. "She weren't twelve
when she climbed up on the knee o' the man wot worked
at the Garden an' 'e 'ired her. She 'as a pretty face, ri'
enough."

Georgiana had done very well in comedy parts, but
lately she had shown signs of wanting to expand her acting
range into serious drama, and Mr. Gifford was willing to
give her the opportunity if she could improve her speech.
He thought she had talent.

Diana was not so sure. Mr. Gifford, she could now
admit, was a kind man and did not like to discourage
anyone. She admired that about him and she liked his
generosity. He treated his actors well, too. She was also
most grateful to him for having invented this position for
her and for professing to be extremely glad that she was at
liberty to accept it. However, she still did not want him for
a stepfather. He was not the equal of her mother in any
way, and it seemed entirely incredible to her that Flavia
Forsythe, who was his superior in birth, in breeding, and
in acting ability, had at last consented to become his bride.

"It will make it easier on the road," had been her
mother's weak excuse. "And I am fond of him. He is
generous, good-tempered, kind, and an excellent actor as
well as manager. Furthermore, now that the wars are at an
end, we are contemplating a tour of American theaters—
Philadelphia, Boston, Washington City, and New York.
Under such circumstances, marriage is not only desirable,
it is necessary."

"And necessity is your main purpose in wedding him?"
Diana had demanded. "What if you should fall in love?"

"I have not been in love for many years." Mrs. Forsythe had spoken coldly and a trifle defensively. "I find it a most debilitating emotion. A marriage based on mutual interest is much to be desired. Mr. Gifford and I share many interests besides our main one, the theater. He is intelligent and pleasant. We are comfortable together, and that, my dear, is a condition which, though you may not credit it, is more desirable than a so-called grand passion."

It seemed to Diana that her mother was endeavoring to convince herself as well as her daughter that she was making the right decision. She longed to argue with her, but such a course might have brought her own unhappy situation to the surface. So far, her mother, beyond briefly decrying the ruin of her fondest hopes for her daughter's future, had remained silent. An argument on the subject of her forthcoming nuptials might have brought the rebuttal that it was none of her business, and if she did not care for the man who would eventually become her stepfather, she ought to have used the discretion she had been taught since babyhood to manage her own life. That her mother had said none of these things was a credit to her self-restraint, and it was up to a grateful Diana to make use of that same self-restraint. A well-earned scolding from her mother coming on top of her own misery would be very hard to bear.

Yet, if her mother married Mr. Gifford—or rather, when she did—Diana would have to find another means of livelihood. She would not be able to bear the continuous proximity of the man, whose background, she feared, was not far above that of Miss Pemberton. Furthermore, his appearance had never pleased her. She found his good looks coarse, and of late, he had developed a taste for spirits. She attributed this change in his habits to his practice of striking up an acquaintance with the local tradesmen he encountered in taverns and inns along the road to his engagements. He called it "good business," and her mother agreed that it was, but after they were married, would he enlist her aristocratic and beautiful parent in such enterprises?

Diana sighed and cast a glance around the battered old building that tonight would be the so-called Theater Royal of Froxfield. She longed to be on the road again toward their destination, which would be Bath, where there was a far more impressive Theater Royal and where they would remain for a week's engagement and more if popular demand equaled Mr. Gifford's anticipation. In Bath, perhaps, her flagging spirits would revive. Mr. Gifford had suggested partaking of the waters to accomplish this end. Of course, he had no inkling of her inner woes. He attributed them to physical problems. Naturally, given his lack of sensitivity . . . She paused in her thinking. She was being unfair. He was not insensitive. He knew nothing about the reasons behind her abrupt departure from London. She had begged her mother not to tell anyone about that. Mr. Gifford, she had to admit, was sympathetic, and informed of Sir Sabin's role in her dismissal, he would have been extremely critical of him, which would mean that his name would be on the actor's lips far more than she could tolerate.

She loosed a sharp little sigh. In the five weeks that she had been away from London, she had been in a state of deep depression. Try as she did to hate Lady Aurora and her mother, she knew that she had been entirely at fault, first by providing Sir Sabin with the lessons and second by the wearing of his beautiful gift. Her mother *had* chided her about that.

Examining the gown, she had said, "Even if they had not had Lady Julia as an informant, they must have suspected that this gown was far and above such monies as your 'aunt' would spend. Look at the way it is made, and that heavy satin. Much as I object to his action, I must admit that the young man has good taste, My dearest, do not weep."

Diana had managed to blink away the threatening tears. "I am crying for my own stupidity, Mama," she had told her. Another sigh escaped her. "Oh," she murmured out loud. "If only I could forget him!"

"Ah, Miss Forsythe, whom do you wish to expunge from your memory? But, of course, I know, and am most sympathetic." Mr. Hornby, the sole other person who was aware of the reasons Diana had returned to the company, took the chair beside her and covered her hand with his own.

She made an attempt to smile into the actor's handsome and gentle face. "Oh, Mr. Hornby, I did not know you were beside me."

"You were deep in thought, my dear."

"I expect I was."

"I need not tell you, I imagine, that brooding on the past is useless and a waste of energy. It changes nothing and can only weary you."

There was a touch of melancholy in his tone and it was also reflected in his eyes. She guessed that he was speaking from his own experience and, again, wondered what it might have been. However, she contented herself with answering him. "No, you need not tell me that. But you may tell me that I was foolish in everything I did. I ought to have abided by my original intention and left his 'education' entirely to you."

"That, I think, would have pleased neither Sir Sabin nor yourself, my dear," he said meaningfully.

"Sure, you cannot believe that," Diana exclaimed indignantly. "I—I only wanted to help him and I offered to oversee his progress in the waltz because I knew his situation."

"My dear Miss Forsythe, for what it is worth, I introduced him to several young ladies who were equally eager to assist him on that count. I do not wish to make you any more unhappy than you are at present, but I am quite sure that Sir Sabin, who often spoke about you, has feelings for you about which he is unaware."

"Surely you are mistaken. To me he spoke only of Lady Aurora."

"I imagine that he believed he loved her, but"—a shade passed over the actor's face—"a man may believe many things and be totally mistaken. They can look to the rose and fail to realize that it is the daisy they prefer. Do not imagine that I am comparing you to that daisy, my dear Miss Forsythe. You are a rose that would enhance any garden.''

"You do not need to tell me that, Mr. Hornby."

"Of course, I do not, but it is true. All too often we do not realize what we want until it is too late. And, my dear Miss Forsythe, I have a feeling that Sir Sabin Mallory, upon hearing of your abrupt and unjust dismissal, will have quite a few second thoughts. He is a young man of sterling character and the actions of Lady Aurora and her mother cannot fail to displease him."

"Do you think so?" she asked eagerly.

"I do, my dear. I should not be surprised if—"

"Ah, Silas, 'ere you are."

Diana looked up quickly to find Georgiana Pemberton smiling down at her companion, who smiled back and rose quickly. "Georgiana, my dear!" He bowed over her hand.

Diana, who had very few friendly feelings for the actress, was amazed to see that her companion's face had changed and that he was looking at the girl with an affection that amazed her. Yet, she reasoned, he could not care for this young woman who was so far beneath him in every way.

"Miss Forsythe," Georgiana said penitently. "Mr. Gifford said as 'ow—as *how* you was right about my *h*'s and I ought to listen to you."

"Indeed, you should, Georgie," Mr. Hornby said with a hint of sternness. "You are fortunate, indeed, to have the tutelage of Miss Forsythe, who is an excellent coach and speaks beautifully herself."

"I know that," Georgiana said almost humbly. She fixed her large blue eyes on Diana. "But in my h'own . . ." She clicked her tongue and shook her head. "In—my—*own* defense, I must say Miss Forsythe, that until h'I . . . *I* learn a part, I am so h'ob . . . *obsessed* with the meaning that I forget all about pronunciation."

"There's nothing to forgive, Miss Pemberton. I do understand. I fear I spoke mainly out of my own frustration. Please forgive me." Diana put out her hand.

"Oh, I do!" Georgiana clasped it warmly.

"And so," Mr. Hornby said merrily, "we are all right and tight. Shall we go walking in this town? There's not much of it, but it is extremely beautiful and it's time we left this musty old barracks."

"You go, do," Diana urged. "I must speak to my mother." She received a grateful look from little Georgiana.

"Very well, we'll go, shall we, Georgie?" Mr. Hornby smiled down at the girl.

"Oh, yes, please, Silas."

Diana watched them walk up the aisle in surprise. They were so ill-matched. Despite his profession, Mr. Hornby was an aristocrat to his fingertips. Again she wondered what had brought him to the theater and why he had stayed. She also wondered what he could have in common with little Georgiana and then forgot him in remembering his words concerning Sir Sabin. He had hinted that Sir Sabin did not know his own mind. Mr. Hornby was a most observant man. Her mother had often told her that, but it little mattered, she reasoned dolefully. Even if Sir Sabin did care for her, he would not be able to find her, and she would not want him to find her. She was gloomily positive that despite what Mr. Hornby had said, Sir Sabin was currently basking in Lady Aurora's good graces. She sighed and walked slowly up the aisle and out of the theater in the direction of the Red Lion, the old inn where most of the company was staying.

Bath. Diana had been looking forward to her first visit to the famous little city, and having arrived, she had dutifully gone on a tour of it in company with Mr. Hornby and Georgiana.

Her companions had waxed most enthusiastic over the beautiful architecture and their visit to the Pump Room. The Roman ruins beyond it had filled Georgiana with awe, for all she had loosed giggles at the sight of those who were either quaffing the extremely bitter waters or bathing in them. She had taken no more than a sip of that liquid that was supposed to be good for every ailment from a quinsy to, as Mr. Hornby laughingly said, foot palpitations!

"But I had thought that an h'affliction . . . affliction of old age, Silas," Georgiana had said.

"Entirely, my love," he had drawled.

As usual, Georgiana had not understood his sarcasm, but she did not appear to notice what Diana would have dubbed a set-down. A moment later Mr. Hornby had put his arm around her waist and given her a gentle squeeze while smiling tenderly down into her pretty face. There was no doubt that he was very fond of the girl, and despite their insistence that Diana accompany them, she had felt extremely *de trop*. Excusing herself, she had started back to the Garrick's Head Tavern, conveniently located next to the Theater Royal.

The streets were crowded with a heterogeneous mass of people: from elderly ladies in outmoded gowns occupying sedan chairs to young bucks on horseback or driving curricles—some elegantly dressed and others in very humble attire. As in London, it was very noisy: the clattering of wheels over cobblestones; the cries of those hawking violets, milk, muffins, and other wares; the neighing of horses and the cursing of coachmen attempting to pass drays. Glad to escape the turmoil, Diana hurried up the stairs of the inn. A second later, she met her mother, who was just emerging from her room, Moira behind her.

"And how are you enjoying the city, my love?" Mrs. Forsythe demanded.

"It is well enough," Diana said, "but I am sure that it cannot be the same as it was under Beau Nash."

Much to her indignation, Mrs. Forsythe burst out laughing. "The Beau, my love, died long before you were born and before your mama was born, also."

"Really?" Beau Nash was actually just a name to Diana, albeit it had been pronounced with considerable affection by several ladies she had seen in the Pump Room that morning. Granted those that mentioned it had been upward of seventy, but they had spoken of the gentleman as if he had recently died.

"Beau Nash, my dear, departed this world in 1762. I was born in 1780."

"You tell your age and ye'll tell anything," croaked Moira.

Flavia Forsythe only laughed the louder. "At thirty-six, I am not an ancient, Moira. Give me your warnings ten years hence and I shall take care to heed them."

Her mother did seem in good spirits, Diana thought as she entered her chamber. She looked young and happy. Was that because she had finally set the date for her wedding to Mr. Gifford? Diana hoped she was wrong. Yet, Mrs. Forsythe could not continue to wear the willow for her husband forever. Did she still mourn the man whose name had never passed her lips in all of Diana's lifetime? Diana suspected that though she had forbidden all mention of him, her mother might yet love him. She could understand that. Indeed, she could understand it all too well. She had seen many young men since leaving London and a goodly number of these had sought to make her acquaintance, but even if her mother would have allowed her to encourage the bucks and the Corinthians who flocked to the green room, she had no interest in them. Superimposed on every masculine countenance were the features of Sir Sabin Mallory. Indeed, he seemed to loom larger in her consciousness with every passing day, to the point that her sleep was troubled and her intake of food so reduced as to move Moira to declare her a victim of the so-called "green sickness."

Diana sighed and settled down with a copy of *Othello*, the play her mother would be enacting on the following night. Undoubtedly, before she went to bed, she would want Diana to run over the lines with her. She had marked some of the passages she found difficult. As Diana started reading them, she wondered dolefully if this activity would be her main occupation for the rest of her days. She quailed at the thought of constant traveling from town to town, indifferent accommodations and mean little theaters. But what other alternative did she have? In helping Sir Sabin to win the lovely Aurora, she had burned all her bridges and broken her heart in the process.

Despite the excitement of an opening at Bath's Theater Royal, a circumstance that had the entire company "on its toes" and eager to present a peak performance, Diana's mood was very little from that of the previous evening, when she had cried herself to sleep only to find her dreams invaded by Sir Sabin. She had stood in the wings for a half-hour, in order to watch the beginning of Sheridan's *The School for Scandal*, a play that her mother and Mr. Gifford had decided was more suited to their combined talents than the author's *The Rivals*, a prime favorite in Bath.

"It is time they had a change," had been Mr. Gifford's comment. "Just because *The Rivals* was written here and has Bath as its setting, every company that passes through must needs present it to the neglect of what I happen to believe is a much finer work."

"I heartily concur," Mrs. Forsythe had said, and winked at him.

He had had the grace to laugh, for, as Diana knew, Sir Peter Teazle was one of his favorite roles just as Lady Teazle was one of the lights of her mother's repertoire. Mr. Hornby was equally pleased with the choice: he would play Charles Surface as opposed to Captain Absolute and Georgiana would be entrusted with Maria, his lady love.

Thinking about Mr. Hornby and Georgiana, Diana was close to envying them, even though it was hard to divine their exact relationship. There were times when she felt Mr. Hornby's attitude to be more avuncular than loving. Yet, on other occasions, seeing them strolling through the city arm in arm, there was no mistaking the fact that they were lovers.

She was thinking of them as she sat in the green room

awaiting the final curtain calls. They were lucky, even if ill-matched. They had found happiness in being together. She could not, however, believe it would last. Mr. Hornby must eventually weary of the girl. She pulled herself up mentally, not admiring the direction her thoughts were taking her. She was being a snob, looking down on poor Georgiana just as Lady Aurora and her ilk had looked down on her as a person to be dismissed out of hand.

That, she realized suddenly, was part of the pain of the situation. A brilliant student, a lady through and through, was how the teachers at school had characterized her and it was also how Lady Marchant had seemed to regard her. Then, and merely because Lady Julia had overheard a conversation in a mantua maker's atelier, they had put two and two together, and without even giving her the benefit of the doubt, they had concluded that she was carrying on a clandestine affair with Sir Sabin Mallory. True, they *had* asked for an explanation, but it had been easy to see that nothing she could have told them would have made any difference. Their minds had been made up well before she had been summoned.

"But it is *he* . . . I am absolutely positive of it!"

Diana looked up startled. While she had been deep in thought, the green room had been filling up with the usual number of gentlemen who came back stage to ogle and woo the actresses. Georgiana, as usual, would have her share of admirers, and so would her mother. Females occasionally came back, smitten by the charms of one or another actor, but these were not so plentiful, not if they were real ladies—and this woman had spoken in tones that were unmistakably cultured. Looking in her direction, Diana noted that she had fine if not beautiful features and certainly an air of distinction, present even in what she guessed was her distress. Furthermore, there was something about her that reminded her of someone. As she looked, the woman spoke again, "And why does he call himself by that name?"

Her companion, a nice-looking man in his forties, appeared equally distressed. "It is not hard to guess, my dear Venetia. He always possessed an elliptical sense of humor. And I would guess that this cognomen was based on Flora's exploits."

"I should not be surprised," the woman called Venetia sighed. "Of course, that must be it. Damn the creature . . . and do not look at me that way, Julian. I cannot speak well of her even if she is dead. I wonder if he knows?"

"Considering the secrecy, even of her burial, I would doubt it."

"You are right, my love. He could not know, else he must have returned."

"He should never have gone away. It was not his doing," the man exclaimed.

"His pride," she said mournfully. "But to turn to this profession." She looked around the green room and, meeting Diana's eyes, gave her a quelling glance and turned away.

Diana blushed, aware that she had been openly interested. The glance she had received reminded her of those she had seen on the visages of the Ladies Marchant and Derwent, a cold back-to-your-place-wench expression that cut her to the quick.

She glanced at the door leading to the stage and wished that she might leave, but if she did, her mother would be hurt. She always wanted Diana's comments on her performance, even though these were invariably complimentary. Consequently, looking everywhere but at the couple, who still stood a short distance away from her, she remained in her corner.

As it happened, Mr. Gifford was the first actor to emerge. He received considerable well-deserved applause from the assembled company. Several gentlemen came forward to congratulate him. Diana heard one of them say, "I was sorry you were not doing *The Rivals*, which is quite a favorite here, but I had forgotten the excellence of this present play. You are one of the best Sir Peters I have had the pleasure to see."

Mr. Gifford looked understandably gratified and Diana was about to rise and offer her congratulations when Mr. Hornby entered the room. Several other men came to congratulate him and he was acknowledging their compliments with his usual, gentle, self-deprecating smile when the woman who had been addressed as Venetia impulsively moved away from her companion and, joining the circle around the actor, put her hand on his arm.

"Arthur," she said brokenly. "Oh, my dearest, dearest Arthur!"

Those around Mr. Hornby had moved back as the lady came forward, and now they edged back still further, exchanging surprised and, in the case of one or two of them, derisive looks. As for Mr. Hornby, he stood still, as if frozen to the spot. It was a moment before he said, "Venetia, my dear."

"Arthur." The gentleman who had been with her also came forward. "Good to see you, at last."

"Julian." Mr. Hornby nodded.

"Oh, Arthur," the woman said. "Flora is dead!"

Though she had no reason for it, Diana tensed as she stared at Mr. Hornby, who was so unaccountably being addressed as Arthur instead of Silas and who obviously had a connection with this top-lofty couple. His face registered nothing. He said merely, "Is she?"

"Silas, love." Georgiana had entered the green room, and notwithstanding the fact that several obviously smitten young gentlemen were trying to waylay her, she made her way to Mr. Hornby's side and caught his arm. She received a cold quelling look from the couple. The actor must have caught their expressions, for despite his obvious shock, he slipped an arm around Georgiana's waist and drew her closer to him. "My dear," he said gently, "I think you must meet my sister and my brother-in-law, Lord and Lady Camperdene."

"Your . . ." Georgiana stepped back. She paled, "H'I'm p-pleased to m-make yer h'acquaintance," she said out of what was obviously deep shock. She would have moved away, but Mr. Hornby held her firmly at his side.

Diana recalling the look visited upon her by Mr. Hornby's sister—his sister?—felt very sorry for Georgiana. Her speech had improved within the last two days, but it was not proof against such an announcement. She noted that Lady Camperdene did not trouble to return the girl's salutation. Without visiting so much as a second look on her, she said, "Arthur, is there nowhere we might talk? We have a great deal more to tell you."

There was a grim look on Mr. Hornby's face. "I am willing to speak with you, certainly, Venetia. However, Miss Pemberton, who is my future bride, must needs be included in a conversation that will probably hold some interest for her."

"Your bride!" Georgiana and Lady Camperdene spoke in unison while Lord Camperdene appeared appalled.

Mr. Hornby looked down at Georgiana. "Did I speak too soon, Georgie, my love? I have been waiting to put this question to you for a long time, but until this moment I could not. You see, my dearest, I did not realize that I was free and could offer for you. Do you want to marry me?"

Tears started to Diana's eyes as she saw the look Georgiana gave him. It was composed of adoration and amazement, as if, indeed, she could not believe what she was hearing. "Want to . . ." she began.

"You are not serious, surely, Arthur," Lady Venetia spoke over Georgiana's faltering words in accents of utter horror.

Mr. Hornby did not seem to have heard her. Diana had the impression that of all the people in the room, he was aware only of Georgiana, still held in the circle of his arm. "Well, Georgie, will you be my wife?"

"Oh, yes, but . . ." she spoke tremulously and with a quick, frightened glance at Lady Venetia's frozen countenance.

Lord Camperdene cleared his throat. "You are not cognizant of your circumstances, Arthur. Flora's has not been the only death in the family. We must talk and it had best be in private." He, too, regarded Georgiana coldly.

Mr. Hornby said steadily, "I agree that we must talk, for there is obviously a great deal more that I ought to know. But unless the lady who has just consented to be my wife is present, I must needs remain in ignorance of the situation."

There was a moment's pause before Lord Camperdene said, "Very well. I suggest we repair to our temporary residence. We are, at present, occupying a house in Camden Place."

"We are at your disposal, Julian," Mr. Hornby said. He took his arm from around Georgiana's shoulders, and possessing himself of her hand, he added, "Shall we go now?"

Watching them and seeing the cold closed look on his sister's face, Diana felt a wave of sympathy for Georgiana wash over her, but in that same moment she realized that Georgiana did not really need her sympathy. Obviously she had a man who loved her and who was willing to prove it in the face of what one might describe as overwhelming odds.

10

Shortly after Mr. Hornby's departure, Flavia Forsythe came out to her usual round of applause and subsequent solicitations from admiring young men. Diana, having proffered her compliments, was aching to get back to their lodgings and discuss the confusing but exciting scene she had just witnessed. However, Mr. Gifford detained her still longer with some adjurations about their forthcoming *Othello,* which would require a special rehearsal the following afternoon, despite the fact that the performance would take place that night. And naturally he had something to say about Mr. Hornby and the advent of his family. Consequently it was well over two hours before Diana could also describe the actor's meeting with his sister and her husband, and in fuller detail than that provided by Mr. Gifford.

Mrs. Forsythe listened with more interest than shock, and as she finally concluded her argument, Diana dared to say, "I am under the impression, Mama, that this comes as no surprise to you."

"It does not," Mrs. Forsythe admitted. Half-regretfully, she continued, "I do know some of his history, and since you were a witness to his meeting with his family, I do not believe that Mr. Hornby will mind your knowing what I know. I only hope that this does not mean we will lose an actor of skill and even brilliance."

"If his sister has anything to say about the matter, I fear we will," Diana sighed. "She reminds me of Lady

Marchant. But no matter, do tell me about Mr. Hornby. And how did he come to confide in you?''

"Questions . . . questions." Her mother held up a protesting hand. "The reason I know anything about him is because when he came to us, I could see that he was an entirely different breed than your average thespian. Furthermore, he had had very little experience in the theater. He spoke of university plays, many of which were in Latin. However, I was impressed by his bearing and his speech, which, as you know, is entirely natural and unaffected. He speaks as many actors wish they might but which takes years of practice to acquire. Hearing it, I will not scruple to tell you that I feared he might be one who, having either run up large debts or committed some other worse folly, was hiding behind greasepaint and footlights.''

"Oh, no," Diana protested. "I would never imagine that Mr. Hornby could—''

"Ah, but you are an innocent when it comes to the theatrical trade, my dear Diana," Mrs. Forsythe said trenchantly. "Men quite as aristocratic in bearing as Mr. Hornby have proved to be miscreants fleeing from the law. We have had Bow Streets Runners lurking in the alleys behind the theater more than once, ready to seize one or another member of our company.''

"Such as Mr. Bryans," Diana murmured with some little satisfaction as she remembered his recent incarceration for debt at the hands of a determined constable who had waited for him as he came offstage.

"Such as Mr. Bryans," her mother acknowledged. "Consequently, though I was most favorably inclined toward Mr. Hornby, I was still on my guard. I did notice that he seemed extremely melancholy. There was a hurt look in his eyes that made me want to soothe him as I might an unhappy child. He did seem very young to me.''

"I would imagine that he is rather older," Diana mused.

"He is. I would put him at thirty-two or -three," her mother agreed, "but this was four years ago. Be that as it may, I did feel it incumbent upon me that I ask him more about his background. At first, he was reluctant to confide in me, but he obviously needed a sympathetic ear, and with a little prodding on my part, he spoke about his wife and another man. His very words were 'I found them together.' Not an uncommon tale, Diana, but there was such shock and grief in his eyes that I could tell her actions had come as a complete surprise to him. I also had the impression that, until the revelation, he had trusted her entirely, surprising in a man." Mrs. Forsythe grimaced. "Usually, it is the other way around, at least in my experience. However, having witnessed his pain, I could not bear to question him further.

"I gave him a side and asked him to read the role of Bassanio, which he did very creditably and surprised me further by essaying one of Shylock's speeches in a manner that sent chills down my back. Yet, at the same time, I was aware that he was not one of us—not an actor. I knew it would take time for him to develop into one, but I discussed him with Mr. Gifford, who, in common with myself, had been impressed with his manner and his speech. Consequently, we decided to give him a chance. It was then that we realized that we did not know his name. I cannot tell you how he replied to our question. He hesitated and then with a most bitter expression, he said, 'Something with a horn in it . . . Horner, perhaps?'

"Mr. Gifford told him that that name had been used in a scurrilous lampoon directed at the Prince Regent and suggested that he use Hornby, and so Hornby he became. He himself added the Silas."

"His sister addressed him as Arthur. She is Lady Camperdene. I wonder—"

"Do not wonder and do not probe," adjured Mrs. Forsythe. "If he chooses to tell us anything, well and good. If not, we must rest content."

"Oh, dear," Diana sighed. She continued, "Can you believe that he has actually proposed to Georgiana Pemberton?"

"And why should he not?" Mrs. Forsythe demanded. "He does not need to question her love for him."

"But . . ." Diana frowned and received a frown in return.

"Many have crossed even wider chasms in their social positions and lived, as the old saying goes, happily ever after, Diana. It is character that counts and also love, and I am of the opinion that Silas Hornby has come to know what love can be through this child. My dearest, why are you crying?"

"I am not." Diana blinked away her tears and then could not help from saying dolefully, "Oh, Mama, why could that not have been true of me?"

Mrs. Forsythe put her arms around Diana. "My dearest, did Sir Sabin mean so very much to you, then?"

Diana reluctantly nodded. "But by—by now, he and Lady Aurora—"

"Why did you help him, child?"

"It was through helping him that I—I came to care for him. I did not know that—that I would feel that way, but, Mama, he is so kind, so good and—"

"Oh, Diana, my poor love. I wish there were something I could tell you. Actually there is. You are a beautiful girl, my dearest, and one day there will be a man who will really appreciate you. You are young yet."

"Young?" Diana repeated mournfully. "In another few months, I shall be *nineteen*. And besides . . ." She paused.

"Besides—what?"

Diana heaved another sigh. "I do not believe I shall ever meet anyone like Sir Sabin again." That was all she could say, she decided. She could not state the real reason for her doubts concerning an eventual marriage, provided that she could ever forget Sir Sabin. She could not, dared not, bring up the subject of her illegitimate birth to her mother!

"You will be surprised to learn that life and love are not entirely over for you yet." Mrs. Forsythe smiled. "No matter how stricken of heart we are, we women have a way of recovering. That might be small comfort at present, but I am sure you will come to agree with me, my child.''

Her mother was looking very tired, Diana thought. ''Perhaps I will,'' she sighed. ''But now I will go to bed.''

''An excellent idea,'' Mrs. Forsythe approved. ''In the morning, everything will look far rosier, I assure you.''

It took Diana quite a while to fall asleep and it seemed to her that she had been sleeping only a few hours when there was a knock on her door. Was it Moira come to rouse her? she wondered and, opening her eyes, looked toward the windows. The curtains had been drawn by the chambermaid, but as always, she had pulled them back, not liking to waken in darkness. Consequently, she could see that it was still very early. The sky was lighter, but the sun was only a streak of red across the horizon. It could not be Moira, coming so early. Someone must have made an error in the room. However, even as that thought crossed her mind, the knock was repeated more urgently. Climbing out of her bed, she went to the door and opened it the merest crack. ''Who is there?'' she whispered.

''Oh, Miss Forsythe, 'elp me,'' came a low, trembling voice. ''H'I do not know wot h'I should do!''

All vestiges of sleep left Diana, for it was Georgiana who stood outside. She opened wide the door. ''Come in, my dear,'' she invited, and saw by the pale light creeping through the windows that Georgiana was cloaked and carrying two bandboxes. ''My dear, where are you going?'' she demanded in shock. ''You cannot be leaving us!''

''Oh.'' Georgiana sank down on a nearby chair. ''H'I feel h'I'm not for 'im.''

Memories came rushing back into Diana's head. ''Tell me what's amiss, child,'' she urged. Inwardly she was surprised at the form of address that she had inadvertently used. Georgiana could give her a good four years and a thousand more in experience, but she seemed so unhappy, so helpless and confused. Her head was drooping; indeed, her whole body appeared to be drooping. ''You must take off your cloak,'' she added. ''You must be passing warm.''

Mechanically Georgiana obeyed her. "I 'ave to leave," she moaned. "An' then 'e can go back to wot's rightfully 'is. 'E cannot gi' it h'all up because o' me. 'Tisn't right."

"Tell me what happened, Georgiana," Diana said gently.

It took quite a while, for the narrative was frequently interrupted with protests of Georgiana's love for Mr. Hornby and with bursts of tears, but Diana finally had a vivid image of what had taken place at the house in Camden Place.

"It were all so fine," Georgiana had said in awed accents.

Diana could actually see her clinging tightly to Mr. Hornby's arm as they had come into a beautifully furnished drawing room. "All 'ung wi' brocade an' crystal over' 'ead an' wi' a rug you could sink in."

Her host and hostess were inclined to ignore the girl but Mr. Hornby had not permitted that.

" 'E kept callin' me 'is wife to be—'im that'd never mentioned marriage before."

"He explained that yesterday," Diana reminded her. "He did not know he was free."

"But 'tisn't right," Georgiana cried. " 'E's one o' *them*."

Mr. Hornby, not to Diana's entire surprise, had a title. He was Sir Arthur Cranmere. " 'E's the same like them wot kept lookin' at me h'as if h'I were a bad smell."

His sister and brother-in-law had gone on to tell Mr. Hornby of the death of his older brother, who had been killed in a hunting accident, dying without issue. Lady Flora Cranmere, who had been caught by her husband, lying with a handsome young groom in the stable loft, was also dead and they had been searching for him in vain. "They want 'im to come back."

"And what did he say?" Diana prompted.

" 'E asked about 'is Cousin John'n they said as 'ow 'e were actin' as caretaker'n Mr. Hornby said 'e could go on wi' wot 'e were doin' because 'e were 'appy wi' this life'n wasn't in no 'urry to go 'ome. But h'I—*I* don't believe 'im. *I* think 'e said all that account o' me, 'cause 'e don't think h'I'd fit in wi' all them grand folk. An' so h'I 'ave to leave 'im," Georgiana sobbed. "An' I want you to h'explain. T-tell 'im that—" She jumped at a sharp knock on the door. " 'Oo's that?" she quavered.

"It might be Moira come to rouse me," Diana said as she hurried to answer the knock. "Who is there?" she asked tentatively, hoping that she was right about the identity of this second caller.

The voice was muffled. "Is she there?" it demanded.

"She is," Diana said in relief, and opened the door to admit Mr. Hornby, who for once was neither calm nor elegant. His clothes looked as if he had flung them on in a hurry. His cravat was untied and there was a night's growth of beard on his cheeks. He actually rushed past her and stood in front of a shocked Georgiana.

"One of the maids said you'd be here," he said angrily. "And why are you dressed for traveling?" He lifted one of her bandboxes and threw it down. His eyes actually blazed. "Would you leave me, also?"

"Oh, Silas," Georgiana wailed. "H'I'm not for the likes o' you. Your sister—"

"Damn and blast my sister," he said furiously. "She's not marrying you. I am. And it is because I love you, you little fool!"

"But, Silas, I'm not yer sort. You—you're not the—the first. I been wi' others," she whispered.

"You have been with me for two years—the two happiest years of my life," he said more gently now. "Who was it left the company and came every day to visit me when I was in Whitecross Prison? It was a sacrifice I begged you not to make, but you'd not heed me. As for the other, I do not care what happened before I met you. All I know's that you've brought me more happiness than anyone I have ever known. I wish to tell you, also, that I am happy in this life, our life, my dearest. I enjoy acting. I am not in the least desirous of leaving the company and I will not, nor must you because"—his voice was trembling

with emotion now—"I do not know what I would do
without you, Georgie, so please, my angel, please marry
me." He sank down on his knees beside her and carried
her hand to his lips.

"Oh, Silas," Georgiana murmured. "H'I—I will if you
are s-sure you are sure."

"My love, my only love," he said still brokenly. "I
could not be more sure of anything in this world. Will you
forgo the banns and marry me within three days' time?"

"H'I—*if* that is what you want, Silas." She looked up
at him out of tear-drenched eyes. "I will." She uttered a
little shriek then, for Mr. Hornby had scooped her up from
the chair, and holding her against him, he pulled open the
door with one hand and carried her out of the room.

Standing in the wings watching Silas Hornby, again
playing the role of Charles Surface, Diana was amazed and
at the same time touched. There was a new texture to his
acting. His Charles seemed lighter, more buoyant than
before, and she did not hesitate to ascribe that to the
presence of his wife.

Somewhat to the disappointment of an excited company,
Mr. Hornby and Georgiana Pemberton had slipped away to
be married in an ancient church of Calne, a village some
nine miles out of Bath. Their only witnesses had been
herself, her mother, and Mr. Gifford. Diana's eyes smarted
and a line from the *Othello* of the other night came to her.
"Mine eyes itch, doth that bode weeping?" Desdemona
had said. Diana knew that this was hardly the sentiment
that should cross her mind in view of their obvious happiness. They had looked almost delirious with joy when they
had left the church. Fortunately, the following day being a
Sunday, the theater was dark and they had an entire day
and night to be together. No one knew where they had
gone, but when they returned, they looked even happier
and Georgiana had displayed a new dignity. She was also
taking considerable pains with her speech, with strong emphasis on finding the right place to put the elusive 'h'.

Sir, I have little to say, but that I will rejoice to hear that he is happy; for me, whatever claim I had to his attention, I willingly resign to one who has a better title.

In her character as Maria, Georgiana had just uttered this speech, and Diana, though rejoicing that every *h* was in place and every *i* free from any additions, found her eyes blurring. Obviously, love, rather than her poor efforts, had been as Georgiana's pedagogue.

Moving back, Diana made her way into the green room, not wanting anyone to see that she was in tears. Fortunately, no one was present as yet and she was able to wipe her eyes and in some part regain an equilibrium understandably shaken ever since the wedding.

Naturally, it had been quite impossible to expunge Sir Sabin from her mind at that time—impossible, too, not to imagine herself in Georgiana's place as she lifted a glowing face for her bridegroom's kiss, a bridegroom who, of course, bore the features of her pupil.

Sitting down in her accustomed chair, Diana was conscious that the green room was both warm and stuffy. Looking about her, she also found it too narrow, and soon it would grow narrower and hotter when it was filled with the people who would come back to congratulate the actors and flirt with the actresses. She wondered at Mr. Hornby's odd decision to remain with the company. Were she in his place, she would like nothing so much as to dwell in a manor house and have horses and dogs. She would also do a lot of walking and riding around the grounds, and she would never go to London. No, perhaps, if she had a house such as that owned by Lord Marchant, she would visit it once or twice a year during the Season. She shook her head, not wanting to think of the Marchant mansion. However, much as she longed to put it out of her mind, she must needs admit that she missed it; more than that, she missed the bright chatter of Rosalie and Eustacia, who had been more than mere pupils. They had been friends! It seemed impossible that she would never see them again. If only she had known . . . But she must not dwell on the other lessons and their unfortunate aftermath.

"Never look back, my love," her mother had advised.

It was impossible to obey that particular command, impossible not to look back to a time when she had taken far too much for granted. She had actually counted herself "one of the family," and thus had failed to consider the consequences of her rash, impulsive, and were she to be entirely truthful with herself, deceitful actions. Yet, how very quickly that tenuous relationship had been severed, how very hastily she had been shoved into her place.

"I must not think about it," she sighed.

She stared around the room again, and seeing a faded portrait of some actress of the past hanging on the opposite wall, she heaved a second sigh. If only she had had talent in acting . . . But that had been denied her, and to remain backstage, to be barred from the one profession where she might have made her mark, seemed a cruel fate indeed, as well as a sad comedown for the proud Miss Diana Forsythe.

"Was I proud?" she asked herself, and knew that she had been. Her dismissal had been doubly hard to take because of that same pride. Despite the fact that she had never known her father, despite the fact that her mother was a member of the despised acting profession, Diana had been proud of Mrs. Forsythe's accomplishments and proud of her own at school. She had had a bright future awaiting her. She had been an excellent scholar and was also a gifted teacher. And though the prospect had not enchanted her, she would have, in time, enjoyed heading her own school. She knew that, too, now that it was too late.

"Pride goeth before destruction and a haughty spirit before a fall," she had read that in the scriptures, and how right it was. She, who had fallen, had been proud and some of that pride had been merely reflected glory—because she was living in a fine house and mixing with the *ton*. She had fallen into the error of believing she belonged there. In other words, she had been a fool and deserved to see all of her plans destroyed and herself brought low.

Applause filled her ears. The play was at an end. How many more plays would she witness, how many more green rooms would she grace? she wondered despondently.

"Excuse me," a masculine voice said tentatively. "But are you a member of the company, young woman?"

Diana looked up to find a tall man—a Corinthian, she decided, from the cut of his well-fitting clothes—standing by her chair. He had a handsome but arrogant countenance and an air of command. Indeed, he reminded her of the men who came to Marchant House. She would not be surprised were he a titled member of the *ton*. She guessed him to be in his mid-forties, and very probably his reason for hurrying back to the green room was because he had an eye on one or another of the two leading actresses. In her present mood, she could only be pleased that he was doomed to a disappointment he might not usually encounter. "No," she began and paused, for he had stiffened and was staring down at her incredulously. Taking a step backward, he said, "Who are you?"

He had turned so pale that Diana, forgetting her prejudices, rose swiftly. "Sir," she asked concernedly, "are you ill?"

"No," he said, his eyes still fastened on her face. Then, much to her indignation, his glance traveled from her head to her feet and back again. He repeated peremptorily, "Who are you? Rather, what is your name?" Reaching out a hand, he clasped her arm tightly. "Tell me," he ordered.

His grip dug into her flesh, hurting her. Caught between surprise and anger, Diana said coldly, "Pray release my arm, sir."

He flushed and his hand fell to his side immediately.

"My excuses, but it was a shock." He continued, "I must have your name, young woman."

Obviously he was used to issuing orders and having them obeyed, Diana thought resentfully. Nor could she approve the imperious note she yet heard in his voice. Still coldly she responded, "I cannot see how that might concern you, sir. I am not an actress."

"Damme, I am not . . ." he began heatedly, and then paused, still continuing to stare at her in a way she was finding not only rude but also most disconcerting. He looked, indeed, like the villainous Osmond when confronted by the presumed Castle Specter. In tones that were much less belligerent, he said, "I beg your pardon. You see, you bear so very close a resemblance to my . . . Please, will you not tell me your name?"

Though Diana was yet taken aback by his high-handed approach, his change of attitude, coupled with his words, told her that it was surprise rather than rudeness that had moved him. She said, "I am Diana Forsythe."

He paled. "You—you are Flavia's daughter?"

"Yes, my mother is Mrs. Forsythe," Diana responded pointedly.

"I beg your pardon," he said shakily, "but—but when will your mother come into the green room?"

"She ought to be here very soon, sir." Diana regarded him narrowly. He was, she thought, looking far from well. "Might I get you some water, sir?" she asked.

He smiled then. "No, that is not necessary, my dear." He continued to stare at her, almost, she thought, as if he were memorizing her features. Then, as if he were talking to himself, he said in a low, shaken tone of voice, "It is amazing. I would never have believed there could be so startling a likeness."

"To whom, sir?" Diana could not refrain from asking.

He hesitated, and much to her surprise, his eyes had become very bright, almost as if there were tears in them, as he said slowly, "To the portrait of my grandmother,

and I now have reason to believe, your great-grandmother.
I am speaking of Felicity Charlton, Dowager Countess of
Lyall. I think . . . Indeed, I am quite sure that I must be
your father, my dear.''

11

Much against his will, Sir Sabin had bedded down at the Castle Inn in Marlborough for the night and an unexpected rainstorm had kept him in that hostelry for the following day. Notwithstanding the fact that a garrulous landlord was ready to entertain those who thronged the taproom with the history of this "new" town—new, at least compared to Bath with its Roman ruins—Sir Sabin found himself patently disinterested in the fact that the legendary and to his mind entirely fictitious wizard Merlin had supposedly given the place its name. Nor could he work up much interest when told that the ruined castle on the mound under which those fabled bones lay, was erected by William the Conqueror. Nor could he mourn because most of the ancient buildings of Marlborough had been destroyed during a fire in 1663. He managed to surprise and anger his worthy host by striding forth from the taproom in the middle of an anecdote concerning a local ghost that seemed to fascinate the rest of that stranded company.

Coming outside, Sir Sabin moved to the edge of the High Road leading to Bath. In less than a day, provided that the weather improved, he would be there, and this time he was almost certain of finding what he had missed in all the other towns through which he had doggedly passed: the Gifford Acting Company, or more specifically, Diana Forsythe. Then, battered by a wind carrying a whiplash of rain, he sighed and strode back into the inn—but not to the taproom. Instead, he sought his small chamber at the top of the house, and keeping his head down so as to avoid the beams, he stretched out on his lumpy bed and tried to sleep.

Unfortunately, sleep did not come easily. He had already slept for the greater part of the morning, whiling away the hours until he would be in the same town, the same theater, where this time he would meet the young woman whose reputation he had inadvertently ruined, the young woman who he missed the more with every passing hour and whom, he had belatedly come to realize, he loved with all his heart!

It had been a realization that had rendered him both happy and miserable. He was happy in the thought of her and miserable at the havoc he had wrought in her life. Would she ever forgive him for having sent her the gown? Unfortunately, much more than that required her forgiveness. There was the matter of Lady Aurora, whom he had never ceased to praise in Diana's presence.

Thinking of Lady Aurora, Sir Sabin shuddered. With all her lessons, Diana had failed to teach him what she was really like. He was, of course, honest enough to admit that he would have resented such instruction even if it had been in Diana's nature to provide it. Moreover, she would never have stooped to anything so petty. Not once had she let fall a word of criticism concerning that petty, spoiled creature he had actually imagined he loved. That love had been banished from his mind as quickly as one might rub out letters written upon a steaming pane of glass. It had gone with the look of smug satisfaction that had gleamed in Lady Aurora's eyes as her mother explained the reasons behind poor Diana's ignominious dismissal.

At Lady Aurora's accusations concerning himself and his possible dalliance with Diana, he had come perilously close to hating the wench and certainly the scales had been lifted from his eyes. He had seen her as she really was: mean and vindictive, a veritable sister to the chit poor Dick had been forced to wed!

"And had I been unlucky enough to marry Lady Aurora, I too might have willingly died to be rid of her," he muttered to himself.

A long sigh shook him. In the weeks he had been searching for Diana, he had been vouchsafed a revelation. At first he had wanted to find her mainly because he wanted, in some way, to make amends for the folly of sending her that gown, which he ought to have known she would have trouble explaining. However, as the days passed and he did not catch up with the company, he realized that he was missing her as he had missed no other person in his life. He could not remember when he first realized that he loved her, but having come to that conclusion, he knew that the emotion was not a new one. Quite possibly, all the time that he had been pursuing that chimera named Aurora, he had been deluding himself. It had been Diana whom he had loved from the first, Diana whom he had looked forward to seeing on those Tuesdays she could spare. And it would be to Diana to whom he would offer his heart, his hand, and all his worldly goods. And he would see that, despite her background, despite her lack of a father she could name, he would give the actress's daughter a secure place in society. Furthermore, he would see that she had twenty gowns all as beautiful as the green-and-white satin, in which she had looked as lovely as the morning star!

In his mind's eye, he could envision the announcement: At St. James's Church, Sir Sabin Mallory to Diana Forsythe . . . " And let the world take notice that Lady Diana Mallory could hold her head as high as—or rather, higher than—the Lady Auroras of this world.

"Oh, God." He stared resentfully at the rivulets of rain running down the uneven windowpane. "Let the storm be over tonight. Let me see her again and let her forgive me for my blindness." There was a wetness in his eyes as he turned over and again sought the help of Morpheus to pass the hours that must elapse before he could be on the road to Bath and Diana.

*   *   *

It was probably better for his peace of mind that Sir Sabin did not know that for the first time in many weeks Diana Forsythe was not thinking sadly and longingly of him. The words blurted out by the importunate stranger of the green room had been shocking, indeed. And before they had really registered, Flavia Forsythe had unexpectedly come into the green room and Diana had been witness to yet another shocking scene.

Her mother, surrounded, as usual, by admiring gentlemen, had been confronted by that same stranger, who had said chokingly, "Flavia!"

Diana, still rocked by his revelation, had seen her mother come to a dead stop and stare at him incredulously. Her greeting had been absolutely without inflection. "Gervais."

Others had come forward to congratulate her, but she had seemed aware only of the man confronting her, the man who had said in a low voice, "Oh, my God, Flavia, what a damned fool I have been. Your daughter, our child, is the very image of my grandmother!"

Early in the morning on the day following her meeting with the man, whose full name was Gervais Charlton, Earl of Lyall, Diana awakened and sat up in bed hugging her knees and thinking of all that had passed the previous evening. It seemed like a dream, a dream that bore an odd relation to the revelations about Mr. Hornby. But to her mind, her situation was even stranger and much more wonderful! Swept away, at long last, was the confusion and the pain, she had barely acknowledged, of almost two decades. From one moment to the next she had acquired a father, a father and an identity! Diana Forsythe was no more. In her place stood Lady Diana Charlton!

"Lady Diana Charlton," she said out loud, and experienced once more the excitement that had well-nigh overwhelmed her when, with her mother, she had gone to the earl's—to her father's house in Laura Place, hired for the season.

Shortly after sitting down to a lovely supper, she had learned that rather than having been born out of wedlock, she was the legitimate daughter of Lord and Lady Charlton of Lyall Hall, outside of Grantham, Lincolnshire. However, she had not been born there. Her birthplace had been, as her mother told her, Dublin, Ireland, whence Lady Flavia Charlton had gone after a furious quarrel in which the legitimacy of the child had been questioned by her irate husband.

After an excited but chastened Lord Lyall had brought his estranged wife and finally recognized daughter back to the Garrick's Head in a post chaise on which his crest was painted in gold, her mother had summoned her into her room and talked for a long time. Through her eyes, Diana could almost see the events that had led up to that terrible final confrontation.

In the beginning, however, the love of Gervais Charlton for the beautiful young actress Flavia Forsythe had been deep and true and overwhelming . . . overwhelming for them both!

They had met in the green room of Drury Lane. The youthful earl, just out of Oxford, had gone to the theater to see Nicholas Rowe's *Lady Jane Grey*, a drama in which the equally youthful Flavia Forsythe had had the title role. By the end of the play, the entire house was in tears.

"Your father came back to assure himself that I had not, indeed, gone to my execution." Mrs. Forsythe had laughed, her eyes unusually soft as she remembered that moment. "He wanted me to come to supper with him. I gave him the same answer I gave all the young men."

"You refused him," Diana said.

She had done just that. Acquainted with the tragedy of her mother's life, Flavia had not wanted to follow her example. However, Gervais Charlton was extremely persistent. He had continued to pursue the beautiful young girl. He had followed the company to Brighton and later as far as Birmingham. His pursuit had not stopped there. And finally, in the town of York, Flavia had agreed to join him for supper.

He had been very respectful, but even though she liked

him, she was suspicious, fearing the day when he would offer her *carte blanche*.

Surprisingly enough, that day did not come. Finding him always respectful, she began to see more of him. His attitude never varied. Never once did he attempt to make free with her. There came a day when she had to admit to herself that she had fallen in love with him. Then, one night he told her he could not live without her and begged her to marry him.

Flavia had been unable to believe her ears, and then, she, who had never made a public display of her feelings, had actually burst into tears. He had looked at her incredulously and fearfully, asking her if that were a refusal.

"I told him I was crying because I was so happy." Flavia had looked at Diana. "I was, too. I was ecstatic. I did care for him so much . . . so very much." Her voice had trembled, but after a moment she had regained her composure. "I told him I would marry him."

Because of his rank, the earl had obtained a special license and they had been wed the very next day—in a small out-of-the way church. Then, after a fortnight, he had taken her to Lyall Hall, a manor house that, he had explained, had been built on the site of a castle razed by Cromwell's forces during the Civil War.

Mrs. Forsythe had described a lovely house rebuilt in 1670 with additions by Robert Adams. A great park had been designed by Capability Brown and there had been a lake. Indeed, her mother's description of the mansion and its grounds had made Diana's mouth water. Unfortunately, however, the earl's mother and sister had been living in that house, and aware of the bride's background, they had loathed the idea of Flavia Forsythe before meeting her and had managed to turn the older members of the county against her. Even the servants were contemptuous of the new Lady Charlton.

"Oh, Mother," Diana had breathed, reaching for her hand.

Mrs. Forsythe had not returned the clasp. She had kept

her hands clamped together so tightly that her knuckles showed white as she described how her mother- and sister-in-law had moved to the Dower House. Gervais had been very unhappy over their decision, but his wife had been relieved. They had both been so patently disapproving, but never when he was present. At such times they had kept up the pretense of liking her. Their removal to the house, they had assured him, was merely so that the newly married couple might be alone.

Hearing a sarcastic inflection in her mother's voice, Diana had asked, "Did he believe that?"

"Not entirely, hence his unhappiness," Mrs. Forsythe had stated. "But I was delighted that they had gone. And, of course, I was still so deliriously in love with Gervais that I did not mind that we were, in a sense, ostracized by the older members of the community. The younger ones took us to their hearts."

Mrs. Forsythe had tossed her head, and for a moment Diana had obtained a vivid picture of the defiant young girl she must have been.

Time had gone on, and though Flavia had asked Gervais to return to London, he had been oddly reluctant. He spoke of preferring the country, and she had not argued. She had found it very pleasant, but she did miss London, and when Sir Guy Harborne, a friend of the family's, returned from that city and came to visit his dear friend Gervais Lyall, she had quizzed him about the places she had known—with emphasis, of course, upon the theaters.

As it happened, Sir Guy had seen her in several plays and was extremely admiring. Furthermore, he loved the theater and was even thinking of constructing one upon the grounds of his own nearby estate.

Mrs. Forsythe had paused in her narrative, staring into space, her eyes stormy. "I think I had not realized until that moment how very much I missed my profession. I was young then and at the height of my career, and it had been hard to give it up. I did not realize how hard until Guy came with his descriptions of theatrical activities in London and about that projected theater, which he also discussed with Gervais. He did not say very much, but I had the impression that he was not nearly as excited as myself. However, when I asked him what he thought about it, he said that Guy would not be setting a precedent were he to erect a small theater. The same had been done on several other estates."

The young Lady Charlton had grown more enthusiastic. Guy had gone ahead with his project and had often ridden over to Lyall Hall to consult with her. One day, he had asked her to go riding, and in the course of their ride he had impulsively asked if she would like to come to his estate and see how the work was progressing. Delightedly, she had agreed, and they had gone without telling anyone. They had intended to be back very shortly, but as luck would have it, a storm came up, complete with thunder and lightning. They had been forced to take shelter in a little keeper's hut on the grounds. Flavia had not reached home until after midnight. When she had arrived, with Guy at her side, the Dowager countess and her daughter were with the earl. He had been looking doubtful and frightened, but when he saw Guy, he grew furious and would hardly listen to her explanations. His mother and sister, naturally, did not believe her.

The pair had done their work well. Once Flavia was alone with Gervais, he had told her that they had said there was considerable talk about her so-called dalliance with Guy. While he did not believe the gossips, he felt that she was acting in far too provocative a manner for her position. He wanted her to curtail her friendship with Guy. Hurt and just as angry as he, Flavia had retorted that she knew from whence the gossip stemmed—the Dower House. She had accused his mother and sister of trying to make trouble because they hated his actress-bride. He defended them, insisting that they did not understand her. Eventually he agreed that they might be troublemakers but still it would be better if she did not see Guy.

Mrs. Forsythe had reluctantly bowed to her husband's

wishes, and for a time they were happy again. Then, one day Guy came to tell her that the theater was in the final stages of construction. He begged her to come and see it. He hoped that she would approve a design to which she had contributed some of her theatrical know-how. She could not resist the invitation and had gone with him. She had found it beautiful, and though she had reached home in good time, she had found a furious Gervais, who had castigated her for seeing Guy again.

She had explained about the theater and begged him to come and see it. He proclaimed himself not interested and said that if she wanted to be a credit to the community, she would not interest herself in such folderol. She had been furious and accused him of impugning her honor. She had added that he had not thought her acting folderol when they had first met, and he had retorted that he had taken her away from all that and now it had followed her.

It was then that she had realized why he had not wanted to take her to London. In his way, he was just as disapproving of her profession as his mother and sister. She, hurt and furious, had said defiantly that she would see Guy when and as often as she chose, and furthermore, she would act upon his stage whenever he wished it! Subsequently, she had appeared in the first production, which had been *Romeo and Juliet.* Though she had been highly praised by her friends, her husband had not even come to see her.

Then, she had found that she was with child. She had been delighted. She had told Guy that she could not act anymore. She was going to settle down and be a wife and mother. He was regretful but understanding. He had also bade her farewell, explaining that he had to leave the district immediately. A dear friend had suddenly become very ill.

Flavia had been relieved. She herself was beginning to think she had acted foolishly when it came to Guy. Gervais had been very cold of late and extremely moody. She realized that she had seen very little of him. She had believed, however, that her announcement must clear the air between them.

"I told Gervais about the child." Mrs. Forsythe had stared into space, speaking in a low voice. "He suggested that I was carrying Guy's brat. He also said that he knew Guy had left home that day, without giving any reasons, but Gervais felt he knew the reason. He knew I had been with him that afternoon and Guy must have left because he had not wanted to fight a duel with a cuckolded husband."

A reflection of the hurt and anger she must have felt was visible in Mrs. Forsythe's eyes. Her tone was grim as she had said, "I did not trouble to contradict him. That night I left the house and in a few days I arrived in Ireland."

"He did not even try to find you?" Diana had asked.

"I imagine he did, but I did not want to be found." Mrs. Forsythe's eyes had grown stormy again. "I loved him, but I could not contend against his mother and his sister with their spite and their lies—or with his jealousy. I do loathe jealousy!

"The servants lied, too. Servants are terrible snobs, my dear, and my background pleased them even less than it did my mother-in-law and her daughter. They spread the word of problems between myself and Gervais. They hinted that I was unfaithful. Think how much they must have made of the time when Guy and I had sheltered in the hut!

"Many of my so-called friends looked at me askance, having been entertained, no doubt, at their toilettes by whispering abigails or chattering valets. Too, I was very proud. I thought that if Gervais had really loved me, he could never have doubted me—and certainly never made so cruel an accusation and . . . Well, there it is, my dear. I hope that you can understand me."

"I do, oh, I most certainly do. They, all of them, were cruel, poor Mother." Diana had flung her arms around her. "But," she had asked a few minutes later, "did you not even miss him?"

Her mother had not answered immediately. She had looked down at her hands. "I missed him," she had finally said in a low voice. "But I did not—could not remain with him, not in the circumstances I have detailed to you. Even if I could have forgiven him for his accusations, even if he had apologized for having made them, I could not stomach the atmosphere of disapproval and doubt that constantly surrounded me. My life was so different from his. I was used to freedom, he was not. And though it might seem strange to you, I was not unhappy once I had returned to the theater. I had you, my love, and I had my work."

Thinking of all her mother had said, Diana had the distinct feeling that there was much she had not said concerning her feelings for her husband. Mrs. Forsythe was not a woman who wore her heart on her sleeve. Fond as she was of Mr. Gifford, she had yet to set a date for their wedding. Was that because she still cared for her husband? It was all a great shame, but much as she tried to banish the feeling as unworthy of her, Diana was just the tiniest bit resentful that she had been, as she saw it, the victim of her mother's pride.

"If she knew I was legitimate," she murmured, "she might have told me so, and spared me all this conjecturing. It would not have hurt to give me an inkling of the truth so that I would not have continued to believe . . ." She paused in her cogitations. She was not being fair. When she was little, she had once asked Moira why she had no father, and she had been told that he was away. Moira had also solemnly adjured her not to put that question to her mother. She had been sorely confused by those statements, and for a time she had hoped her father would come back. When she was older and wiser, she had reached the conclusion that she was illegitimate, but she had never told her mother of those beliefs. Consequently, she had no right to blame her for all the mistaken notions she had harbored. Thinking about the situation now, she would try not to resent her mother for not telling her the truth. In common with Flavia Forsythe, she would not look backward but only forward to the father who had been so quick to acknowledge their relationship.

"Lady Diana Charlton," she whispered, and wondered how long it would be before she was used to her new name and her new status?

The rain had ceased an hour after sunrise, and late that afternoon Sir Sabin Mallory rode wearily into Bath. The highway had been muddy and deeply pitted from the rain. Consequently, he had not been able to gallop like the wind as he would have chosen to do. Instead, his journey had been plodding and, given his state of mind, extremely wearisome. Furthermore, he had slept very badly the night before, mainly because he had been struck by an idea that had not occurred to him earlier. He had naturally assumed that Diana had returned to her mother and the Gifford Company—but had she? He had been so positive of that, but now he was fearful that she might have gone somewhere else. Perhaps she might not have wanted her mother to know what had happened. Yet, where could she have gone? And, if she were in Bath, as he prayed she would be, what was her state of mind? And how would she receive him? In discovering that he loved her, he now had to contend with the possibility that she might not feel the same way about him. Yet, she *had* always seemed extremely glad to see him, and when he had danced with her at the ball, he had thought he had discerned a special quality in her smile and a softness in her eyes whenever she had looked at him. Yet, was that true?

By the time the hour of seven had been banged out by the town clock, Sir Sabin had learned that Miss Forsythe was, indeed, with the company. He had also discovered that she was residing at the Garrick's Head. However, upon hopefully inquiring for her, he had been told that she was out. Now, as he made his way down the aisle toward his seat in the pit, he wondered when he dared go back and see her. She had told him that it was her habit to sometimes sit out part of the play in the green room. Since the

work in question was *Othello*, he wondered if she might
not repair to the green room that night. She had also told
him that the play was a prime favorite of the company and
often done, which might mean that it was overly familiar
to her. Possibly, he could go back after the first act.
However, it transpired that Mrs. Forsythe was an excellent
Desdemona and Mr. Gifford, whose acting had not always
pleased him, was proving to be a fine Othello, so fine that
he had decided to remain for the second act, in which the
actor had surprised him with his displays of jealousy.
These were really most effective—one might almost believe that he was not acting. Mr. Hornby was also telling
as Cassio.

Finally, the play was at an end and the applause was
deafening. The actors took call after call. A farce followed, but since none of the principal players were in that,
Sir Sabin thought it safe to go back. Coming into the green
room, he found it quite crowded. Most of the actors were,
as yet, present, but he did not see Diana. Then, he heard
her laughter. At least, it sounded like her laughter—though
in her situation, it seemed unusual that she would be in
such a good mood. Still, it had been several weeks ago
and one could not suffer forever, he reasoned.

His heart was once more beating in his throat as he
made his way toward that sound. He came to a dead stop
as he sighted her. She was wearing the gown—the very
gown that had caused all the trouble—and around her
throat was a necklace that at first sight appeared to be
made of green fire, but of course, the stones were emeralds, emeralds and diamonds. She was standing very close,
very, very close to an aging Corinthian. He, in turn, was
staring down at her ardently, his arm encircling her waist.
As Sir Sabin watched, the man bent to drop a light kiss on
Diana's forehead.

Sir Sabin stood as though turned to stone. He did not
know what to think—or rather, he did, remembering that
Diana came from a long line of unmarried females with
noble protectors. And obviously she had found one too.

No matter that he had to be at least in his forties if not older; he was able to buy her the necklace she was flaunting. And the way he was looking at her, as if he could not believe that she was real. She did look beautiful, incredibly beautiful—this, in spite of the fact that she was boldly smiling into her companion's face. How quickly she had learned the wiles that courtesans use to entrap elderly fatuous men. No doubt, she had more jewels at home. Then, as he stared at them, her elderly admirer—to call him by his rightful name: seducer, keeper, whoremonger—moved away and Sir Sabin strode in the direction of Diana.

"Miss Forsythe," he said between gritted teeth.

She looked up in amazement. "Sir Sabin!" she exclaimed. "I did not know you were in Bath. Oh, how came you to be here?"

She ought to have sounded chagrined or shamed, but instead she was *smiling*, smiling at him delightedly, an expression that proved that she had no shame.

He said coldly, "I arrived today."

"Have you come to take the waters, then?" she asked.

"No, I did not come to take the waters. I came because—because I thought you might be here with the company as, indeed, you are."

"You came—you came to see *me*?" she asked incredulously, and flushed.

Seeing the flush, he divined it as shame. Finally, she had the grace to be ashamed, as indeed she should be, parading in that indecent finery. "Yes, I came to thank you for the lessons," he bit the words off.

"The lessons?" she repeated. "But how did you know I was here?"

"I have ways of finding out," he answered. She would never know from him how he had followed the company from town to town, how many false leads he had been given, how many weary miles he had traversed for nothing, nothing, nothing!

"Oh, I am indeed glad you have come," she exclaimed. "I have something wonderful to tell you."

Had she no shame at all? Was she actually about to boast that she had found a protector? "That is not necessary," he said between his teeth. "I saw him. I little thought that you, of all people, would succumb to the blandishments of a man old enough to be your father."

"But . . ." she began, and then her flush deepened. "You are saying that—that—"

"I am saying that I find your actions particularly reprehensible, dallying with that old man in a public gathering. Obviously, you are completely shameless. I will leave you now, Miss Forsythe, if that is what you still call yourself. And I thank you for having taught me one more lesson."

Diana's eyes had grown very large and she was also considerably redder than before. She slapped him smartly across the face, and her head held high, she turned away.

Sir Sabin, aware that quite a few people were staring at him, said between his teeth, "Thank you for that lesson too, Miss Forsythe." He turned on his heel and strode from the room.

"And what, my dear, was that all about?" The earl returned to Diana's side. "Did it," he continued, "require such public retribution?"

Her father's eyes held censure, but Diana was still quivering with the almost physical pain she had encountered so swiftly upon the surge of fury following those cruel words from a man she had feared never to see again. She said in a low voice, "He insulted me. Unforgivably."

"Ah, then, perhaps I should have his name and send my seconds?"

"No," she said quickly. "It is not necessary. He—he is quite beneath notice."

"That is precisely what I would have said." He looked at her closely. "But do I perceive tears in your eyes, my love?"

She shook her head. "I—I am so angry," she said in a low voice.

"You are more and more like the lady you resemble so closely. I did not have the privilege of knowing her well, but it was said that strong passions, whether they were of grief or anger, brought tears to her eyes. You will have to see the portrait, and soon. I shall issue orders that it be removed to my London house. I must be in London soon and you will stay with me, my dear Diana."

It was not a request; it was a statement that ruled out all argument. Diana, however, was not excited by the prospect. She was still thinking of Sir Sabin's reprehensible conduct and his entirely, never-to-be-forgotten-or-forgiven accusation!

Anger boiled up again, bringing with it the threat of further tears, tears of anger, too, especially when she recalled her utter joy in seeing him. She gritted her teeth. To think that she had spent so much time mooning over this most unworthy individual ever since they had parted on the night of the Marchant ball, now over two months into the past, and then to have him equate her with—with any common doxy! That was a straw in the wind, to be sure. Indeed, it was a whole haystack. He had naturally assumed that because of the background she had been so unwise as to reveal to him, she, as in the case of her mother and grandmother before her, was a loose woman! But her mother was not, and had never been, a loose woman. And she, Diana Charlton, had been born in wedlock and was just as legitimate as Sir Sabin Mallory, whom she hoped to God that she would never, never see again!

Flavia Forsythe, moving to Lord Lyall's side, had not seen Sir Sabin, but she knew her daughter well enough to realize that she was in the grip of some strong emotion. She looked concernedly at Diana and then up at the man she had once called husband, and she saw, somewhat to her relief, that he was smiling. "What has happened?" she asked curiously.

He shrugged. "A young man of our daughter's acquaintance, I have not the details, but I gather words were exchanged.''

"Who was he?"

"I do not know. However, I am sure it was of no moment, a teapot tempest, my dear Flavia. But enough, my dear. When can we have a meeting in private? There is so much that I should like to say to you. Why must you remain so elusive?''

She said gently, "I have not been elusive, my Lord. I am in the midst of a season. We are rehearsing for our next presentation. Not all my repertory is at my fingertips, as it were.''

"Must you address me as my Lord?" he complained, his eyes caressing her face. "Might I add that I thought you a splendid Desdemona, but it pained me to see you throttled. I felt it almost as a physical constriction in my own throat. I have been a fool, but as I have explained, I am older and certainly wiser. My mother is dead and my sister is wed and living in Inverness. My wife died when my son was born, and quite truthfully, I never really felt as if she were my wife.''

"That is unkind to her memory, surely," Flavia remonstrated.

"I acknowledge that fact, but she was selected by my mother and I . . . Well, suffice to say that I could not have been in my right mind at the time of our quarrel.''

"You did not give the impression of hysteria or drunkenness, my Lord, but . . ." Flavia shrugged. "All this is water under the bridge.''

"Is there no hope?" He looked down at her, his eyes catching and holding her own gaze.

"We should not be having such a discussion here.''

"How can we not, when you'll not see me in private?"

"I have been busy, and you have Diana.''

He swallowed. "Are you going to marry that actor?"

"I am betrothed to him, as I have told you," she said steadily.

"I have the feeling that Diana does not like him.''

"She does not need to like him. She will not be marrying him."

There was a pause before he said very hesitantly, "Might I ask you: could she, at least, be with me in London?"

"I think that an admirable idea."

"Do you, indeed?" he demanded eagerly.

"Yes. She is not happy here. I did not realize how unhappy she has been until quite recently. And nor had I realized how very bitterly she resented not knowing the identity of her father."

"At first, I resented the fact that you had not told her," he said slowly "but at this point I find myself very glad that you did not, for she might have grown to hate me as much as you do."

"I do not hate you, my Lord, but many years have passed. I live another life and have my commitments. I cannot push them aside. Mr. Gifford has been kindness itself to me and to Diana, too. I cannot repay him with cruelty."

"And if there were no commitments?" he asked softly.

"But there are, my Lord," she said firmly.

"Ah, my dear, I had wondered where you were. I did not see you at first." Mr. Gifford had come to her side. He seemed in a good mood, as he usually did after the rain of compliments that had fallen upon him from so many people in the green room, but Flavia noticed a tenseness in the arm he placed with studied casualness about her waist. He added, "Good evening, my Lord."

"Good evening, sir," Lord Lyall said coolly. "You turned in an admirable performance."

"You are kind to say so, my Lord."

"I am not kind, sir, when I say that you have mastered the role. It is no more than the honest truth."

"Then, I am doubly flattered, my lord." The actor bowed.

Lord Lyall turned back to Flavia. "I will bid you good evening. May I hope that Diana will come to supper with me?"

"She has my permission," Flavia said. "You must ask

her.'' She watched as he strode to Diana's side. She saw
her daughter look up. Was she forcing a smile? She had
been looking a little distrait before. Undoubtedly, that was
contingent . . .

''A penny for your thoughts, my love,'' Mr. Gifford
said.

''I was thinking about Diana,'' she responded.

''Were you?'' he asked pointedly. ''And not of Lord
Lyall?''

Flavia gave him a sharp look. ''You asked a question,
sir. I answered it truthfully. Might I add that you have
removed Othello's makeup.''

''My dear.'' He was smiling more easily now. ''Surely
you cannot believe me jealous.''

''I hope not,'' she said coolly, ''for that is one emotion
I cannot abide.'' Moving away from him, she looked
toward Diana and found that Lord Lyall was slipping her
cloak around her shoulders. Flavia came to her side, ''My
dearest, I will wish you a good evening.''

''Thank you, Mama.'' Diana was still having trouble
smiling. She did appear a little more cheerful as she
added, ''Father has asked me if I will come to London
with him. He has told me that you approved.''

''I do, most heartily.'' Flavia smiled.

''You see,'' Lord Lyall said, ''I was telling you the
truth, my dear Diana.''

''I did not doubt you, sir. But it is all so—so strange
and wonderful.''

''For me, too, my dear child,'' he said huskily. ''I only
wish . . . But enough!'' He bowed over Flavia's hand. ''I
will bid you good night, my dear Mrs. Forsythe.''

''Good evening, my Lord,'' she said, and watched him
as he proudly escorted Diana toward the door. She was
conscious of a stinging in her eyes, but she preferred to
blame it on a combination of weariness and the strong
lights of the stage. She had a bright smile for Mr. Gifford
as she came back to him.

Part Two

12

London in July. Diana had seldom been in the city at that time of year. In June, the theaters closed and the actors went on the road—that is, if, in common with the Gifford Company, they were not on the road already. They might also rest, as Mrs. Forsythe and Diana had also done from time to time at their little home in Chelsea Village.

This summer, Diana would be staying at Lord Lyall's stone mansion at 22 Berkeley Square. Lord Lyall's driver, she found, was particularly skillful in bringing the traveling coach with its eight sweating horses through the cluttered streets. Of course, he was aided by a footman and two postboys and by his horn and a pair of lungs from which issued a sound as loud as any trumpet, scattering the sheep in the street and ordering other coachmen to make way, make way. Such methods roused anger in pedestrians and other drivers, but they were effective. They reached their destination quickly.

An obsequious footman assisted Diana to the street. Her father, standing on the sidewalk, offered his arm. He looked warm but happy, his green eyes, the same color as her own, glowing with pride.

Having had over a month to recuperate from her confrontation with Sir Sabin, Diana was feeling better. She was glad of her father's decision to remain in Bath even after the company left. Staying with him in his lovely house, she had had an opportunity to adjust to the radical change in her circumstances and also to become better acquainted with him. Now, there would be another meeting, with her half-brother, Lord Anthony Charlton, who had been visiting a friend from Eton. He had just graduated from that school, and in another two months he would be bound for Oxford. As she took her father's arm, she directed a nervous glance at the paneled front door with its shining brass knocker, wondering how the lad would feel about this sister who had been unknown to him until the letter dispatched to the house where he had been staying.

She had half-expected to find him in the hall, but when she came in, she was greeted by a large group of servants lined up to meet her. She was introduced to each and found that she had an abigail named Sophia. She had an impression of smallness, pale-blond hair and pale-blue eyes. The girl seemed shy, so shy that she could not manage so much as a glance at Diana's face but looked to the side or to the floor. Diana, caught in her own shyness, yet managed a welcoming smile. Then, as they went up the stairs to the first floors, she heard her father ask, "Where is Anthony?"

"He is here, sir," she heard a hesitant young voice answer from above. There was a clatter on the stairs, and in a second a tall, slender boy of sixteen joined them. Diana met eyes that were a greenish hazel set under dark brows. His hair was chestnut in hue and his features irregular. His mouth resembled that of his father but was wider, and his nose was less Roman. He was, she decided, quite startlingly handsome.

"Good afternoon, sir. Welcome back." He had a quick, shy glance at Diana. "And—and may I bid you welcome, too" He seemed to want to say something more, but shyness, she decided, was impeding him.

"Good afternoon, Anthony," Lord Lyall said cordially. "You had my letter?"

"Oh, yes, sir."

"This is your sister, Diana. And, my dear Diana, might I present your brother, Anthony."

"Diana . . ." The boy had another look for her and a

tentative smile. "Good afternoon, I—I do hope you had a pleasant journey from Bath."

"Good afternoon, Anthony. Oh, yes, we did—and the coach so well-sprung." She wondered immediately if she should have said that. He would think her unused to such luxuries, which indeed she was. She also wondered what he must think to meet a sister whose existence had been unknown to him until the arrival of that letter. Would he resent her? She hoped not.

"You two must become acquainted," Lord Lyall said. "Anthony has had the particulars of the situation in the letter I sent him and ample time to recover from his surprise, have you not, my boy?"

"Oh, yes, sir, I am quite recovered." A grin that Diana guessed was habitual appeared and disappeared. He stared at Diana. "I hope you are quite recovered also, Diana. It must have been very odd at first—the situation."

"It was," she agreed wholeheartedly.

"And for me as well," Lord Lyall admitted. "We will have to compare sensations—but later. Diana, I am sure, would like to cleanse the dust of the road from herself."

"Oh, I would," she agreed gratefully.

"Good. When you are rested, someone will show you to the library."

Sophia preceded Diana, bringing her to a chamber hung in green-and-white chintz and furnished with a four-poster twice the size of the one she had had at Lady Marchant's home. Her room was equally immense and beautifully appointed. What particularly pleased Diana was the fact that it was located on a corner of the house and consequently had windows to the front and side. There was a large fireplace surrounded by white tiles. Over the mantel-shelf hung a beautiful Chippendale mirror. Looking into it, Diana had a sense of unreality, as if she were caught in a dream from which she could not rouse herself. She had had that feeling more than once in the past weeks, but it was not a dream: little Sophia was waiting to assist her out of her clothes and into the peignoir she had just unpacked.

She saw the abigail staring at the garments in her bandbox and guessed that the girl was surprised at the paucity of clothes. Or perhaps she was not surprised; undoubtedly the other servants had told her the strange story surrounding her new mistress. Servants knew everything about everybody and Diana was positive that members of the *ton* returning to London would soon be advised of the tale by their valets and abigails. She would be a nine-day wonder until some new *on-dit* displaced her. She could not think about that now. She would have her bath and then she would join her half-brother in the library.

She wondered about Anthony. She had been drawn to him, but what would he feel about this interloper who had suddenly appeared from nowhere? She had been thinking about that off and on ever since they had left Bath. Had he known that his father had been wed more than once? She doubted that. She did not think he resented her, but one never knew.

An hour later, Diana, informed as to the location of the library by a smiling butler, came into a large room with floor-to-ceiling cases of books, a sight that thrilled her. Though she had been given free access to the library at Marchant House, she had been careful not to abuse the privilege. She had taken only what was necessary for the instruction of her pupils. She also remembered being questioned by the housekeeper as to the whereabouts of a book she had not taken. The woman had regarded her suspiciously, as if she had doubted Diana's word when she assured her she did not have it. Servants, she had been quick to learn, always resented and distrusted governesses, particularly those who were accepted as "part of the family," though only in a limited sense. She had had her share of being slighted by those resentful minions. That would not happen again, not to Lady Diana Charlton!

As she moved farther into the room, her half-brother startled her by rising swiftly from a high-backed chair near the desk. "Ah, you are looking more the thing," he commented.

"I thank you," she said shyly.

"You are certainly very like . . ." He paused. "I can imagine that Father was exceptionally startled when he first saw you. He must have thought he was looking at a ghost. Do you believe in ghosts?"

Diana shook her head, not entirely understanding him. "At least," she said, "I have never seen one."

"Nor have I. There is a suite of rooms at Eton that none will take because it is said to be haunted. I have been through it night and day and heard nothing."

"I have often thought," Diana said candidly, "that those who do hear or see spirits have partaken of the bottled variety before the experience."

He laughed. "It is said that the Blue Ruin can make you see a whole legion of 'em. Have you ever tasted Blue Ruin?"

"No, never, have you?"

He sent a wary glance over his shoulder toward the door. "I have, though you must not betray me to Father. It was last year. One of my friends smuggled it in and all of us had a bit of it, after hours. I cannot say I liked it."

"It is well you did not," Diana said severely. "It would have been terrible to have developed a taste for it."

He made a face. "I cannot imagine that anyone could do that, though I suspect that those who do swill it down in the grog shops around Covent Garden, say, wish to forget about being hungry and poor."

"I think that is true." She nodded, liking him for his understanding.

"Something ought to be done to help them," he said. "One day I will be in the House of Lords, though. I would rather it would be the House of Commons. I should think that would be more interesting, would not you?"

Diana was visited by a most unwelcome memory. Sir Sabin, too, had wanted to alleviate the lot of the poor through legislation. She said diffidently, "I confess to not knowing much about politics."

"Ah, well, *you* do not need to know about them, unless

you marry someone connected with the government. Should you like to see the portrait?''

She was considerably startled but also grateful for his swift change of subject. "The portrait?"

"It is here." He pointed toward the fireplace. "Come and look just to assure yourself that you are as alike as I believe you to be."

The portrait hung over the mantelpiece. Diana, raising her eyes to the tall dark woman shown standing next to an Irish setter, could have been looking at a mirror image of herself. She expelled a quavering breath. "It is unbelievable!"

"Is it not?" Anthony grinned. "It might have been yourself who sat for that painting, or rather, stood for it. I am glad it was not, for then you would be dead. I much prefer you to be here. I liked you the minute I saw you. What did you feel about me?"

Diana turned away from the portrait. She was conscious of a rush of happiness and realized that up until this moment she had yet been wary of him, fearing that he might, after all, resent her.

"I felt the same about you," she said shyly. "And now I like you even more. I have always wanted a brother."

"And I have always wanted a sister. Do not be in a great rush to marry, Diana, though I cannot imagine that you will be single very long."

An image of Sir Sabin flew into her mind, prompting Diana to say quickly and positively, "I have no desire to marry anyone. I doubt that I ever shall."

"You will," he said positively. "Just wait until you are presented at court. The invitations will pour in and—"

"Desist, I pray you!" Diana held up a protesting hand. "Let us cease to contemplate the future and come to know each other."

"That is an excellent suggestion," he approved. "I will tell you about me and you can tell me all about your life. I understand that your mother is an actress. I do enjoy the theater. Have you ever appeared on the stage?"

He had many more questions, and in answering them, more of the strangeness of her new position vanished. She hoped that the recurring memories of her encounter with Sir Sabin in the green room would vanish, too. Unfortunately, she was not entirely sure of that, but at least she would have plenty of distractions!

"A ball at Carlton House, Aunt Eugenia! I never, never dreamed that I should be invited," exclaimed a young girl as she walked toward the grand ballroom of that beautiful but overly decorated palace. "I do feel that I have at last arrived."

"My dear," drawled the older lady at her side, "a little less enthusiasm, I beg of you."

Sir Sabin Mallory, who was directly behind that pair, smiled wearily. It was amazing how quickly one did tire of these balls and of the routs, the races, the card games, and the small select dinners and suppers that filled the days and nights of unattached gentlemen such as himself. Of late, he was even tired of testing his prowess in fisticuffs at Cribb's Parlor or in shooting matches at Manton's, endeavors at which he excelled to the point that he had won several bets on the strength of them.

He could, however, remember when he had shared that girl's enthusiasm. Actually, it was less than a year ago that he had had his first invitation to Carlton House, coming there with Lord Marchant, who had secured him the card. That had been a period for firsts, he recalled. He winced as he thought of some of the gaffes he had made, not having had the benefit of Mr. Hornby's instruction at that time. Fortunately, he had not known many people. Now he had a tolerably wide acquaintance with various members of the *ton* and could number among them Lord Alvanley, Bruell, and Byron. Alvanley had secured him this invitation. It had been one of several for this evening. Indeed, the table in the hallway of his London house, also an inheritance from his late uncle, was filled with invitations, many of them having arrived while he was at his home in Yorkshire. In the months that had passed since he had been to Bath, he could have been out every night and most of the day.

Hostesses, particularly those with marriageable daughters, invited him to dinner, balls, and even the theater. However, for himself, he preferred the snug little dinners given by one or another of the new friends met at White's, Brooks, or Boodles. He had gone to quite a few of these, but he had always found himself bored and wanting to leave. He had also attended another Opera House Masquerade, had flirted with a pretty nun, but when it had come time to invite her home, he could not bring himself to oblige. He forbore to dwell on the reasons for this, even though his dreams were still not free of a certain green-eyed lady who had proved so manifestly unworthy to receive the heart and hand he had been prepared to offer her. He grimaced, wondering why he was still allowing that encounter in Bath to plague him. Perhaps it was because it was late November and would soon be December, an anniversary of sorts. He sighed and entered the ballroom. He expelled another sigh as he looked upon all the lovely women in their rich gowns. He could not see the Regent, though Alvanley had said, "For reasons best known to himself, Georgie will be in a white uniform. If you see what appears to be a walking snowstorm or perhaps the English equivalent of one of those Siamese elephants, which, I understand, are white, make your bow to his Highness."

Sir Sabin smiled at the recollection. He positioned himself against the wall and scanned the chairs where several determinedly smiling young women sat with their eyes wistfully fixed upon the dancing couples. Occasionally, he had performed an act of kindness and asked one or the other to dance. However, while their surprise and eagerness had touched him, the reason for their lack of partners was generally all-too-apparent. Then, as he stood there indecisively, he glimpsed Lord Marchant across the floor. He had not seen his Lordship in several months, and still glancing in that direction, he saw Lady Charlotte. She was looking a little heavier than he remembered, and he wondered if she were already with child. At that moment, the music ended and he made his way toward the couple. He was pleased to see Marchant. Despite the fact that he was not welcome at his London house, they were still friends. That was apparent because, since they had not met since his wedding, there had been a note from him inviting him to a dinner at his club—it had come while he was in the country.

Just as he reached him, the majordomo announced, "Lord Lyall and Lady Diana Charlton. Glancing toward the doorway, Sir Sabin came to a halt and wondered if he were seeing aright as a tall man, whose features he recognized immediately, mainly because they were imprinted on his brain, and a tall young woman with dark hair done in the latest style and wearing a gown of white lace which must have cost her protector a pretty penny . . . Protector? But that, he realized, was not possible. She had been called Lady Diana Charlton. Did that mean that the man had *married* her?

"Sabin, well-met!"

He turned to see Lord and Lady Marchant behind him. Dazedly he smiled and bowed over Lady Charlotte's hand. They exchanged pleasantries, and then, being unable to contain himself a moment longer, Sir Sabin said, "She has done very well for herself, has she not?"

"Who, my dear fellow?" Lord Marchant said confusedly.

"Lady Diana Charlton," Sir Sabin replied coldly. "I presume the gentleman with her is her husband?"

"Her husband!" Lady Charlotte regarded him with considerable surprise. "Oh, no, he is not. Is it possible that you've not heard the tale?"

"The tale? Concerning them?" Sir Sabin questioned.

"Lord, where have you been, man?" Lord Marchant laughed. "It is akin to Aladdin and the Wonderful Lamp or, perhaps, Cinderella—but no, neither of these really suffice." As he paused, the musicians had started playing a waltz and Sir Sabin saw a tall, heavyset young man purposefully take Diana in his arms.

"Do not keep him in suspense, I beg you, my love," Lady Charlotte urged, her soft voice causing Sir Sabin to cease following Diana with his eyes and turn back to his friends.

"What is this tale of wonder?" he asked.

"Tell him, dearest," Lady Charlotte prompted again. "You know more about it than anyone."

Meeting Sir Sabin's interrogative glance, Lord Marchant nodded. "I expect I do. My sisters, Rosalie and Eustacia, that is, are yet in communication with Diana, and she, you see, is the long-lost daughter of the Earl of Lyall." As Lord Marchant recounted the circumstances attendant upon the meeting of Diana and her father, Sir Sabin grew cold. "There it is," the earl concluded. "Is it not as fabulous as I suggested?"

Sir Sabin felt actually dizzy. At least, the candles in the brilliant cut-glass chandeliers as well as the sconces on the sides of the walls seemed to meld together. It was a moment before he could say faintly, "Fabulous, indeed. Is it really true?"

"No one seems to harbor any doubts," Lord Marchant responded. "My sisters and several other people of my acquaintance have seen that portrait—they say it is amazingly like her." He gave Sir Sabin a narrow look. "Good God, man," he exclaimed, "you'd best sit down. You resemble my sister Aurora when she heard the news, though I do not believe you'll be emulating her hysterics. Mama was also much exercised—"

"Sir Sabin," Lady Charlotte interrupted, "are you quite well?"

"No, yes—yes, I am." he stared at the girl across the floor, managing once more to follow her with his eyes as she moved gracefully through the patterns of the dance. She was so lovely. He was wafted back to the green room at the Theater Royal in Bath, and he was seeing once again her delighted smile as he approached her. And he had believed her to be without shame and had said . . . He shuddered at the memory of his accusations. He had well-deserved that slap across the face. More memories flooded into his mind. It was not difficult to recollect all that he had told her. He had thought of those moments often enough and traced to them his current ennui, his feeling that nothing in life mattered very much to him. Something inside him throbbed and ached, his heart, of course, and it was an actual physical pain—or was it? He was not sure. He was too confused.

"Are you quite yourself, Sir Sabin?" Lady Charlotte gave him another anxious look.

He managed a reassuring smile. "Quite, thank you. If—if you will excuse me." Without waiting for her answer, he bowed and moved away, coming to a stop near a tall window. It was no use trying to ignore them, those memories that were yet pouring into his head or, rather, swimming up to the surface of his mind. They had never been fully exorcized. They had lain there, rising at odd moments, each with their burden of pain. Anything could bring them back: a green gown worn by a stranger, a dark head, a theater marquee.

Once or twice he had thought he had seen her in the crowds of London and had followed her only to find that he was mistaken. But he would not see Lord Lyall's long-lost daughter on the public street—his *daughter*, and he with his accusations that had so effectively blotted out the bright, welcoming light in her eyes, the happiness that had illumined her face when first she had seen him. Had she looked happy?

Yes, his memory told him. She had looked very happy to see *him*, and he had assumed that she had capitulated to the persuasions of the man beside her, the man who had been looking at her so fondly. And he, he had wanted to tear off the gown he had given her and wrench apart her necklace, scattering the emeralds to the four winds. He blinked against tears that blurred the candlelight again. He

had to see her, had to speak to her, but of course she
would not want to speak to him—not ever again.

In that same moment he saw her on the floor with that
fat young man, and now the music was coming to an end.
Her partner had led her to the edge of the floor. He bowed,
muttered something, and then moved away toward the
chairs; for the nonce, Diana was alone. Was it possible
that she did not have another partner? No, they were
forming a cotillion and she had been approached by another young man. He led her onto the floor and Sir Sabin
watched as she went through the paces of the dance. She
was looking so incredibly beautiful but, he reasoned, no
more beautiful than she had been when first he had met
her.

Thinking of all the times they had been together, he
castigated himself for having been a damned fool—thinking
about, dwelling upon the insipid Aurora, who, once her
beauty left her, would have nothing. Diana would always
be beautiful. There was such character in her face. He had
to see her again, had to speak to her, even though he was
quite aware of the futility of such an effort.

He moved around the ballroom and, as he did, felt a
breeze stir his hair. Looking over his shoulder, he saw the
portieres swaying and, beyond them, the doors open on a
small balcony. It would be overlooking the gardens. He
. . . His thoughts came to an end with the music. He stood
still, watching the dancers as they came off the floor. He
had no trouble spotting Diana. He thanked God that she
was tall—so tall, so graceful, so beautiful! Her partner was
bowing to her and now someone else was approaching her,
damn him. A tall young man. He spoke to her. She smiled
and shook her head. He moved away and Sir Sabin saw
Diana glance at the chairs. He, too, looked in that direction and saw the heavyset young man speaking with an
elderly lady. He was bowing now. Evidently, he had been
given a second waltz with Diana. Hardly aware of what he
was doing, Sir Sabin strode forward, managing to make
his way through that vast throng and reaching Diana's

side. The first notes of the waltz were in his ears, and out of the corner of his eye he saw her probable partner making his way in her direction. With a veritable pounce, Sir Sabin was upon her. He caught her in his arms and whirled her onto the floor. To his surprise, he met with no resistance and then he heard a gasp.

"You," she murmured, and tired to pull away from him.

He had the impression she had been thinking of something else and had hardly noticed the man who was to have claimed her for the waltz. He did not have time to speculate on the reasons for that. If he were to relax his hold on her for an instant, all would be lost. He gritted his teeth and, clutching her, whirled her about, narrowly missing another couple. Ignoring her stream of whispered protests, he managed to guide her toward the balcony, and in another few moments he had achieved his objective. They were outside and the wind was blowing cold.

Diana glared at him and tried to extricate herself from his determined grasp. "How—how . . . This is unbelievable. Let me go, Sir Sabin. At once!"

He tightened his grasp. "You must listen to me, Diana," he exclaimed.

Her eyes seemed enormous. They were filled with anger. "Why?" she demanded in a low voice. "Have you thought of any more insults you can heap on me?"

"I wish to beg your pardon and—"

"You may not have my pardon, sir," she retorted. "I find you entirely insufferable, and your behavior in Bath . . . what you told me—"

"I thought—I thought . . ." To his utter shame his voice broke. "I came to ask you to marry me."

"Really?" Her gaze was even colder than before, her tone edged with doubt.

"It's true," he cried. "And I thought—I thought . . ."

"You do not need to tell me what you thought. You were most explicit at the time. And what might you mean by saying you meant to propose to me? What of the beautiful Lady Aurora?''

"Damn Lady Aurora! I was blind. Diana, why do you think I was in Bath? I came looking for you. When I could not find you in London, I followed the Gifford Company from place to place, always, always missing it. By the time I rode into Bath, I'd not slept . . . But what is the use of offering these excuses? I thought . . . you know only too well what I thought. And since that time, I—''

"You have discovered that I am better connected than you had imagined and—''

He put a hand across her mouth and dropped it immediately, saying, "Do you think that matters to me? I could wish you were not. I could wish that now, this very night, I could take you from this place and we could be wed. You may believe me or you may not, but I do love you. I think I have loved you ever since we met again, only I was such a damned fool, I did not realize it, did not realize that those Tuesdays when we were together were the bright spots in my life. I only knew that when Lady Aurora and her mother told me what they had done to you, because of my miserable error . . . If Lady Aurora had been a man, I would have challenged her on the spot for all she implied. Oh, God, God, God, Diana, can you not forgive me? I do love you with all my heart.''

There was a long silence as she stared at him. It was he who broke it, saying hopelessly, "Very well, Diana, when I came after you, I did not take into account that you might not feel the same about me. I assumed, which I should not have done, that you might. And I expect that if you ever did have such feelings for me, I have managed to kill them. I will take you back. It is passing cold out here.''

"No,'' she said quickly. "Not yet.'' She looked up at him and he saw that her eyes were very bright. "You hurt me grievously, Sir Sabin. I cannot deny that. But I do forgive you.''

"Oh, my dearest, can you be so generous?'' he asked huskily.

"I must be," she began.

"You must be?" he interrupted. "I do not understand."

"You would understand if you'd let me finish what I was about to tell you." She moved a little closer to him. "If I do not forgive you, I will continue as unhappy as you seem to be."

"Diana, oh, my dearest," he said unbelievingly. "You do care for me."

"Yes, I do . . . very much," she said in a low voice.

"Oh, God, thank God, I was so afraid . . . But no matter!" He drew her into his embrace, and releasing her an enchanted moment later, he said, "You must marry me, and soon. Will you, Diana?"

"I will, but you must speak to my father."

"I will go to him tonight."

"No, no, you will need to write to him. Our direction is 22 Berkeley Square."

"I will wait upon him tomorrow."

"He may not be able to see you so soon. He has many engagements. But I hope that he will see you as soon as possible."

"My love, my love." He brought her hand to his lips, kissing it fervently.

"My dearest, you'd best take me back. My partner will be wondering what has happened to me."

"That heavy young man?"

She nodded. "His name is George Soane, Lord Burford. I am given to understand that my father and his had been friends since childhood. Consequently, we see him quite often."

From her tone, Sir Sabin divined that she was not quite pleased with his Lordship. However, he forbore to comment, saying merely, "I will return you to his arms, but may this be the last time."

She hesitated, frowning slightly. "On second thought, my dearest, let me go back alone, lest you risk censure that may be repeated to my father."

"Your father . . . It is an amazing tale. I had it from
Marchant tonight."

"Is it not?" she said happily. "He has been so kind
. . . but enough! I must go. Stay here a moment, please."
Before he could protest, she had slipped away, and when
he entered the ballroom again, he saw that she had re-
joined Lord Burford, who was looking angry. He was one
of the sort whose anger colored his face an unbecoming
red. Gazing at his heavy features, Sir Sabin grimaced and
did not acquit Lord Lyall of sentimentality. It could only
be that which must have moved him to believe the young
man worthy to partner his daughter.

A week after the ball, Sir Sabin, having written to Lord
Lyall presenting his offer for his daughter's hand, was
admitted to the mansion on Berkley Square by a servant in
green livery. He came into an immense hall. The floor was
black-and-white marble, and there was a domed ceiling
from which hung a chandelier that rivaled those at Carlton
House. On either side of him were marble pedestals topped
with alabaster busts. One was a particularly beautiful head
of Dante and the other was that of a woman who may or
may not have been Pallas Athena. Mounting a circular
staircase, he was shown down a long hall to a pair of doors
that opened on the vast library. Over the huge fireplace
hung a portrait that, at first glance, he took to be Diana. A
second look, however, revealed that she was wearing a
hooped gown. Her dark hair was worn in a modified
pompadour, close to her head. However, the features and
the eyes were so similar to Diana's that he could understand the amazement with which Lord Lyall must first
have viewed her. He could also imagine her amazement—
she who had once told him she believed herself illegitimate, a situation she had seemed to treat lightly enough.
Yet, knowing her, he was very sure that she had been
unhappy about it. And now . . . Cinderella had risen from
her cinders and lived in a palace.

The house was very like a palace, and as he glanced

about the chamber again, he was less admiring than intimidated by the many fine books and paintings, the inlaid tables, and unless he were deeply mistaken, a Cellini cup on the mantelpiece. At least, it resembled one that Mr. Hornby had pointed out to him in the British Museum. With his newly acquired knowledge of art, this evidence of wealth and culture only pointed up his own position. He was not poor, and in his visit to his home he had seen several paintings, the worth of which he could recognize, but there had been nothing to equal the grandeur about him—and this was only one of his Lordship's dwellings. In aspiring to the hand of his daughter, he might seem like an arrant fortune-hunter.

He was not reassured by the entrance of his host. Seen at closer range, Lord Lyall was younger than he had appeared in Bath or at the ball. He was a very handsome man, and now Sir Sabin saw a definite resemblance between Diana and her father. They were both dark and Lord Lyall's eyes were also green—a cold green, Sir Sabin thought uncomfortably. His other features were also similar to those of his daughter, save that his nose was longer and more Roman and his lips less full. It seemed to Sir Sabin that there was a grimness about his countenance, an expression he could only hope was habitual rather than predicated on his presence.

Bows and greetings having been exchanged, Lord Lyall indicated a large leather chair that stood on the other side of a long desk. He himself took a thronelike chair behind the desk. Sitting down, his Lordship bent a look on him that to Sir Sabin's mind bore an uncomfortable resemblance to that of a presiding judge rather than the man he hoped might be his father-in-law.

"I understand that you wish to marry my daughter," his Lordship said in the cold measured tones he might have used to sentence some malefactor to prison.

"That is true, my Lord. I have long had . . ." He paused as his Lordship held up a hand.

"I beg you will not give me the details, Sir Sabin. I must tell you that your hopes regarding my daughter cannot be realized."

Though the announcement had the force of an actual physical blow, Sir Sabin realized that he had been expecting no less. "My Lord, I know that you must be aware of what passed between Diana, uh, your daughter and—" Again he was silenced by his Lordship's upraised hand.

"Sir Sabin, I am not interested in anything that may have passed between you and my daughter. She will soon be betrothed to a young man who is the son of my oldest friend, one whose rank is comparable to her own. I trust that you understand me, sir."

Sir Sabin flushed. "Though my rank is not comparable to yours, my Lord, our family is an old one and . . ." He paused as he met his host's cold stare.

"Had I not been aware of your lineage, Sir Sabin, I would not have consented to receive you. Yours is, as you say, an old family, and a good one. But it is my wish that my daughter ally herself with George Soane, Marques of Burford, and I might add that years ago his father and I agreed that were we ever to have children of a similar age and of the opposite sex, they would marry. Lord Burford, my friend, is unfortunately dead. However, his son is most eager to wed my daughter, and thus I am able to honor my promise."

Sir Sabin had an immediate picture of the young Marquess of Burford in his mind's eye, and also there were Diana's words concerning that, to him, repellent individual. It was with considerable difficulty that he managed to swallow the hot arguments that rose to his lips. He could not refrain from saying, however, "How will he know that your promise has been honored, my Lord?"

"I will know, Sir Sabin," Lord Lyall responded.

"But—"

"I beg that you will not weary yourself and me with further argument, sir. My daughter has been apprised of my decision and I promise you that she has every intention of abiding by it.''

Sir Sabin grew cold. A most unwelcome suspicion arose in his mind. Had Diana, intent on punishing him for his hot words uttered in Bath, only pretended to encourage him so that she might subject him to his present humiliation? Looking into the earl's implacable countenance, he could infer nothing from it save the fact that, as far as he was concerned, the interview was at an end. He rose, "I thank you for your courtesy in seeing me, my Lord. I will bid you good afternoon.''

"Good afternoon, Sir Sabin." His Lordship had also risen. "My man will see you out.''

As he descended the front steps of the house, Sir Sabin had a hollow feeling in his chest, and though he was not generally inclined toward metaphor, he had no difficulty in attributing the sensation to the figurative loss of his heart. Again he wondered bitterly if Diana had urged her father to grant him this interview because she had fully anticipated the outcome.

Possibly, he might have felt more sanguine had he known that from a window of her chamber, Diana had witnessed both his arrival and his departure out of eyes red from weeping. The matter of Sir Sabin's proposal had occasioned her first serious disagreement with her father. It had also brought home to her a most unpleasant and daunting truth. Had she been plain Diana Forsythe, she would not have hesitated to slip out of the house and follow Sir Sabin to a place where they could converse, unobserved by servants. She would have told him that no matter what her father decreed, she loved him and would wed no one else.

Unfortunately, she was no longer plain Diana Forsythe. She was Lady Diana Charlton, and in the months that had passed since she had risen to this eminence, she had found herself hedged in by those rules that must needs govern the smallest action of a lady of quality. She could go nowhere unaccompanied. She could not pick and choose her friends.

All were subject to her father's approval, which had ruled
out Miss Martin and any of the Gifford Company with, of
course, the exception of her mother. She did have her
father's permission to visit her mother's Chelsea home,
since Mrs. Forsythe refused to enter the house on Berkeley
Square. However, she must make that brief journey with
Sophia, her abigail, in attendance and she had an uneasy
feeling that the girl was required to report all her movements to her father. Consequently, it would be very difficult to get word to Sir Sabin, especially now that the one
other person who might have helped her—her half-brother
Anthony—was at Oxford. She had not known him long,
but they were much in sympathy. Furthermore, his youthful Lordship chafed at his father's restrictions as much as
she herself.

Her only recourse was through her mother, but were she
to express a desire to see her mother—say, today—her
father, with whom she had had a stormy session over the
matter of Sir Sabin's proposal, would immediately suspect
her intentions. But, on the other hand, there had to be
some way of letting Sir Sabin know that her sentiments
were not those of Lord Lyall.

She started at a slight scratching at her door. "Yes?"
she called.

Sophia came in and bobbed a curtsy. "If you please,
your Ladyship," she said in her soft, almost inaudible
voice, "your father would like to see you in the library."

Diana regarded her abigail with the opprobrium generally visited upon all messengers who bring bad news.
Though she had learned to love and honor Lord Lyall,
neither sentiment was uppermost in her mind at present,
and she had no desire to hear a description of Sir Sabin's
dismissal. Nevertheless, her father's wish being tantamount
to a command, she had perforce to nod and say, "You
may tell him that I will be there directly, Sophia."

She received a sidelong glance from the girl, who never
looked directly at anyone. "Would you like me to straighten
your hair, your Ladyship?"

Diana exhaled a long sigh and glanced at herself in the mirror, disliking Sophia's elliptical reference to hair that bore evidence of having been ruffled by nervous hands before, during, and after her father's interview with Sir Sabin. She said, "I will attend to my hair, thank you, Sophia. You may return to his Lordship."

"Yes, milady." The girl curtsied and withdrew.

With a sigh, Diana, feeling more alone than ever, ran a comb through her disordered locks and came out of her chamber. She was experiencing one of her bad feelings and she wondered whether or not it was contingent on her father's meeting with Sir Sabin or on something else. She hoped that it was the former. She had had enough unhappiness for one day.

Coming into the library, she found Lord Lyall standing by the portrait and looking up at it. Diana, too, regarded it, marveling anew at the resemblance. Certainly it was amazing, but she hoped that there the likeness ended. She now knew a little more about her great-grandmother, who had died when she was not much older than she had been when the portrait was painted.

The full name of the lady in the portrait was Harriette L'Estrange. A widow at the early age of seventeen, she had married into the Lyall family when she had been six months into her nineteenth year. That she had not waited out the full term of widowhood had been considered scandalous, and when, no more than two years later, she had died in childbed, there had been many who had averred that she had had no more than her just deserts. Her second husband had never married again. In recounting this history, Lord Lyall had said sadly, "That is a characteristic of the Lyall family—we love but once."

Diana sighed. She was quite sure that she, too, could never love anyone except Sir Sabin. She had told her father as much and was prepared to repeat that statement even in the face of his increased disapproval.

"Ah, here you are, my dear," he said, turning toward

her. "I have something I must needs discuss with you. Pray sit down." He indicated the chair by the desk.

Diana did not take it immediately. "Sir Sabin, did he arrive?"

Lord Lyall shrugged. "Yes, he arrived punctually."

"And you refused?"

"As I told you I would, my dear. But let us speak no more about that. Now, as I asked—"

Diana lifted her chin and gazed straight into her father's eyes. "I love Sir Sabin and—"

"My dear," he interrupted coolly and firmly. "I grant you that he is a pleasant-spoken young man. His family is good. However, he can scarcely aspire to your hand. You are a Charlton of Lyall."

"When I was a Forsythe of nowhere, Sir Sabin—" Diana began.

"That was not your fault," the earl interrupted. "Your mother and I . . . But I will speak no more of my folly and her anger. That is in the past and you, my love, are back where you should be. I understand that this is all very new to you, but I must compliment you on your deportment. You are every inch a Charlton, and you must never forget that."

"I have tried, but Sir Sabin—"

"The subject of Sir Sabin has been dismissed," he said frigidly. "It is time we talked about your future husband."

"My future husband," she repeated, feeling cold and frightened.

"I beg that you will allow me to finish, my dear. I have had another offer for your hand, one that pleases me and that I believe you must accept."

"Another offer?" She looked at him in stunned surprise. "But I know so few—"

"You know this young man quite well, Diana. I am speaking about Lord Burford."

"Lord Burford!" she exclaimed. "No!"

Her father's eyebrows rose. "My dear, an excellent family, a marquess."

She actually shuddered as she mentally contrasted the porcine visage of Lord Burford with Sir Sabin's fine features. "No," she repeated. "No, I beg you'll not ask me to marry him."

"My dear, it is a matter that was agreed upon before you were born. Let me tell you . . ."

She listened to his explanation with mounting impatience, and at the end of it she paced back and forth across the long room. "I cannot fulfill your promise to the dead. I do not like him. I shall never like him," she said in a low but passionate tone of voice.

"Diana, Lord Burford is not precisely handsome, but I beg you will not judge by outward appearance alone. I assure you that when you get to know him better, you will appreciate his finer qualities."

"I shall never—" she began.

"Hear me, my love," her father's voice cut across her protests. "We are invited to Burford Castle for the holidays. You will come to know him then, and I am sure you will agree with me."

"I will never agree," she cried passionately. "I love Sir Sabin! I will always love him."

"You are certainly magnanimous, Diana," her father said sarcastically.

"Magnanimous?" she repeated. "I do not understand you."

"Do you not?" he inquired sarcastically. "Is he or is he not the same young man who, in so many words, called you 'whore?' "

Diana paled as she remembered that scene at the green room in Bath's Theater Royal. However, the earl had never once referred to it. Despite the fact that he had been standing only a few feet away, she had had the feeling that he had been so absorbed in his conversation with her mother that he had not really noticed Sir Sabin, for all he had spoken about sending his seconds. She said numbly, "But he believed—"

"I do not care what he believed," Lord Lyall said icily.

"But you should care, since those beliefs concerned your character or, rather, the lack of it. Meeting him, I was hard put not to tell him that I remembered him for the villain he was. However, I would not give him the satisfaction of letting him know that I had heard his accusations. I recognized him the minute he crossed the threshold, and I was astounded to think that you would actually pay heed to his suit. I can also tell you that it gave me considerable pleasure to put him in his place."

"You do not understand," she said numbly.

"I understand, my dear, that this young man is not worthy of your attention and you must understand that I will never countenance your marriage with him. Burford might lack his physical attributes, I grant you, he is not handsome, but he has character and he is from a family that has made its mark in the history of our country. You do not know him."

"I do not want to know him," Diana exclaimed. "Sir Sabin—"

"Enough of Sir Sabin," he rasped. "Let him find himself another governess. He is not worth your little finger. But I shall not press you to wed Burford. I will ask only that you come with me to his house for the holidays. If at the end of our sojourn, you are still of the same mind, I will not mention his offer again. Will you not come? You will find the castle much to your liking and your brother will be with us, too. There will be other guests as well. Young Burford, as you will discover, is an excellent host and enjoys good company."

He was actually pleading, and much as she was minded to refuse the invitation from one whose society became irksome after five minutes, let alone as many weeks, the fact that her father had, in a sense, capitulated, warmed her. She did owe him a great debt, and also beneath his surface coldness she divined loneliness and a need to be understood as well as loved. If her mother had been a little more patient . . . But she must not, in pitying her father, criticize her mother's actions. Though she had been with him only a little over five months, she had had more than a taste of his arbitrary humor, his sense that he alone knew how she should conduct her life.

Her mother was a free spirit. She had rebelled against restraint as much as anything when she had cultivated Sir Guy. And there was much to be said for her point of view. But her father was waiting for her answer. She said, "I will come to Burford Castle for the holidays."

He looked gratified and responded, "I knew you would agree with me, my dear, once you thought it over."

Diana opened her mouth and closed it on a burgeoning retort. She had wanted to say that she agreed to nothing save the fact that she would spend the holidays at Burford Castle—but perhaps that was what he was implying and there was no need to invite another argument. Yet, she was not entirely sure. She felt a great longing to see her mother and would see her as soon as possible!

13

The dark-green post chaise with its four beautiful chestnuts and its crested door drew curious looks from the pedestrians on Cheyne Walk in Chelsea. Some stopped to look as a footman in green livery put a set of steps down in front of the door he had just opened. Their curiosity turned to admiration as the tall, beautiful girl in the stylish green coachman's coat descended. One lady actually groaned with envy as she saw and immediately attempted to memorize the velvet bonnet that framed the new arrival's lovely face.

Diana, unaware of all this attention, looked back at her abigail, who was just about to descend. She said, "Sophia, my dear, I do not believe you are well-acquainted with this village, are you?"

Sophia said in some suprise, "No, milady, I am not."

"I thought not," Diana said with a trace of satisfaction. "Well, I will have William drive you around. Perhaps you would like to see the Royal Hospital with its statue of King Charles, and there are other points of interest."

The girl looked surprised and somewhat disturbed. "But I should go with you, milady. The master has said—"

"It will be passing dull for you," Diana interrupted, "cooling your heels in our small kitchen. Moira, my mother's abigail, is not very talkative. Should you not prefer to see the sights?"

At the word "kitchen," the abigail's gaze, generally so wavering, had become fixed and her expression was unusually miffed. Obviously, Diana had struck a nerve. Sophia was not the sort of servant to appreciate chatting with those she considered her inferiors. Her attitude toward Moira had caused the latter to dub her that "persnickety wench." Now, seeing the play of emotions on Sophia's face, Diana judged her badly pricked by the horns of a dilemma. More than ever, she was convinced that the girl had been bade to listen and report. However, she would not be able to countermand orders that relegated her to the kitchen. Meeting Diana's eyes, Sophia's own pale orbs reflected defeat.

"You are kind to suggest it, milady," she said in her soft little voice. "I should very much like to see the village of Chelsea."

"Good." Diana smiled. "I am sure you will find it delightful." Moving to the coachman, she gave him his orders and added, "You may return in an hour or so, William, but be sure that Sophia sees Ranelagh Gardens."

"I will that, your Ladyship," he said. "Though it is a bit of a distance."

"No matter. If you are later than an hour, I shall not mind, William."

Diana stood at the wrought-iron gate of her mother's house for a moment, admiring the swiftly flowing Thames, bright under the late-autumn sun. She had never appreciated the view half so much as she did today, and was quick to trace the reason. She had rid herself of the undesirable presence of Sophia, "creeping Sophia," as she had nicknamed her in her own mind. She realized that her action in relieving herself of the girl's presence would be duly reported to her father. However, he could scarcely complain about what she, if asked, would describe as a kindness to her servant.

Moving to the front door, she lifted the brass knocker and let it fall against its plate. That portal was opened immediately, suggesting that Moira was lurking just beyond it. "Oh, Miss Diana," the old woman breathed as she moved back to let her come in. "If you doesn't look splendid . . ." She flushed. "I mean, your Ladyship."

"Dear Moira." Diana bent to kiss her. "Miss Diana always, to you, and do not let me hear any more nonsense. Where is Mama?"

"She is here." Mrs. Forsythe, wearing a morning gown of pale-pink muslin and with her golden curls falling about her shoulders, looked amazingly young and pretty, her daughter thought lovingly. She flung her arms around her mother and held her tightly. "Oh, I have missed you, Mama. It seems ages and ages since last I saw you."

"It has been all of a fortnight," Mrs. Forsythe said softly, "but it has seemed overlong to me, too, my dearest. But do you not look splendid!" She sent a rather wary glance around the room and then said, "Sophia is not with you?"

"Not at the moment, Mama."

"Ah, and how did you manage to dispense with her?"

"I had William give her a tour of Chelsea, for which I shall undoubtedly be castigated by my father—but at least she is not here to listen and report."

Mrs. Forsythe nodded. "I am glad of that, my love. I cannot bear the chit. And I agree with you, I am quite sure she is a paid observer. Your father has not changed."

"No, he has not," Diana cried passionately. "Oh, Mama, I do wish . . . Oh, I do not know what I wish." Diana had not expected to weep, but the pain she felt over Sir Sabin's dismissal had not lessened in the last week. On the contrary, it had increased with every passing day.

"Ah, my love, come." Her mother led her up a small pair of stairs and into the sitting room that lay just off her bedchamber. Indicating the rather shabby sofa that had stood in its corner as long as Diana could remember, she said, "Sit down, my love. No, first let me take off your coat, else you will be far too warm." She glanced at a fire burning on the hearth. "Ah," she added as she helped Diana out of her coat, "Another new ensemble, I see, and so becoming too. But, no matter, tell me what's amiss, my darling."

"Mama!" Diana seized her mother's hands. "Do you know about Sir Sabin?"

"Sir Sabin?" Mrs. Forsythe frowned. "I've not seen him since Bath, when, as I remember, he was less than kind."

"He did not mean it, Mama!" Diana let Mrs. Forsythe's hands fall. She took a turn around the room. "He did not mean it," she repeated. "It was natural, or maybe it was not natural, that he would think . . . Oh, dear, I do not care about that. He has apologized, Mama, and he has asked me to marry him and, oh, I do love him. I think I have loved him ever since he carried me home on that January day." More tears ran down Diana's cheeks as she brokenly described the scene at the ball and her father's reception of Sir Sabin's proposal, as well as his counterproposal. She added furiously, "I will not marry Lord Burford, never in this world. I do not care what Father says. I find him horrid. And the idea of spending two hours in his company is so irksome that I shudder to contemplate the holidays."

"As I said, your father has not changed," Mrs. Forsythe sighed. "However, by his lights, I expect it is only natural he would want you to make an advantageous marriage, my love. I do seem to remember Lord Burford—I am speaking of the father, of course. He was pleasant enough. We saw him infrequently, for he was not a well man. Still, it does not follow that the son—"

"His son is tiresome and jealous, ridiculously jealous," Diana cried. "The other evening I was detained, as I explained, by Sir Sabin and came late to the waltz that, at Father's urging, was the third one I had granted Lord Burford. You have no idea how very unpleasant he was, and he remained in the dismals for the rest of the evening."

"You forget, my love, that he has reason to be jealous, however much I deplore the emotion, and you may be sure that I do." Mrs. Forsythe was silent a moment, staring into the fire, as if struck by an unhappy memory of her own. She shook herself slightly and added, "But you are very beautiful, a matrimonial prize, my love. And from all you say, Lord Burford, as a friend of your father's, is eager to press his advantage.''

''He has pressed his advantage—he has offered for me already. However, I have refused it, and Father has concurred, though I am sure he hopes that I will relent. I will never relent. Oh, God, I almost wish I had never come to Bath.''

''I do believe, my child, that that is an exaggeration.'' Mrs. Forsythe put both hands on her daughter's shoulders and looked into her eyes. ''Is it not?'' Before Diana could answer her, she continued, ''If you are unhappy with your father, you may return here.''

''Oh, I could not,'' Diana said almost without thinking, and then flushed. ''I mean he—he has been kind to me. And I could not repay him in such coin.''

''That is well-spoken, my love. And I do agree with you. Furthermore, you do not have to honor his wishes when it comes to your marriage. I wonder that he is so desirous of pushing you into a match at this present time, save that he must wish to see you creditably settled.''

''I would be creditably settled with Sir Sabin,'' Diana cried. She continued mutinously, ''He has no right to order my life this way.''

''There speaks an echo of my own self, some nineteen years ago, though now it seems more like a hundred and nineteen. My dearest, as your mother, I tell you that you need not marry at your father's command. No one can compel you to accept Lord Burford's offer.''

''But if I agree to join him for the holidays . . .''

''My love, he is not issuing an invitation to the altar. Accept it as it stands, and do not allow yourself to be intimidated by him or by your father. The Burford estate, I might mention, is very large. Anyone who is visiting there can easily lose himself or herself on the grounds and, in consequence, avoid uncomfortable confrontations.''

Diana suddenly giggled. ''You are suggesting . . .''

''I am *saying* that if you wish to remain unharmed, keep

out of harm's way," Mrs. Forsythe said coolly. "You have always been a resourceful girl. There is no reason for you to change because you have suddenly been elevated."

Diana loosed a long breath she hardly realized she had been holding. She caught her mother's hand and held it. "You are right. I am still me, am I not, in spite of all these horrid restraints and Sophia. She cannot intimidate me, either. But I do wish I might have another abigail. Unfortunately, Father tells me that she is the daughter of his mother's housekeeper and raised on the estate. He considers her training exemplary."

"And probably he entertains feudal feelings regarding his servants, but you are dealing with the matter well enough. I do hope she will enjoy her visit to the Royal Hospital."

"I gave orders that William take her considerably farther." Diana winked.

"You see," Mrs. Forsythe said triumphantly. "But, my love, I do understand that these months with your father have been difficult. Any change is difficult, especially when your affections are involved."

Diana's smile fled. "I do love Father, but Sir Sabin . . . I never dreamed that he would come to love me . . ." She paused and then said, "Will you do something for me, please? Will you let him know that my sentiments remain the same, no matter what my father told him?"

"Yes, my dear, of course I will," Mrs. Forsythe said gently. "And . . ." she paused, and a slight frown creased her forehead. "If for some reason you do feel too intimidated by your father, let me know. It may be that I can talk some sense into him."

"Oh, will you?" Diana cried.

"You may be assured of that, my dear."

"And you will get word to Sir Sabin as soon as possible?"

"I will get word to Sir Sabin," her mother promised.

There was another question that Diana longed to put to her mother, but she was not sure how to phrase it. Finally, she said, "I have given you very little opportunity to tell

me about yourself . . . the marriage to Mr. Gifford. Have
you set a date?''

Mrs. Forsythe looked down. "Not yet, my love." She
added dryly, "You may be sure, however, that we will not
make a runaway match of it. You will have fair warning
and it may even be . . ." She shrugged.

"What?" Try as she did, Diana could not keep a shade
of hope from creeping into her tone.

"I do not know. I beg you will not tax me on this
matter, my love.''

"I do apologize," Diana said quickly. When her mother
used that particular tone of voice, the questioning period
was at a definite end. However, the hope remained. She
went on to talk of other things, none of which she remembered once she had parted from her mother and joined a
sulky Sophia in the post chaise. All she remembered was
that Sir Sabin would soon know the state of her heart and
that her mother stood firmly behind her—her mother, who
might or might not marry Mr. Gifford. There was another
hope contingent upon that possibility, one that she scarce
liked to consider, but she thought philosophically, was that
not the nature of all hope?

The nearest town to Lord Burford's estate was Fakenham
in the county of Norfolk, but as Mrs. Forsythe had told
Diana, the grounds were extensive and would have all but
encompassed that village.

The castle itself had proved disappointing. It consisted
of little more than a ruined keep and a few shattered walls.
For the rest, the manor house that had replaced it was
relatively modern, having been built in the early eighteenth
century and finished toward its middle with funds brought
into the family by Alice Polson, the heiress of a Cornishman
grown rich on coal. Dating from that time, the Burfords
had prospered considerably.

Diana had seen the portrait of the heiress in the long
gallery. Clad in sumptuous pink satin and wearing her hair
powdered over a cushion, she had been heavy-featured, a

marked contrast in looks to the slender, even wispy man
who had married her and to his equally slender forebears,
with their long elegant bodies and high-bred faces repeated
through the centuries with only a change in costume. Her
son and grandson, unfortunately, bore a close resemblance
to her.

Diana had had ample time to study the paintings in the
long gallery. By reason of tall windows ranged on one side
of the room, it was chilled by the breezes that crept
through rain-warped wood, and not often visited. Consequently, in lieu of losing herself on the grounds white with
a heavy and unexpected snowfall, Diana had often sought
sanctuary there.

Much to her regret, his Lordship enjoyed the library,
thus proving an effective deterrent to her presence there,
amid a large and varied collection of volumes. She had
managed to snatch a few books, one being a relatively
ancient description of Norfolk and Burford Castle, during
the period when it was still standing. The other volume
was an eighteenth-century reprint of Reginald Scott's *The
Discouerie of Witchcraft*. Though that treatise, exceptionally forward-looking for its period (1584), scoffed at the
idea of witches, Diana quite wished there were some truth
in the superstition, and herself a practitioner of the craft
and able to go sailing off via a broomstick back to London.

On a day several weeks after her arrival at the so-called
castle, Diana curled up on a long sofa, which she had
pushed closer to a small fire on the hearth of her favorite
refuge, sent a mutinous glance at the Burford ancestors to
her right and left, and wished their descendants at the
bottom of the ice-covered pond in the Italian garden.
Though it was useless and frustrating to dwell at length on
her situation, she was growing more and more uncomfortable. It seemed to her that the fabled sword of Damocles
was poised within inches of her head. Though she remembered her mother's promise and her every intention of
acting upon it, Mrs. Forsythe seemed very, very far away

and she, a lone warrior, faced a determined antagonist who had already shown himself capable of unfair fighting.

She smiled wryly, remembering her father's heartening mention of "other guests." Ostensibly, due to a series of mishaps and cancellations, she, her father, and brother, arriving at Lord Burford's estate, discovered that the "guests" invited for the holidays consisted of themselves— with her half-brother due to leave for Oxford in a month's time, which, she remembered unhappily, was up tomorrow.

There were two other people at the castle. They were Lord Burford's first and second cousins, Miss Celia Bray and Mr. William Polson. Miss Bray, a faded woman some forty years old, acted as his hostess. Timorous and unassertive, she had evidently been ordered to produce praise for her cousin whenever she encountered Diana. She did so with the coordinated precision of a mechanical doll, the while clasping and unclasping her hands and smiling brightly. Mr. Polson, who served as estate manager, was, if possible, even more of a sycophant than the lady. He nodded approval of every word uttered by his relative and, in common with Miss Bray, dropped globules of praise whenever possible.

Diana smiled and frowned. Though they were the only two people in the house, it was amazing how they appeared to multipy. She was always meeting one or the other around a corner or on a stair. She half-suspected that the servants were bidden to watch and report her whereabouts to them so that they might trap her with their ceaseless encomiums on the subject of her host, who was also far more in evidence than she would have deemed possible in a mansion so large.

She shuddered. While Lord Burford had not made any mention to her of the offer of marriage he had discussed with her father, she had never felt so intimidated. Even at school, the vigilance of teachers instructed to oversee their lively young charges and to report any infraction of rules could not approach that of the trio at the mansion. She felt outnumbered, outmaneuvered, and surrounded—not unlike a tower under siege that must soon fall to a stronger enemy, one who was determined on capture and was aided at every turn by his cohorts and by her father, whom she knew stood firmly in Burford's camp. Her only ally was her youthful and sympathetic half-brother, who, on the occasions when they were alone, kept her laughing at his imitations of his host, Miss Bray, and Mr. Polson. They were as accurate as they were amusing, and they were not his only contribution to her well-being. He had promised to send a letter to her mother, explaining her plight. That missive was currently reposing in a book under the crocheted throw that was lying over her lap.

She had started to write it the previous afternoon, shortly after having extracted the promise from Anthony to post it in Oxford. She had been in the midst of an impassioned plea for rescue when she had looked up to find Sophia standing by the desk. As usual, the abigail had entered so quietly that she had not been aware of her presence until that moment. She may or may not have seen the opening sentences, but Diana was of the opinion that she had, for that evening, apropos of nothing, Lord Burford had suddenly said, "My dear Diana, it occurs to me that you may want to write to your mother or your friends. If you have any such communications, please leave them on the table in the hall and my man will take them to the village. A stagecoach leaves the Blue Crown every other day, even in this vile weather.

Diana winced. She was reasonably positive that any letter she left in that suggested spot would be carefully perused by his Lordship and, very probably, her father. She cast a hunted glance out of the window at the chill vista that lay before it, keeping her pent inside with no hope of straying away from the house for even so much as an hour unless she wanted to catch her death of cold. It was very cold here, even inside, when there was no fire laid on. Indeed, she could imagine that such arctic regions as Siberia could hardly be much colder.

Of course, her feelings were exaggerated, but faced with

Lord Burford's languishing glances and his constant praise of herself and, what was even worse, her father's constant praise of *him* and his steady refusal to heed her protests that she had no interest in the man, could not care for him, and would never change her mind on that score, she had more than an idle suspicion that her father had come to the conclusion that, in time, she would be worn down by the process of attrition.

A quavering sigh escaped Diana, not the first she had loosed that afternoon. Then, she tensed, hearing footsteps coming down the hall. It might be her brother, who had promised to join her here as soon as he could. However, it might also be Sophia. On several other occasions, she had invaded Diana's several refuges, this being her favorite because it was most inaccessible and cold enough to repel the abigail. Yet, coming into the long gallery, the card room, also little used, or the back parlor, Sophia would ask if she might do anything for her and, being summarily dismissed, would go quietly out, only to be replaced by Lord Burford. Diana was beginning to loathe the very sight of the girl and to resent her father deeply for what she did not doubt was his encouragement of her surveillance. However, on occasion, she had wondered whether or not it was Lord Burford who might not be the instigator in that quarter. Either way, it was two against one.

She glared at the portrait of Lord Burford's late father. Inadvertently, he was responsible for her situation. He had been Damon to Lord Lyall's Pythias. He was the reason that her father had decided Lord Burford was the perfect husband for her. As previously noted, they did resemble each other, and she was positive that Lord Lyall did not see beyond that resemblance to the overweening self-satisfaction of his heir. Now she sat up, tensing as the door was pushed open, but even before the visitor entered, she relaxed. Sophia always knocked or, rather, scratched upon the surface of the door. Anthony never did. She smiled brightly at him as he entered and came over to the sofa.

Grinning at Diana, he commented, "You resemble a stag at bay, my dear sister."

"I am glad to see you. I was so afraid you might be—"

"Burly Burford or the Mad Marquess." He nodded. "How is that for the title of a play? Shall I suggest it to Mr. Gifford?" Before she could respond, he continued, "Quick, where's the letter? One never knows when Silent Sophia will come stealing in."

"Did you pass her in the hall?" Diana inquired in some alarm.

"I did not, nor did I notice the Bray or the Polson. Perhaps *they* are making love in the stable loft and will be frozen to death. Is that not a 'consumation devoutly to be wish'd?' "

"You are entirely outrageous." Diana giggled as she produced the letter and quickly handed it to him.

He slipped it inside his jacket and his grin widened. "I will now leave this on the table for Burford's man to pick up on his way to his Lordship in the library."

Diana sighed. "It is too demeaning to be so underhanded, but Sophia, you do not think that Father has encouraged her to follow me and alert Lord Burford to my whereabouts."

Anthony's grin vanished. "No, I do not. He would never stoop to anything like that. He would think it beneath him. I would not put it past his Lordship himself. Yet, on second thought, even he has his pride. Unless he thinks that all is fair in love and war."

"Love?" Diana grimaced. "I could never love him. Why cannot Father understand that?"

Anthony moved to the portrait of the elder Lord Burford. "Because of him," he said.

"That ridiculous promise," Diana exclaimed.

"Not entirely that. They do look amazingly alike, and I know that Father misses him sorely. They were like brothers, you see. I remember him. He was very kind—nothing at all like his son. I hold that our lad must harken back to the coal heaver's daughter."

With a reproving glance, Diana said, "Do not be a snob. Remember that I, your half-sister—"

"Hails from gentle folk and is as beautiful as you are good and should not be subjected to the likes of Burford for an hour, let alone all these weeks. Despite his sartorial splendor and these, his noble ancestors"—Anthony made a sweeping gesture—"the man's a clod!"

Diana laughed and said, "Oh, dearest Tony, I shall miss you. I do wish you were not leaving."

"I wish I were not, also, but 'love's messengers must be swift!' Who knows? I might not even consign this to the post at all."

Diana started. "What might you mean by that?"

"I have a hankering to meet your mother. I might place it in her hands, instead."

"But you can't, can you?" she asked, trying to keep her eagerness from seeping into her tone. "I mean, you are due back at school."

"It is not a full day's journey between Oxford and London." He bent to kiss her lightly on the forehead. "Do not give up hope, my child," he said with a ridiculously avuncular air. "Help *will* arrive to free the captive maiden. Remember that there has been no official announcement as yet."

"He has offered," she sighed.

"You've not accepted."

"And I never will," she cried. "I cannot see why he remains so determined when I've given him no encouragement at all."

"As to that, my dear, you've but to look into your mirror."

Diana groaned. It was her face or, rather, her striking resemblance to her great-grandmother that had wrought the immense changes in her life, and now, would it be her face that would come between her and happiness? "I will never marry him," she cried in answer to that silent question.

"I am glad of that," Anthony said. "Half of him would be too much, I'm thinking."

"What can you mean?"

"You are not usually so dense, Diana. As you are my half-sister, he'd be my half-brother-in-law." He pretended to shiver. "Ugh, what a horrid fate!"

She found she could laugh. "I will miss you, Tony. I do wish you could stay longer."

"No, you do not, my dear. You wish that I would leave even as early as tonight so that you will know that help is on the way." His smile had vanished and he looked unexpectedly sober. "I hope your mother will abide by her promise. Father might listen to her persuasions." He sighed. "He can be amazingly wrongheaded, though. And all the time he will believe himself totally in the right."

She was conscious of a chill. "I know that myself from my own experiences, and from those of my mother as well."

Anthony moved to her and put his arms around her, holding her tightly. Pressing his mouth against her ear, he said urgently, "Be very strong, Diana."

14

Diana had good cause to remember her conversation with Tony in the long gallery, a scant two days after she had bade him a regretful farewell and seen the post chaise bear him down the rutted driveway. She was, as usual, sitting in that same chamber, enjoying the winter sunshine that brightened the tall windows. It was a beautiful day, and with Anthony on the road to Oxford and, hopefully, beyond, she could for once enjoy the shadow of the trees across the white snow and in her immediate vision the clusters of red berries on a holly tree. It reminded her of the old carol, her mother had been wont to sing to her when she was little:

> The holly and the ivy,
> When they are both full grown,
> Of all the trees within the woods
> The holly bears the crown.

She blinked at a sudden wetness in her eyes. She did miss her mother. She had never valued her enough, she thought. Rather then resenting her for not having revealed her heritage, she should have examined the reasons behind that reticence more thoroughly. Her mother was strong-willed, true enough, but never unjust and certainly never blinded by sentiment. She would not have forced her to endure the company of a man she could not abide out of loyalty to a late friend. She tensed. She had heard the door open, but looking around, she found it closed. She was still alone. She stretched out on the couch and continued to stare at the felicitous combination of sunshine and snow beyond the windows.

She must have drifted into sleep, Diana realized, for the loud knock on the door scattered a host of images. "Yes," she called, hoping for once that it would be Sophia or, failing that, her father. However, it was Lord Burford who entered and came to stand near the couch.

"Ah, my dear, I thought you must be here. I am told that you favor this chamber. That, I might add, pleases me mightily." He rubbed his hands together.

Diana found the gesture peculiarly repellent. She regarded him narrowly. There was no way to tell him that she favored this chamber mainly because he visited it so seldom. Earlier that morning, however, she had told him that she was going to rest in her bedroom. She wondered how he had happened to come and seek her here, and remembering the opening door, she divined that, as usual, Sophia had alerted him. Did curses really return to "plague their inventors" as was contended in Shakespeare's *Macbeth*? If they did not, she had one for Sophia, whose vigilance must be counted extraordinary. But she was constrained to comment on Lord Burford's remark—something she was unwilling to do, she was not quite sure why. She said, "Yes, I do find it pleasant." She wished that she might have added a qualifying, "when I am here by myself." However, she must needs remember the courtesy due him as her host and her father's friend.

To her regret, he drew up a chair, and positioning himself beside her, he said, "Your father and I have discussed your preference for this room. He finds it very heartening that you are already taking such an interest in my family. I imagine they would have been equally interested in you, my dear. I am indeed sorry that my mother has gone to her final resting place. I am sure she would have agreed that you were a most worthy successor."

"A worthy successor?" Diana repeated faintly.

"But, of course," he said easily. "I must tell you, my dear, that when I initially offered for you, I was not cast down when your father told me that you wanted to give the matter more consideration. I realized that I, too, had been impulsive. In consequence, I must explain that I practiced a little stratagem for which I pray you will forgive me. When I invited you and your family here, I said that there would be other guests present. That was not true. I wanted the opportunity to see you as much as possible without the encroachment of others, and I have. I must tell you that in the past weeks I have become convinced that you are eminently suited to be my wife. You are beautiful and dignified. I can think of none other that could grace this home. Consequently, I am happy to tell you that I am doubly convinced that you will be the next Marchioness of Burford."

Diana rose swiftly, and moving away from him, she said incredulously, "Am I to consider this in the light of an offer, my Lord?"

He rose. "You may, if you choose," he said indulgently. "However, I must remind you that I had already offered for your hand. When I told your father of my decision this morning, he pronounced himself delighted. He has accepted in your name. It remains only for the banns to be read."

"And have I nothing to say about these plans?" she inquired icily.

He appeared mildly surprised. "Surely, you are cognizant of the depth of my feelings for you, my dear."

"And what of my feelings, my Lord?"

He favored her with a complacent smile. "I was told that you might offer some resistance to my proposal. Your father has suggested that you discuss this matter with him. You will find him in the library and—"

Diana, not troubling to listen to anything more he might tell her, sped out of the room. She reached the library in minutes and pulled open the door, slamming it behind her. Standing just beyond the threshold, she glared at Lord Lyall, who had just risen from his chair, a frown on his face. "Is it true—" she began.

"My dear," he interrupted, "that is hardly the way a lady should enter a room."

"I have begun to believe that I am not a lady," she retorted. "I have begun to think that I am considered a puppet without the power to think or act for myself, else I surely should have been consulted concerning Lord Burford's second offer, rather than having him present it to me as if it were a foregone conclusion that I marry him."

Lord Lyall's frown deepened. "Sit down, my dear. I think it is time that you understand exactly why I have given my sanction."

"You said that you would not," she flared. "You told me that if I were not of a mind to accept him as my husband, I would not be constrained to do so."

"That was before I had an opportunity to see you together. Though you might not agree with me as yet—"

"I will never agree!"

"Though you might not agree with me as yet," he repeated in cold, even tones, "I have seen you with Lord Burford, and as I anticipated, you complement each other. Furthermore, this house is an admirable setting for you and you could not expect a higher position in society."

"I do not love him," Diana cried hotly.

"Love is not generally for us, my dear. And yet, I happen to know that Lord Burford is very much in love with you. He has told me, too, that he knows you will be compatible. He is also pleased that you have taken such an interest in his family. He mentioned that you are often to be found in the long gallery."

She could not restrain a bitter laugh. "That is true. And may I tell you why I have gone there? Because early in my stay here, I discovered that wing was very seldom visited. Furthermore, the light is good and I could read there undisturbed by Lord Burford, Miss Bray, or Mr. Polson. However, of late, he has often sought me out there and, generally, fast on the heels of Sophia. Did you perhaps ask her to follow me and alert him to my whereabouts?"

Lord Lyall flushed a deep red, and rising swiftly, he

said angrily, "Can you imagine that I would stoop to so dastardly a device?"

"If I am wrong, I beg your pardon, Father. It has just seemed odd to me that Lord Burford's appearances have invariably been preceded by Sophia, who, I will not scruple to tell you, I dislike. But that is aside from the point. I am not drawn to Lord Burford. I find him overbearing and generally unpleasant."

"He can be tactless, I admit, but I blame that on his youth. His father—"

"He is not his father," Diana cried. "Why do you continue to equate him with your friend?"

"If you would give me leave to finish what I was about to tell you, I will explain why. When he was George's age, he was inclined to be overbearing and impatient. However, as the years went on, his true character emerged. I cannot believe that his son, who so resembles him physically, does not have a lion's share of his good qualities as well. He is intelligent. He is well-read. He and I have had some fascinating discussions on many diverse subjects. You must give yourself an opportunity to know him better."

"I do not want to know him better, Father. I do not want to marry him. I do not love him!"

"Love, my dear, as I have just suggested, is ephemeral. Character is what counts—character and substance, both of which are possessed by young Burford."

"I have told you—" she began.

"My dear, let us not argue, please. I want you to weigh his proposal pro and con for the next few days—"

"While the banns are read in church, perchance?"

"The banns?" he repeated. "What do you mean by that?"

"He told me that you having accepted in my name, it only remained for the banns to be read!"

"Ah, youth," Lord Lyall said indulgently, "ever impetuous. I will tell him that he must continue to put a harness on his ardor. I'll not have you rushed into marriage quite so hastily. However, I do want you to consider the advantages of the match.''

''I tell you—''

''And I tell you!'' her father broke in. ''I will not consider arguments given to me on the spur of the moment. I will tell young Burford that he is only endangering his chances by his eagerness. He'll listen to me. And I think that in the next few days, you'll see another side to him.''

''If he had six sides, Father, none of them would please me.'' Without giving him a chance to respond, she went out of the room. Feeling as frustrated as she ever had in her entire life, Diana went slowly up the stairs to her chamber. Truly, she thought bitterly, her father was seeing Lord Burford through a glass, darkly—or rather he was not seeing a shadowy image, he was seeing his dead friend and not his son at all. She stared out of the window at the cold snowy ground. The thought of escape was in her mind, but the snow prevented it, just as it would prevent anyone who might hope to talk some sense into her father from coming here.

''Oh, God, what can I do?'' she said out loud.

There was the sound of footsteps coming across the floor from the inner room. Sophia appeared in the doorway. ''Might I be of help, your Ladyship?'' she said in her small, soft voice.

Staring at her, Diana's suspicions came to the fore again. Seized by a sudden inspiration she said, ''I have a mind to visit the ruined tower. I have been wanting to see if for quite a while, but this is the first fair day. Would you like to come with me, Sophia dear?''

The girl glanced out of the window. There was a view of the tumbled structure from there. She shivered. ''If your Ladyship wishes, I will go, of course, but—''

''But you would rather not,'' Diana interrupted. ''Then, you must not. I will go alone.''

''It is very cold out there, your Ladyship.''

"I shall be glad of the fresh air," Diana replied. "And I have always been interested in antiquities."

"I will fetch your cloak. And you'd best wear your pattens, too," Sophia said solicitously.

"Thank you, Sophia, I will."

There was something sad about the tower, Diana thought as she gazed up at its broken walls. Then, shivering, she moved into a crevice that offered some little protection from the frosty wind. Looking, she saw an arrow slit that was still intact. She could imagine the archers, their crossbows in readiness as they prepared to battle with some approaching enemy. They must have thought themselves impregnable. A slight laugh escaped her. She, on the other hand, wanted to be discovered by the enemy, and since it was far colder than she had anticipated, she hoped that she would not need to wait long.

"My dear Diana, what are you doing out here?"

She started and bit down another laugh, a triumphant laugh. Two prayers had been answered. Her hiding place had been discovered by the enemy in question—as it could never have been had he not glimpsed it from the upstairs windows—and who would have alerted him to her presence there? However, he had asked her a question.

"I have always been interested in ancient buildings," she said, trying to keep her teeth from chattering.

"So your father tells me," he said heartily. "I myself have the same interest. As a boy, I often played here."

"It would be pleasant, particularly in the summer," she remarked.

"Yes, indeed," he agreed. "But I am fond of the frost and ice as well. Perhaps you would like to hear about Sir Yves de Beaufort, my ancestor. I prefer the name 'Beaufort' to Burford myself, but it was anglicized in 1420 when . . ."

She barely listened to what promised to be a lengthy recital. Though she was growing colder by the minute, she had accomplished the purpose that had brought her into the tower. One enemy had suffered defeat and would soon be dismissed.

On a morning three days after her discussion with her father, Diana, looking out of the window in her room, saw to her delight more evidence of the unexpected thaw that had set in yesterday. Rather than an undulating blanket of white stretching as far as she could see, there were patches of yellowed grass, brown earth, and irregular pools of water. The sky was clear and in the distance the sun was rising. The change in the weather was not the only reason for her current happiness—the weights had been lifted from her heart or, rather, the tightness from her chest, if she were to be specific about the physical manifestations wrought by her state of mind. The day before yesterday, she had finally seen the last of Sophia!

The girl's dismissal had taken place after her father and Lord Burford had had words concerning the latter's unofficial employment or, rather, deployment of the chit, whom he had bribed to follow and disclose Diana's whereabouts.

Sophia, subsequently questioned by Lord Lyall, had burst into tears and admitted her complicity, adding in pathetic tones, "I thought as you wanted it, too, my Lord."

Lord Lyall had been furious. "Can you imagine," he had demanded, "that I would actually *pay* you to spy on my daughter? You will leave my employ immediately and I will have you driven to the Blue Crown, where on the morrow you may catch the stagecoach to London."

Diana felt singularly free. She had not realized how very much the abigail had disturbed her. It was only after she had been relieved of her presence that she understood that Sophia had been a veritable thorn in the flesh. That she had also been relieved of several pieces of jewelry—trumpery trinkets, the pearls and emeralds having been locked away—did not distress her. The absence of Sophia more than compensated for her loss.

There was also a coldness existing between her father

and Lord Burford that Diana prayed would continue. However, much to her disappointment, Lord Lyall had not responded to her suggestion that they cut short the visit. He had cited the bad roads and he had also mentioned the recent disappearance of a stagecoach in a blizzard not far from the town. Still, he had not brought up Lord Burford's qualifications for marriage, and the latter had been keeping out of her way of late, presenting to her a most chastened face whenever they met in one or another of the corridors.

Unfortunately, last evening he had been more in evidence and his attitude at that time had suggested he had not lost hope. Today, she might be able to avoid him by going riding. Even if he joined her, there was not much he could say during a fast canter.

Slipping out of bed, she went to the armoire, savoring anew the unexpected pleasure of being able to dress without the help of Sophia. True, her gowns were more complicated than those she had been wont to wear as a governess, but fortunately her riding habit presented no difficulties.

Coming downstairs an hour later, Diana, going in the direction of the dining room, was startled by masculine laughter. Through the open door, she glimpsed her father and Lord Burford. The overlay of chill so evident lately was gone from her father's tone as he said complacently, "I cannot approve your methods, my boy, but I am inclined to agree that the end justifies the means. I can remember a time when your dear father and I—it was when he was courting your mother and she . . .''

Diana stayed to hear no more. The sensation of being trapped rushed over her again. Her father was still seeing his dead friend rather than the latter's living son. And now what would happen? Diana came to a decision. As she was her mother's daughter, she would follow in her foorsteps, and as soon as she might!

On returning to her chamber, Diana had a moment of real regret. She had learned to love her father and he had been uncommonly kind to her, but she would not be a sacrifice upon the altar of sentiment. If he could forgive Lord Burford's bribing of Sophia, there was very little hope that he would ever see the man for what he really was: an arrogant, overbearing fool!

Going back to her armoire, Diana examined her garments. She would not take all of them, she decided, only the few that she could put into one bandbox. She was extremely thankful that Sophia had gone, else the little wretch would have lost no time in alerting the men downstairs. She was also glad that Lord Burford had inadvertently offered aid of his own. There were no guests, who must certainly have asked questions had one or another of them caught her as she attempted to slip through a side door. Fortunately Miss Bray slept late and Cousin William occupied a house somewhere on the grounds. The servants could be avoided, if she were careful. She was also thankful for her years on the road with her mother. She had learned to pack quickly and efficiently, and in less than an hour, she was ready to leave. However, she would need money, she remembered belatedly. She was not sure how much she had, but her father had given her twenty pounds before leaving London. She had made a few purchases in the village, but she was rather sure that she had eighteen pounds and a few pence left—enough to buy a ticket on the stagecoach and to hire a hackney to take her back to her mother's house once she arrived in London.

She lifted her little purse from her reticule. To her surprise, it seemed considerably lighter than she had expected. Opening it, she found that it was empty. Diana loosed a long quavering sigh. Sophia had not contented herself with trinkets alone, she realized despairingly. She had left her without so much as a groat!

She had just finished unpacking her bandbox and was hanging up the last of her garments, when there was a knock on the door. She tensed, hoping that it was not Lord Burford, but surely he would not seek her out in her very chamber! She moved into her sitting room and opened her door the veriest crack, pulling it wider as she saw her father standing there.

He was looking anxious, but his face cleared as he said, "Oh, you are dressed. I thought you might be ill, my dear. Are you going riding, then?"

"I thought I might."

"May I join you, my dear?"

"Of course," she replied, guessing from his expression that he had much he wanted to say to her. And did he intend to plead the cause of Lord Burford yet again, she wondered unhappily. Still, no matter what arguments he produced, she would not capitulate, and sooner or later the latter must wear of his vain pursuit.

They were waiting for their horses to be saddled when a footman came hurrying into the stables. "My Lord Lyall," he panted, holding out an envelope, "this came for you from the Blue Crown."

Lord Lyall looked understandably surprised. However, he produced a coin, and after handing it to the man, he opened the letter, scanning it quickly. His eyes widened. Turning to Diana, he said with something less than his usual calm, "I must leave. I fear you will need to ride without me, my dear."

"Where are you going?" she demanded in a surprise equal to his own.

"Someone I know must see me on a matter of great importance. They have come a long way." He spoke, she noted, hurriedly and evasively, not meeting her eyes.

Her surprise increased, and added to it was alarm, for he did look so disturbed. "Am I not to know the name of this person who summons you?" she asked.

He shook his head. "It is not important that you know, my dear. Ah, here we are," he added as one of the grooms led out a sleek black horse. In another moment, he was mounted, and urging his horse forward, he was out of the gates in seconds.

Diana stared after him with considerable concern. At that moment, she was heartily glad that she had not fol-

lowed her original intention and stolen away from Burford
Castle without a word. Arbitrary or not, she knew that she had
come to care for her father a great deal more than she had
realized. And what was this message that had caused him
such great concern?

"May I help you to mount, milady," the groom asked,
leading her horse forward.

"Yes, yes, of course," Diana replied, looking with
approval at the gray he was holding. Once in the saddle,
she refused his offer to ride with her and guiding her horse
out of the stables, she started toward the path that would
take her to the highway and eventually to the Blue Crown.

Diana had passed through gates held open by a surprised
gatekeeper and had made the turn onto the highway when
she suddenly espied a solitary rider coming in her direction. His horse was mud-splattered—not surprising, considering the condition of the roads. His hat, she noticed
nervously, was pulled down to shade his features, which it
did, most effectively. She regarded him narrowly, hoping
that he would pass her, the while she unwillingly thought
of highwaymen, not so prevalent upon the roads as for-
merly, but still a hazard. Urging her horse into a canter, she
passed him only to hear the sound of hooves behind her—
following her? Casting a quick glance over her shoulder,
she saw to her horror that the rider had, indeed, turned and
was coming after her. The gates were not very far away.
She could turn back, but while she was debating this
possibility, she was still urging her horse forward. In
seconds, her pursuer had caught up with her. He reached
for her reins, saying in a low, amused voice, "Where are
you going, my dear? Would you not like to have some
company upon this lonely road?"

"At such an hour in the morning and you say you
cannot find her?" Lord Burford glared at Miss Bray, who
had obviously dressed hastily and was, as usual, clasping
and unclasping her hands in an excess of agitation.

"She—she is not in her c-chamber, Cousin George,"

Miss Bray said. "One of the servants did see her going in the direction of the stables with her father. She was dressed for riding."

"Lord Lyall received a message requiring him to go to the village. I hope she did not join him. Send Browne to the stables and find out if that is where she went." Lord Burford shook his head. "And her mother coming here!"

"It is early for a call," Miss Bray said.

His frown deepened. "She is on her way to an engagement, it seems." He had another glare for Miss Bray. "Go and find Lady Diana, damn it!"

"At once, Cousin George." Miss Bray hurried out.

Lord Burford took a nervous turn around the room, glaring at an inoffensive Chinese vase. The message that Diana's mother had arrived at the gatehouse and would like to see her daughter had come as a most unwelcome surprise, reminding him as it did of that old scandal mentioned briefly by his father. He was of two minds. In offering for Diana, he had decided to overlook the fact that her mother was an actress and no better than she should be, at least according to the *on-dit* that had circulated at the time.

Diana was so incredibly beautiful and her manners were excellent. Lord Lyall had told him she was the product of a select boarding school. Furthermore, he had said that Mrs. Forsythe would soon be on her way to America. Consequently, her presence at his gates was a shock. It was a great shame as well as an unfortune coincidence that Lord Lyall had been called away at this precise moment because he was unaware of what he should do. He had not wanted to receive the lady, but to have her turned away would have been extremely awkward. He was, however, doubly glad that he had not invited other guests at this time. One never knew. . . . He could only hope that he would be agreeably surprised. It also occurred to him that he ought to meet the lady who would eventually become his mother-in-law. Despite Diana's unaccountable refusal to accept his offer, he was very sure that she would not continue to defy her father's wishes. It would be only a matter of time before he received her acquiescence and could tell his many creditors that he would soon be in receipt of a large dowry, one that would fill coffers much diminished by deep play at a dozen hells before he had seen the error of his ways and the depressing depletion of his resources. It had been that more than any other consideration that had moved him to say to his servant, "I shall be delighted to receive Mrs. Forsythe and her friends."

He thought the man looked at him quizzically, but perhaps that was his imagination!

As he waited in the drawing room, Lord Burford was startled by the voices of two females. Both were much louder than he had expected. An imperturbable butler opened the doors and announced, "Mrs. Flavia Forsythe, Miss Georgiana Pemberton, and Mr. Silas Hornby."

Thanks to years of rigorous discipline and his own innate courtesy, Lord Burford managed to subdue the exclamation that rose to his lips. He smiled politely at a trio, the likes of which had never crossed the threshold of that magnificent chamber. To say that he was appalled at the appearance of the two women was no exaggeration. Although it was not later than ten in the morning, both were clad in satin gowns and wearing ornate necklaces, bracelets, and earrings. The colors of their garb were an affront to the eye. The older of the pair was clad in purple, the younger in a bright yellow. As for their faces, it was only too obvious that the high flush on their cheeks was artificially produced. Both had blond hair, elaborately arranged in puffs and curls. The color, again, had to be spurious.

They were accompanied by a man who looked to be in his thirties. His garments were also a serious affront to good taste. Obviously, he had thought to ape the dandies but in a way so exaggerated as to be ludicrous. The points of his shirt collar were longer than Lord Burford had ever seen; they practically reached his nose. His cravat was exaggeratedly folded, and stuck in the center of it was a diamond pin, undoubtedly paste! For the rest, he was wearing ballooning blue Cossack trousers strapped to brightly polished boots. His cane was topped by a huge silver ball. In common with the ladies, he was looking around the room with every appearance of awe.

Lord Burford cleared his throat and with some difficulty managed a weak but cordial smile. "I bid you welcome, Mrs. Forsythe," he said faintly, fixing his eye on the older of the two females.

"La, you're the one wants my girl?" she responded in stentorian tones.

"I—" he began.

Before he could continue, the other female said, "I 'ear as yer a marquess."

"That is correct," he said coldly.

"An' yer goin' to marry 'er," the older female said in accents of great surprise. "You're a goin' to gi' 'er yer 'eart'n yer 'and. Wot do you think o' that, Georgie?" She fixed a wide stare on her companion.

"She done all right for 'erself, I'd say." The girl nodded. "Don't you agree, Si?"

"All right, I should say." He looked at Lord Burford. " 'Tis a grand place you 'ave 'ere. 'Twas worth comin' outa the way to see it, right enough."

"I told you we 'ad to come. 'Tisn't often we see the like o' these. Only 'tis different wi' you, Mrs. Forsythe," the female named Georgie commented.

"Oh, yes, I lived in one o' them grand 'ouses when I were wi' 'er father. Can't say as I liked it much. Too dull by 'alf. But Diana's different. She likes a nice 'ouse, always did. Not much for the stage is Diana. 'Tis damned lucky 'er pa took a fancy to 'er'n is showin' 'er around the way 'e's been doin'."

"Aye, she's fallen on 'er feet right enough." The female named Georgie sent a glance around the room. "I been h'admirin' all them paintin's an' them screens. Looks like they come outa China. My pa, 'e were a sailor'n went to China. 'E come back wi' all sorts o' things: little shoes wot them China females wear, like doll shoes, they is on account of they does funny things to their feet. All embroidered they was.''

"Are you a patron o' the arts, yer Lordship?'' Mrs. Forsythe looked at Lord Burford.

He swallowed. "My father collected—''

"Ah, yer father, seems like I knew 'im when I were wi' 'is Lordship. But wot I were goin' to say's that I 'ope you'll come to the theater'n get all yer friends to come, too. We'll be performin' at King's Lynn next week'n we'll see they 'ave free seats.''

"I thank you," he began, not sure of what more he must say. He had the feeling that he was living in a nightmare. As he stared at his visitors, he tried in vain to imagine Lord Lyall with these vulgar females, but he could not. And the older one, he hated to couple her with Diana, had said something very telling. She had said that she had known his late father while she was living with Lord Lyall, suggesting that no marriage could ever have taken place. He himself was sure of that. And that meant that Diana was Lord Lyall's by-blow, his bastard daughter, whom he was trying to pass off as legitimate. And how could she, with a mother like that, be anything else? Obviously, the creature must have been a young man's folly, and how had she managed to produce a daughter as beautiful as Diana? As beautiful and as aristocratic, at least she gave that impression!

Yet, did he really know her? He had seen precious little of her during her weeks at the castle. Was she avoiding him for fear she would make a slip? That did seem a logical explanation. And where was the chit? And where was Lord Lyall? He cast a frantic glance in the direction of the doorway, willing one or the other to come and shed some light on this horrendous situation.

Hard on these chaotic thoughts, Mrs. Forsythe added, "Meanwhile, where is Diana and where's 'er pa? I'd like to see 'im again. It's been a long time since we was together. You know where 'e's gone?'' She fixed a suspicious eye on Lord Burford.

"I have no idea, ma'am."

"How come 'e don't call you milady? Or won't you be a milady until 'e's wed yer daughter?" Georgiana suddenly inquired.

"I don't think it works that way," her male companion observed.

"I don't think so neither," Mrs. Forsythe said. "Ohhhh," she suddenly shrieked. "There you are, dearie. I see 'e's gone'n found you." Mrs. Forsythe turned a smiling face toward Diana, who entered with Sir Sabin.

"Oh, Mama," Diana exclaimed in accents almost as ringing as those of her parent. "I could not believe you was really here. But he told me you were." To Lord Burford's horror, Diana ran to the female and clasped her in her arms. "Oh, I am delighted."

"And I am delighted for you, dearie. You didn't say as you was dwellin' in an 'ouse o' this size. Why it must be bigger'n Carlton 'Ouse."

"I told you it was very grand, Mama. You should see the picture gallery. Why, he has ancestors all the way back to Adam, practically."

"It ain't a castle," the other female suddenly said. She directed a censorious look at Diana. "You said 'twas a castle."

"It was. There's a lot o' ruins outside, but most o' the castle fell down."

"I likes a castle wot looks like a castle," the younger female insisted.

"It can be restored," the man said knowledgeably. "Like wot Sir 'Erbert Wapole did to Strawberry 'Ill. It were a regular 'ouse until 'e added all them arches and such'n made it Gothic."

"I am particularly partial to the Gothic." Diana smiled at Lord Burford. "When we are wed, can we make some changes?"

Lord Burford was very red in the face. "No!" he exclaimed. "And as for my—my offer. It is still under discussion with your father."

"Oh, I thought it was all settled." Diana looked surprised.

"Ye ain't lookin' to back out, are ye?" Mrs. Forsythe demanded.

"I—I'll be damned if I . . ." Lord Burford was panting as if he had just run a cross-country race, and his small eyes were hot with fury as he actually screamed, "I have been vilely traduced! I—I . . ." His whole body seemed to swell as more words piled onto his tongue emerging only as an incomprehensible "ough!" Then, turning on his heel, he rushed from the room, an action that spared him the sight of five people convulsed with laughter.

"Oh, oh, oh, it was best he left when he did." Mrs. Forsythe was the first to recover her equilibrium. "Else he surely must have succumbed to apoplexy! I vow I was becoming quite concerned over the poor man."

"It was as fine a scene as you have ever played, ma'am," Mr. Hornby said. Finally controlling his own laughter, he made her a low bow.

"Oh, Mama, dearest Mama, how may I ever, ever thank you?" Diana moved from the circle of Sir Sabin's arm to kiss her mother once again. Caught between laughter and tears, she continued, "I was so afraid. He'd not give me a moment's peace and he bribed Sophia . . . But enough!" She turned to Georgiana. "And you, too, were splendid, Georgie."

"I was glad to help. Eee, but 'e were a wrong'un all right." She flushed and cast a nervous look at her husband. "I mean . . ."

He seized her hand and brought it to his lips, saying as he released it, "Your description is entirely correct, my love, and must stand."

"I think we'd best leave before we are asked to quit the premises, and in no uncertain terms," Mrs. Forsythe advised, and then stiffened as Lord Burford's voice boomed through the hall.

"What do I mean, my Lord? What do I *mean*?" he yelled. "I am t-talking about your by-blow, your baseborn daughter, whom you tried to foist on me. That woman—

that trull as much admitted she was your doxy. You may not value your heritage, my Lord, but I would rather rot in debtor's prison than have that creature's whelp to wife. And as for you, my Lord, I want you and that pack of—out of here before I exercise my rights as justice of the peace and throw the lot of 'em in jail."

"Oh, dear." Mrs. Forsythe exchanged a rueful look with her companions. "I thought Gervais must remain away longer, but he was never one to cool his heels in fruitless waiting." She paused as they heard footsteps coming back down the hall. "Ah, my loves, and now for the finale," she added with an impish grin. As Lord Lyall appeared in the doorway, she sank into an exaggerated curtsy. "My Lord," she shrilled, "I wondered where you'd got to?"

"Flavia!" He had been looking both perplexed and angry. His eyes widened. "What is the meaning of this?"

She rose gracefully. "Cannot a mother come to see her dear daughter?" she asked blandly.

"Done up for some low farce?" he demanded furiously now.

Flavia looked at her companions. "My dears," she said, "will you wait for me in the coach?"

"Hold. What are you doing here?" Lord Lyall glared at Sir Sabin.

Sir Sabin stood very straight. He did not take his arm from around Diana's waist. Instead, he held her even closer. "I wish to marry your daughter, my Lord."

"And I, Father," Diana said firmly, "will have no one else."

"We will discuss that later," Lord Lyall rasped.

"They have my consent," Mrs. Forsythe said. "Or do you want to subject your daughter to the same manner of marriage I endured?"

He paled. "You say this to me, who loved you with all my heart?"

"It is not love that seeks to snare and confine a free

spirit," she retorted. "I was no more than a possession to you, my Lord."

"That is not true," he cried. "I say again I loved you with every fiber of my being. And once you loved me, too."

"And I repeat, it is not love that seeks to possess and confine."

As they faced each other, Mr. Hornby, his arm around his wife, tapped Sir Sabin on the shoulder. He nodded and with Diana followed the other outside.

"Flavia," Lord Lyall spoke in a voice that was not quite steady. "how can I tell you what my life has been since you left? There's not been a day that I've not missed you. But obviously you did not care for me in that same way."

"Did I not?" she demanded. "When I gave up all that I had striven for since a child? The stage may mean nothing to you, but it was all I knew and was hard for me to leave my friends—my friends who were kind to me and loved me—to go to a strange place, where I was quite aware I would not be welcome. But I—I cared for you. I adored you, and so I put all behind me and came away. But I did not know you'd keep me like a prisoner, never to go to London, never to visit my friends, thrust into a home where I was regarded as a *rara avis* indeed. Your mother and sister whispered about me and only Guy understood how much I loved the theater. Oh," she sighed. "What is the use of going on? You did not understand me, my Lord, and for all your talk of love you still do not understand me or your daughter, either. You are quite willing to thrust her into a loveless marriage. Why? Because of your pride, the same pride that kept me held fast in Lincolnshire. You have learned nothing, nothing with the years, but your son, thank God, is wiser than you."

The protests that had been forming on his lips were scattered by her mention of Anthony. "My son?" he said blankly.

"It was he who told us about Lord Burford. He saw through him. You did not."

"My friend—"

"He is not his father. He is nothing like him. How could you not see it? I saw it instantly."

He loosed a long sigh. "I—I fear I did not want to see it, Flavia," he admitted. "It was hard for me when Edmund died. Besides you, he was the one person in the world I really loved. And I had promised him that if I ever had a daughter . . . I was a damned fool, not to see him as he really was. Oh,.God, I feel as if I have lost Edmund twice, but it seems I must face a much greater loss."

"You'll not lose Diana by letting her marry the man she loves," she said gently. "You will lose her only if you stand in her way."

"I am not talking about Diana. I am talking about you. When do you leave for America?"

"I am not going to America, Gervais."

"Not going? But I thought . . . Has Gifford changed his plans, then?

"No, I am sure he will go."

"You"—he swallowed a lump in his throat—"you are not going to marry him?"

She shook her head, and bringing up one hand, she lifted her necklace so that he could see her throat. "We have parted."

He stared at her throat in amazement and horror. "Those black-and-blue marks—what put them there? He did not . . . ?"

She nodded. "He came near to strangling me in our last *Othello*. It was after your son had come to see me. He appeared to believe . . ." She shrugged. "I loathe jealousy, as I think you know."

"Oh, my God, Flavia." Impulsively he put his arms around her, holding her against him. "Oh, my darling, I am sorry, but I could not know what Anthony intended. Oh, Flavia"—he suddenly released her and fell to his knees—"could you not come back to me? I know I have been wrongheaded and may be so again, but I will try to change; with your help I might succeed. I do love you so much.''

"I love you, too, Gervais. It was why I could not bring myself to wed Mr. Gifford, for all his kindness. And he was kind until—''

He rose. "Never mind Gifford," he said harshly. "Though I've a mind to call him out.''

"No!''

"But I will not," his voice had grown soft again. "I want nothing to mar our happiness. We will live in London, my Flavia, and go to the theater every night, if you so desire. My love, say you will marry me, I beg you.''

"I need time," she demurred.

"I will give you time . . . five minutes!''

"Oh, Gervais!" She produced a watery laugh. "Very well, yes, I will marry you, for I cannot go on missing you for the rest of my life.''

Diana awakened when the first sunbeams came through the small window of the Golden Cross, the inn to which she and her parents had come last night. She moved and was, at first, startled to find something obstructing those movements. Then, memories poured into her mind, and turning, she looked very fondly down on that obstruction: upon long lashes under dark brows and at a nose she admired excessively and a mouth that she prized still more. There was a white line running down the forehead of the obstruction, and it looked to her like a scar—from an old wound? Where had he received it? There was still much to know about the man she had loved for such a long time. She wished that he would awaken so the instruction might begin. But she did not wish to hurry the process. Yesterday had been incredibly hectic, full of alarums and excursions.

Diana smiled as she remembered her fight when the possible highwayman had caught up with her and seized her bridle rein. Then, to have him push back his hat to reveal the beloved features she had feared never to see again! However, she shuddered as she recalled Lord Burford's face, so empurpled with rage as he stood in the carriageway "to speed the parting guests" that she feared he must burst a blood vessel before her mother's hired coach rolled away. It had been a tight squeeze for six people, but no one had minded in the least.

The minister of the church in Fakenham had been almost as shocked as Lord Burford when her father had come in with what the elderly man could only have characterized as a "bedizened female" and demanded a special license, or, rather, two special licenses, a privilege his rank enabled him to obtain.

However, despite his prejudices, the minister had produced them; later he had performed the ceremonies with a dignity that her mother, now Lady Lyall again, had called beautiful. It had been beautiful, Diana thought, her eyes blurring at the memory, and then laughter shook her as she pictured their wedding feast at this very inn. She had hardly recognized her father, so young and happy he had looked as he exchanged toasts with Mr. Hornby and little Georgiana. Everybody had been staring at them, and Lord Lyall, usually so dignified, had not minded in the least—because, it had been a wonderful, wonderful end to a day that at the outset had promised very little.

"Oh," Diana whispered, her mind going back to that candle-lit church. "It was lovely."

Sir Sabin stirred, and she looked at him apologetically. "Oh, my dearest, did I wake you?"

His eyes were wide open now and they rested on her lovingly. "I was not asleep. I was afraid to breathe for fear that I would awaken you, my love."

"And all this time, I feared to rouse you."

His arms were around her. "We will need to get to know each other better. And I think I will enjoy those lessons most of all, but . . ."

"But, what?"

"But, my beloved pedagogue, I will not allow you to confine them only to Tuesdays."

About the Author

Ellen Fitzgerald is a pseudonym for a well-known romance writer. A graduate of the University of Southern California with a B.A. in English and an M.A. in Drama, Ms. Fitzgerald has also attended Yale University and has had numerous plays produced throughout the country. In her spare time, she designs and sells jewelry. Ms. Fitzgerald lives in New York City.

Her lips were still warm from the imprint of his kiss, but now Silvia knew there was nothing to protect her from the terror of Serpent Tree Hall. Not even love. Especially not love. . . .

ANDREA PARNELL

Lovely young Silvia Bradstreet had come from London to Colonial America to be a bondservant on an isolated island estate off the Georgia coast. But a far different fate awaited her at the castle-like manor: a man whose lips moved like a hot flame over her flesh . . . whose relentless passion and incredible strength aroused feelings she could not control. And as a whirlpool of intrigue and violence sucked her into the depths of evil . . . flames of desire melted all her power to resist. . . .

Coming in September from Signet!